ChangelingPress.com

Irish/Tank Duet

Harley Wylde

Irish/Tank Duet

Harley Wylde

All rights reserved.
Copyright ©2020 Harley Wylde

ISBN: 9798623087119

Publisher:
Changeling Press LLC
315 N. Centre St.
Martinsburg, WV 25404
ChangelingPress.com

Printed in the U.S.A.

Editor: Crystal Esau
Cover Artist: Bryan Keller

The individual stories in this anthology have been previously released in E-Book format.

No part of this publication may be reproduced or shared by any electronic or mechanical means, including but not limited to reprinting, photocopying, or digital reproduction, without prior written permission from Changeling Press LLC.

This book contains sexually explicit scenes and adult language which some may find offensive and which is not appropriate for a young audience. Changeling Press books are for sale to adults, only, as defined by the laws of the country in which you made your purchase.

Table of Contents

Irish (Devil's Boneyard MC 4)	4
Chapter One	5
Chapter Two	19
Chapter Three	41
Chapter Four	53
Chapter Five	67
Chapter Six	81
Chapter Seven	95
Chapter Eight	108
Chapter Nine	120
Chapter Ten	131
Epilogue	143
Tank (Dixie Reapers MC 9)	155
Prologue	156
Chapter One	163
Chapter Two	176
Chapter Three	191
Chapter Four	205
Chapter Five	216
Chapter Six	229
Chapter Seven	244
Chapter Eight	255
Chapter Nine	271
Epilogue	286
Harley Wylde	289
Changeling Press E-Books	290

Irish (Devil's Boneyard MC 4)
Harley Wylde

Janessa: I've been in love with Seamus since the day I met him, even though I was fourteen at the time. Now that I'm an adult, I'm ready to go claim my man. Maybe I was stupid thinking he'd wait for me, or maybe I just really wanted a fairy-tale ending. Seeing another woman in his arms hurt like hell, so I ran… straight into trouble.

Irish: I met a girl years ago, one who had me spellbound despite her young age. I kept my distance, knowing it was so damn wrong to be attracted to her, but looking in her eyes I could tell she had an old soul. Now she's back and all grown up, so what did I do? Something stupid. I kissed another woman. When I hear Janessa's been attacked, it feels like someone has ripped out my heart. Whatever it takes, I'll make it up to her, and I will get justice for her one way or another.

Chapter One

Janessa

"I'm not a child anymore, Mom. I'm tired of waiting," I said, my arms folded as I squared off against the only woman I remembered calling Mother, even if she hadn't given birth to me.

"Janessa, I don't think it's a good idea. You know how your father feels about this."

"Mom." I sighed and closed my eyes. "I know I'm young. I get it, I really do. Dad wants to protect me from the world, especially after what happened. But he can't, and I don't want him to. I'm nineteen and I'm ready. More than ready. Other women my age are off starting their lives, but Dad wants to keep me locked up at the compound forever."

I could understand my dad's fear, I really could. He'd found me abandoned in an asylum by my grandparents, and if the woman I now called Mother hadn't sacrificed herself for me, some horrific things would have happened to me. In my dad's place, I might feel the same way, but after five years of living under his thumb, I was starting to feel like I was suffocating. I wanted to go places, do things without a Reaper watching over my shoulder. Mostly, I wanted Seamus.

"Janessa, it's not..." My mom shook her head. "What do you know about Seamus? You met him once. Five years ago. I know the two of you shared some sort of moment, and you flirted shamelessly with him while we were in Florida. That doesn't make you soul mates. You were a teenager!"

"He's part of Devil's Boneyard, Mom. It's not like he's a bad guy. The Devils are practically family to this club, and you know how they feel about women and children. He's not the Antichrist! Why can't you understand that I need to do this?" I asked. Maybe I didn't know him, not really, but I remembered that spark I'd felt and I needed to see if it was still there. I hadn't experienced it any other time, no matter how many boys had asked me out on dates, usually before they realized I was a biker's daughter. Not that I'd ever accepted any of those offers.

"Seamus was patched in, Janessa. He goes by Irish now," Mom said. "We'd better get used to using his new name. He's not the same man you met before. He's gone a bit wild and he… Janessa, I've heard stories. I'm trying to protect you!"

"Maybe I don't want you to protect me," I said. "I'm tired of being locked up in this compound and not having a life. I want to *live!* Why can't you understand that? And I don't care about any rumors. Seamus was a good man then, and he's good now. I just know it."

"Why couldn't you have ever dated boys your age?" Mom muttered. "No, not my daughter. Always mooning after some biker who's more than a decade older than she is."

"Guess the apple doesn't fall far from the tree," I said with a smirk. "How much older is Dad than you?"

"Shut it, missy," she said, but there was a smile curving her lips.

I knew my dad was about a dozen years older than she was, but Kalani loved my dad and he absolutely adored her. Sometimes they were a little nauseating with how in love they were. But at the same time, Kalani deserved happiness, and I was really glad my dad had married her. She was the best mother I could have ever asked for, far better than the one who had given birth to me.

"You know if I wait until Dad gets here, he'll lock me in my room and throw away the key. Probably bar the windows too."

"Janessa," Mom said with that warning tone only mothers seem to have.

She never liked it if I said anything negative about my dad. After he'd saved her life, they'd fallen in love. If Mom went anywhere and didn't let my dad know about it, he tended to panic that something evil had happened. Some might have felt smothered, but not Mom. I think she loved the fact someone cared that much about her.

"What? It's true! I know bad things happened to both us, you more so than me, but he acts like if we aren't under constant watch someone is going to snatch us and run. I can't breathe anymore!"

Mom bit her lip, but not before I saw it quiver. Great. I was going to make my mom cry. The woman who had sacrificed herself to keep me safe when I was younger. I owed her everything, and instead I was screaming at her and whining about life being unfair. I was a bitch. If anyone knew about life not being fair, it was her. She'd been dealt a shitty hand until my dad had come looking for me. If we hadn't been in that room together, if she hadn't protected me, then she might never have escaped. It sickened me to think those people would have gotten way with all the horrors they'd inflicted on people over the years.

"I'm sorry," I said. "You know I'd never do anything to hurt you, Mom. I love you, and I love Dad. The two of you are the best parents I could have ever asked for, but I'm old enough to live my own life now.

You might like it when Dad keeps you overly safe, but I feel the need to escape sometimes."

"I know," she said. "I know you're all grown up. No matter what I do, I can't make you that sweet fourteen-year-old who needed me."

"I still need you. I always will, but I'm going, Mom. If it doesn't work out, I'll come back, and Dad can lecture me all he wants. Promise."

"I never could stop you once you got an idea into your head," she said. "If you're really doing this, then you make sure you say goodbye to Noah. He won't understand if you just disappear. Clayton might be confused either way, but you can say bye to him too if you want."

I nodded and went to get the bag I'd packed. I'd already put a few things in my truck earlier. Even if she'd said no, I'd had every intention of leaving. I'd always lived by the theory it was better to beg forgiveness than ask permission. On my way to my room, I stopped in my brothers' doorway. Noah was pushing a train around the track Dad had put together for his last birthday, and Clayton was making a mess with his blocks.

Dad had met Mom the day he'd rescued me. He'd saved both of us, and he'd fallen for Mom. I'd only been fourteen at the time. They'd gotten married, and it hadn't been long before she was pregnant with my brother. Noah was only four, and even though there was a huge age gap between us, I loved the little squirt. Best baby brother I could have ever asked for. Clayton was a good kid too, especially since he was only three. Mom had gotten pregnant with him almost right after Noah. I never understood why they hadn't had more kids. Mom was the best mother ever, and even though Dad could be suffocating I knew he meant well.

"Hey, kiddos!"

Noah grinned at me but didn't get up, and Clayton didn't even acknowledge me. That wasn't unusual for him, though, not when he was focused on something. I'd wondered a few times if he might be autistic or something, but after the hell Mom had been through at the asylum, I knew she'd never get him tested. Not willingly anyway. Men in lab coats still scared her.

"Hi, Nessa," Noah said.

"I'm going to take a little trip and I wanted to say goodbye, but I'll come back soon. You going to be extra good for Mom while I'm gone?" I asked. "Both of you."

"I'm always good," Noah said, then went back to pushing his train. Clayton glanced at me and quickly looked away, but I knew he'd heard me.

Noah wasn't wrong. He hardly ever gave our parents trouble. If ever there was a perfect kid, it was probably Noah. Maybe they hadn't had more kids after these two in fear they would be complete terrors. How likely was it that they'd have another easy baby? Even when he'd first been born, Noah'd not woken much during the night and hardly ever fussed, and Clayton had been pretty good too. It was as he'd gotten older that I'd started noticing some differences that didn't quite add up. He didn't have the all-out meltdowns I'd heard were sometimes associated with autistic kids, but there were other things, like not making eye contact and how unusually quiet he could be.

I stepped into the room long enough to give them each a hug, and then I went to my bedroom and grabbed my bag. I looked around the room that had been mine the last five years. It was filled with happy memories, but I was ready to make more. The bag was heavy, but I carried it through the house and out to the small truck my dad had bought for my high school graduation. I might not have said how long I would be gone, and I had my reasons. I was hoping that Seamus, or Irish as he was now called, would have missed me as much as I'd missed him. With some luck, I'd only be coming here long enough to tell my parents I was moving to the Devil's Boneyard territory.

I settled my bag onto the passenger seat before getting behind the wheel. My purse was already in the floorboard, and I had a cold drink and a bag of snacks in the console. I put the truck in gear and pulled out of the driveway before Mom changed her mind and came after me. When I reached the gate at the front of the compound, Diego waved me through, not even questioning where I was going. I hoped my dad didn't give him hell for it later. As far as Prospects went, Diego was one of the good ones. I expected them to patch him in sooner rather than later. He'd make a good addition to the Reapers family.

I made it through town without a single Dixie Reaper trying to stop me, which meant no one -- meaning Mom -- had told my dad yet. I'd worried she'd call him as soon as I pulled away from the house. He'd be angry with her, for half a second. I'd never seen him angry with her for very long. Anything that hurt Mom, upset Dad, and he'd do anything to make it right. Even when he was the one at fault.

When the highway opened up before me, I pressed the accelerator a little harder, watching as the needle on the speedometer rose to about five miles over the limit. Any faster and I knew I'd chance getting pulled over, and the fewer problems I had leaving town the better. With my luck, the one officer who was friendly with the club would be the one who stopped me, then I knew Dad would find out quickly that I was leaving town. The drive to the Florida panhandle wasn't all that long, just a two-hour trip from the Reapers' compound. This far south, the weather was still warm despite the fact it was nearing winter. I rolled my windows down and enjoyed the breeze in my hair.

I made it into the Devils' territory in less time than I should have, probably because my foot had gotten heavier once home was no longer in my rearview mirror, but when I reached the compound where I'd stayed with my parents five years ago, the place looked deserted. The gate was open and there wasn't a single bike in sight. The warehouse-like building looked haunted and like it hadn't been used in a while. What the hell was going on? I knew the Devils were still in this area. Several of them came to the Dixie Reapers compound a few times a year to visit.

I shut off my engine and got out. The few homes inside the fenced area were dark and appeared empty as well. If they weren't here, then what was I supposed to do? I could ask someone around town, but I knew that bikers tended to get a bad reputation, and I wasn't certain the townspeople would be helpful.

"Looking for Devil's Boneyard?" a voice asked from behind me.

I turned and saw a guy in a cut straddling a Harley. How the hell I hadn't heard him ride up was a mystery. Having been around bikes the last five years, I was usually aware when a biker was nearby. Devil's Boneyard was stitched on the front, along with the name Ashes.

"Yes, I was looking for… Irish." It was going to be an adjustment, remembering not to call him Seamus. It was the first name that came to mind when I thought of him.

Ashes grinned. "You and every other woman around here. You can follow me over to the compound. Cinder bought a bigger piece of land, put up a new clubhouse, and a bunch of homes. Guess you haven't been around lately."

Every other woman? What exactly did that mean? Had Mom been right when she said I shouldn't have come here? I'd thought… I didn't know what I'd thought. I'd spent the last five years dreaming of the day I would be old enough that I could be with Seamus. Maybe it had been wrong of me to assume he'd felt the same. I'd thought we'd had a connection, that deep-down knowing you'd met your soul mate. Sure, I'd been a kid, but it wasn't like I was going to remain one forever. I really, really hoped my mother hadn't been right. Maybe I was being stupid.

I got back into the truck and followed Ashes to the other end of town and through the gates of a much bigger compound. It rivaled the size of the Dixie Reapers' home. I pulled my truck to a stop at the end of the clubhouse. This one was made of wood and had a long porch across the front, similar to the one back home. It was much more inviting than the one they'd had before. A row of bikes took up most of the space, and I discovered I was really damn nervous. I rubbed my hands up and down my thighs, then got out of the truck and walked up the steps to the porch.

"You want Irish, he's in there," Ashes said, giving a nod to the front door. He pulled out a pack of cigarettes and lit one. "When he breaks your heart, I'll be here waiting."

The man gave me a wink and I gathered my courage. Pushing open the front door, I stepped inside and came to an immediate halt. Naked and mostly naked women paraded around the place, and several people were having sex out in the open. Did this sort of thing happen at home? Is this why my dad refused to let me go to the clubhouse except on family days? My cheeks burned as I scanned the space, looking for the man I'd dreamed about every night. A loud booming laugh caught my attention and I saw him. Irish. He was at the table in the corner, a skinny blonde on his lap and a redhead practically sticking her naked breasts in his face.

Nausea made my stomach churn as I quickly turned away. I bounced off a hard chest and tried to focus on the cut that now filled my vision. *Stripes*. Oh hell. It was the Russian who visited the Reapers with Scratch, often enough he'd know exactly who I was. I looked up and sure enough, the massive man was scowling at me.

"This is no place for little girls. Especially a Reaper's daughter." His accent was thick, but I understood every word.

I squared my shoulders. "I'm not a little girl. I'm a grown woman."

"Is that a fact?" he asked. He waved a hand at the room. "Unclaimed women in this clubhouse are fair game. What are you going to do when one of my brothers decides he wants to have a little fun with you? Your daddy isn't here to protect you right now."

"They won't hurt me," I said, though I wasn't feeling quite so confident as I scanned the room again. These weren't the men I remembered, the ones who had helped us when trouble was after my mom. The men laughing and drinking seemed more like the type to take what they wanted.

Stripes sighed. "Janessa, does your dad know you're here?"

"No."

"Great," he muttered. "You're here for Irish, aren't you?"

I nodded.

"He's not the one for you, little girl. That one is wild and doesn't stick with one woman for an entire night, much less a lifetime. He's screwed more pussy than anyone in this room over the last few years. When you turned eighteen and he didn't come for you, it should have been a hint to keep away."

My eyes burned with unshed tears. It hurt, hearing that he hadn't thought of me once. He'd been whoring his way through the local women, and I'd been pining for him, not even going on a date because I'd felt like I would be cheating on the man I'd thought I loved. I'd turned down every offer I'd had in high school, even for prom, knowing I was meant to be with Seamus. Now I felt like an idiot. How had I been so stupid? Mom had warned me over and over, but I hadn't listened. I'd been too damn stubborn. Spark? Apparently, that spark I'd felt had been one-sided, or maybe just teenage hormones in overdrive. I'd made Irish my fairy-tale prince. Instead, it looked like he was just a regular frog.

"Go home, Janessa," Stripes said, his tone softer than before, more fatherly. "This isn't the place for you."

"I can't," I said. Going home would be admitting defeat and admitting that my parents had been right. I might have told my mom I'd come right back if things didn't work out, even promised as much, but how could I face her? And my dad... he'd be so disappointed, and so very angry with me.

"I can call Scratch, see if he can give you a place to stay for the night. Then you can go home tomorrow," Stripes said.

"Has he even noticed I'm here?" I asked, my voice breaking a little.

Stripes looked over to the table in the corner. "*Nyet.*"

I gave a nod and turned to go. At the door, I hesitated and looked back one last time. Seamus turned to look my way and our gazes locked. His eyes went wide after a moment, and I knew he'd recognized me. I might be older now, but I still looked mostly the same. And just as quickly, he turned to the blonde in his lap, and kissed her. I bit back a sob, refusing to cry in front of the Devils, and I hurried out to my truck. I practically ran Ashes over in my haste to get away. I didn't care where I went, but I needed to escape.

Thankfully, the biker didn't laugh or make fun of me for being so stupid. The end of his cigarette glowed as he watched me flee. I'd been humiliated, and I'd never live it down if my family found out what happened. Who would ever want to date someone as pathetic as me? I knew I'd done the wrong thing. If I wanted to be with Irish, I needed to fight for him. And I might have, if the blonde had made the move and not Irish. He'd made it very clear that he wanted nothing to do with me.

Stupid. Stupid. Stupid.

I revved the engine and peeled away from the clubhouse. The Prospect manning the gate threw it open as I barreled past. My truck fishtailed as I pulled onto the street and steadily picked up speed. Instead of heading back to Alabama, I pointed my truck farther south. I'd always wanted to visit the beach. Maybe I'd go check it out. Anything to keep from going home and telling my mom she was right. Anything to keep from seeing Irish with those women. Anything to make the pain stop.

The tears fell down my cheeks and made my vision blur. I hastily wiped them away and focused on the road again. A dark shape was in the middle, stretching from one side to the other. A scream built in my throat as I saw the gator and realized there was no way to avoid it. I jerked the wheel of my truck and went careening off the road. The truck slammed into a tree, my head banging into the steering wheel. I felt something warm and wet on my face, and my body ached.

I pushed open the door of my truck and stumbled out into the tall grass. I staggered as I made my way back toward the road, hoping the gator was long gone. The last thing I needed was to attract its attention with the blood running down my face. When my feet hit pavement, I didn't see any sign of the gator, or any other cars for that matter. I began walking, back the way I'd come, in hopes that I could find help. I hesitated, my brain feeling fuzzy, and it seemed like I was forgetting something.

Phone. I had a phone in my purse. I turned and froze when I saw three men standing in the middle of the road, right where the gator had been previously. My vision was going in and out, but I noticed they were wearing cuts. I couldn't make out the name of the club as I swayed. Maybe they were Devil's Boneyard and would help me. When the first man grabbed me, I knew I was wrong. I still couldn't read his cut, but there was a skull engulfed in flames. I hadn't seen those colors before and I knew it didn't bode well for me. Admitting I was a Reaper's daughter could possibly save me, or make things a lot worse.

"Looks like we found something to play with," the man said as he handed me off to one of the others.

I was fighting hard to stay conscious, but when a closed fist met my ribs, I gasped and nearly gave in to the urge to pass out. I didn't know what they wanted with me, or who they were, but I knew I was in some serious trouble. I never should have run off the way I had, never should have come to Florida to begin with. And I damn sure shouldn't have come here unarmed. They hit me again, and again. The world was spinning and all I felt was pain, everywhere. I vaguely registered the fact they were cutting my clothes, not caring if the blades sliced into my skin too.

I whimpered, hoping I was wrong about their intentions for me, yet unable to fight back. I'd been taught to do whatever it took to get away, if I were ever attacked, yet here I lay unable to lift a finger against the men. My dad was going to be so fucking pissed, and my mom... God, my mom was going to freak the hell out. It might even cause her to have flashbacks of all that she'd been through in order to protect me before. I heard the men laughing, then a boot met the side of my head. I must have blacked out, at least for a minute or two. When I opened my eyes again, they were just standing around me, staring and talking. I couldn't make out any of the words they were saying. There was a stench of piss in the air, and while I hurt everywhere, I didn't think they'd raped me.

The three men turned and walked off. I couldn't see them the farther away they got, but I used that moment to drag myself toward my truck and my phone. The grass was crisp and cool against my body and I whimpered as pain sliced through me with every inch I got closer to calling for help. I heard the crunch of boots and glanced back to see one of them coming for me again.

He hauled me up and slammed his fist into my head, sending the world spinning and I choked on blood. I sagged to the ground and a moment later I heard three motorcycles start up. They didn't pass me so they must have gone the other direction. I struggled to move and cried as my battered body tried to obey my commands. I managed to drag myself a short distance before I had to stop. Time had no meaning. It was still dark when I finally reached my truck and managed to get my phone.

I pressed 9-1-1 but couldn't even hold the phone to my ear. I knew my GPS was turned on. It was something my dad had forced me to agree to when he'd given the phone to me. In the event there was ever trouble, he wanted someone to be able to track me. Now I was grateful that I'd agreed and had never shut it off. I gurgled as blood filled my mouth, and I could hear a woman talking. My eyes slid shut and I finally gave up, sinking into the darkness. My last fleeting thought was that I hoped someone found me before the local wildlife thought I'd make a good snack.

Dad was never going to forgive me, or ever let me leave the house again.

Chapter Two

Irish

Fuck me! I hadn't seen Janessa Rodriguez in so damn long. It still blew my mind that she'd walked into the Devils' clubhouse. I felt like a complete and utter shit for hurting her the way I had, but it was the right thing to do. If her dad even thought I'd looked at his little girl with any kind of interest, I'd be a dead man. Even though I'd kissed the slut sitting on my lap, after Janessa had walked out, I'd dumped the woman on the floor. I was disgusted with myself.

The years had been really fucking good to her. She still had a pretty olive complexion and dark hair that looked so damn soft. She'd sprouted breasts that were more than a handful since the last time I'd seen her, and hips that screamed she was definitely all woman now. All it had taken was one look and I'd been hard as hell, and not for the woman who had been in my lap.

Janessa had been gone a few hours now, and I figured she was back home where she belonged. I closed my eyes, trying to block out the image of her standing in the doorway, all those gorgeous curves. But it was the look of anguish in her eyes that would haunt me forever. I hadn't been a saint a day in my life. After meeting the Reaper's daughter, I'd felt like I was in a downward spiral. She'd been just a kid, a teenager, and my reaction to her had sickened me. So I'd started screwing any woman who offered. Now I was wishing I hadn't done that.

I'd never counted on her showing up here in Devils' territory. It had been five years, and I knew she was a grown-ass woman now, but I'd figured her daddy would have her locked up somewhere secure. Away from men like me. Hell, he might have even asked a Reaper to marry her just to keep her safe. Did he even know she'd come here? She had to have been looking for me. I just didn't understand why. Yeah, she'd plagued my thoughts since the day I'd met her, but surely she hadn't been waiting for me all this time. Had she? I'd known when she turned eighteen because my VP had made sure I was aware. Maybe he'd thought she'd be the one to tame me, or had just hoped for some sort of reaction. I hadn't made it a secret that I didn't plan to settle down. Even knowing she was legal, I'd not had the courage to go after her, though, and had kept my distance. Now I was second-guessing that decision.

The clubhouse doors flew open and Scratch came inside. He never showed up on party nights, not since settling down with his wife and kids. The look on his face told me something was seriously wrong, and all my brothers went on alert. But he ignored every last one of them and came to me. I just couldn't tell if he wanted to hit me, or console me.

"We need to talk," Scratch said. "Somewhere quiet."

"Something wrong, VP?" I didn't think I'd screwed up lately. Well, other than hurting Janessa.

"Church. Now."

His tone demanded I obey. I followed Scratch to the back of the clubhouse and through the double doors at the end of the hall. I took a seat and Scratch leaned against the opposite wall, staring at me with his arms folded and a fierce look in his eyes.

"Did I do something?" I asked.

"There's been an accident."

I sat up straighter. "Clarity? The kids?"

The VP had an awesome wife and kids, and any one of us would lay down our lives for them. But if Clarity were in trouble, I didn't think Scratch would be standing in front of me.

He shook his head. "My family is fine. This isn't about me, son. It's about you."

"I don't understand. You know I don't have any family here, except the Devils. What's going on?"

Scratch rubbed at his beard, then sat down in his usual seat. "A blue truck was found along the road heading out of town. It had gone off the road and crashed into a tree. The driver isn't in good shape, but there are signs that something else happened."

I still didn't have a clue what he was talking about. I didn't know anyone with a blue truck. I wished he'd just tell me what the hell was going on. The suspense was going to drive me crazy.

"The truck had a Harley Davidson sticker on the back. And Alabama plates," he said.

My gut clenched and I gripped the table. The only person I knew who had been in this area with Alabama tags would have been Janessa.

"The Highway Patrol called Cinder, but he didn't answer, so they tried me next. They thought maybe the driver was related to someone at the club. They found a wallet in a purse. What I want to know is what the fuck Janessa Rodriguez was doing in Devils territory unannounced, and why didn't someone tell me she was here?"

Oh, God. It suddenly hurt to breathe.

"Janessa," I said, my voice cracking. "Is she... will she be okay?"

"Someone beat that poor girl half to death, ripped up her clothes…"

I couldn't help it. I leaned over and threw up.

"She wasn't sexually assaulted," Scratch said, "if that's what you're thinking. The assholes did piss on her, though. Cut her up, beat her all to hell. They're hoping to run DNA and figure out who did this to her, but if they aren't in the system, then it won't do much good. In the meantime, they haven't been able to contact her next of kin."

My heart felt like someone was trying to rip it from my chest. I stood and pulled my keys from my pocket. "I'm going to see her," I said.

"Son, the only reason I can think of for that little girl to be here at all was to come see you. What the fuck happened? Why was she on a road headed south and not going back home? Or an even better question, why the fuck wasn't she with you?"

South? I didn't know. I'd seen how devastated she was when she'd left, and it was my fault. I'd done that to her. I'd thought she'd go home, get on with her life and find some guy her dad would approve of, maybe go off to college or some shit.

"She came here," I said. "I didn't talk to her. I was… I was with someone. A club slut. She saw the two of us and she left."

Scratch cursed and leaned back in his chair. "When Tex wants to remove your balls, I'm not standing in his way. That was a shitty thing to do, Irish, and you damn well know it. That girl was completely hung up on you from the moment she laid eyes on you. Hell, anytime I go see my daughter and grandkids, she still asks about you, even though you never went after her when she turned eighteen."

I hadn't known that. Yeah, he'd brought up Janessa from time to time, but I hadn't known that she'd asked about me, still thought about me. I'd figured when she turned eighteen and I kept my distance that she'd move on. Scratch had only brought her up in passing after that point, almost as if he were feeling me out, but I hadn't understood why. Until now.

"She's at the county hospital. You know I have to call the Reapers, right?" he asked.

"Just… give me enough time to see her. Wait twenty minutes before you call. I know it's a lot to ask, but I need to make things right with her. Is she awake?"

"No. She was unconscious when they found her, and when I got the call, she hadn't woken yet. You need to prepare yourself. From what I hear, it's pretty bad."

I gave a quick nod, then stood up. I stared down at the puke on the floor but Scratch waved me off.

"I'll have a Prospect clean that up. Go see your woman and hope you don't have to say goodbye while you're there," he said. "And, Irish?"

I met his gaze.

"Despite what you think, that girl *is* your woman. Don't fuck it up again."

The thought of Janessa never waking up, of her dying, made me want to throw up again. I rushed through the clubhouse, not stopping even as my brothers called out to me. I got on my bike and drove like a bat out of hell all the way to the county hospital. When I got there, I ran inside and stopped at the information desk.

"I need a room number for Janessa Rodriguez."

The nurse tapped on her keyboard, then gave me a narrowed-eye look. "You her family? It says here she can't have visitors except family."

"She's my… fiancée."

I'd worry about the lie later. Right now, I needed to see her, needed to know that she was still alive. The nurse didn't look like she believed me, but she made a grumbling sound and then motioned to the elevators down the hall before handing me a slip of paper. "Fourth floor. She's in ICU room 3."

I tried not to run, since it was probably frowned upon in a hospital, but I did walk really damn fast. When I got to the ICU, there was another desk with more nurses. It was like trying to get through a bunch of watchdogs in scrubs. I showed them the piece of paper in my hand and I was waved past. Finding room three wasn't hard. My hand shook as I slid the glass door open and stepped inside. I pulled it shut behind me, hoping for a little privacy.

Machines beeped and there was something strapped over her mouth. I couldn't hold back the tears as I looked at her poor, battered face. There were cuts down her arms and peeking out of the top of her hospital gown. I eased down into the chair next to her bed and reached for her hand, holding it gently for fear of hurting her more.

"I'm so fucking sorry," I said. "I never meant to hurt you. I only wanted you to go home."

And that wasn't even entirely true. I'd known it was best for her to go home, but I damn sure hadn't wanted her to leave. Not really. It had been hard not getting up and running after her, holding her tight and kissing her the way I wanted. I'd thought about Janessa way too fucking much over the years, feeling like a sick bastard because of her age. I'd known when she turned eighteen, but no matter how much I'd wanted to go to her, I'd held back. The Devil's Boneyard and Dixie Reapers might have some family connections between the clubs, but it didn't mean that Tex wanted me anywhere near his daughter.

"I need you to wake up, sweetheart. I need you to fight and come back to me. I swear I'll make it up to you," I said, watching her face for any sign that she might be listening.

Someone walked in and I saw a nurse checking the machines.

"She can hear you," the nurse said. "Keep talking and maybe she'll wake up."

I wasn't so sure about that. My voice might just make her want to sleep forever, and after the way I'd treated her, I wouldn't blame her in the slightest. I'd been an asshole, even if I'd thought I was doing it for the right reasons. If that was the last moment we shared, I'd never forgive myself.

"Please, Nessa," I said, my voice hoarse and my throat tight. "Wake up and talk to me. Call me an asshole. Tell me to go to hell. Anything."

"I take it the two of you fought before this happened?" the nurse asked. "We know she was in an accident, then attacked, possibly by whoever caused her to go off the road."

"She was running. From me," I admitted, my heart being ripped in two just acknowledging that. "She never should have been on that road. I pushed her away, broke her heart. If I'd known…"

The nurse gave me a soft smile.

"I wish I could take it back," I said. "If she doesn't wake up, I'll never forgive myself."

"The nurse at the information desk says you claim to be her fiancée. She wasn't wearing a ring when they brought her in," the nurse said, an eyebrow arched like she didn't believe me for a moment.

"I haven't gotten her one yet. The proposal was spur of the moment. She deserves the perfect ring."

The lies were coming easier, but I'd do anything to remain with Janessa.

The nurse still didn't look completely convinced, but she let the matter drop. She looked at the monitors again, checked whatever liquids were going into Janessa's IV, and then she left the room. I didn't know how long I'd have before Tex showed up and kicked my ass. I'd deserve whatever he did to me, and I'd take it. I just hoped I had some time with Janessa before he got here, maybe even see her open her eyes at least once.

The minutes ticked by, but my girl didn't even move, other than the slow rise and fall of her chest. At one point, I started to fall asleep, until blue lights started flashing and an alarm went crazy. I looked at the monitors and couldn't hold back my cry as I saw the screen showing her heartbeat was a straight line.

Nurses and doctors rushed in, pushing me out of the way. One of those carts you see in the movies was rolled in, and I was shoved into the hall, where I slid down the wall and didn't even bother to hold back my tears. I sobbed like a damn baby as they worked on the woman I'd only ever admitted to myself that I loved. The blue light went off and the alarms stopped. Two nurses came out of the room and one stopped in front of me.

"You can see her again," she said.

"Is she…" I couldn't even bring myself to say the word *dead*.

"We were able to bring her back. She's stable for the moment," the nurse said.

I stood and wiped the moisture off my cheeks, then went back into Janessa's room. I reclaimed the chair I'd sat in before, and took her hand again. I talked to her until my voice was hoarse and I didn't know what the hell else to say. Light was coming in through her window, and still no one had shown up. I didn't know what to make of that. It made me wonder if maybe Tex didn't know just yet. Whatever the reason her parents hadn't arrived, I was going to enjoy what time I had with Janessa, and for the first time since I was a kid, I was going to pray really damn hard. I'd pray that she'd wake up, that she'd open her eyes and be okay. Even if she slapped my face when she opened her eyes, I wouldn't care. I just wanted her back, wanted to know she would live. Nothing else mattered.

I talked to Janessa about anything and everything. Well, not quite everything. I left out the women and club business. Even when my throat was sore, I just sipped some coffee and kept talking. Hours passed. At one point, I would have sworn her fingers twitched, but nothing else happened. I waited, hoping she would wake up. I convinced myself I'd imagined it and started talking about my favorite movies and why I liked each one. When I felt her fingers twitch again, I knew it had to be real. I pushed the call button and waited for a nurse.

"Everything all right in here?" a blonde nurse asked as she entered the room.

"Her fingers moved. I thought they had earlier and then figured I was just imagining it, but they just moved again."

She gave me a warm smile and moved closer to check on Janessa. She checked the solutions hanging on the pole, then watched the monitors a moment. Did she think I'd made it up? I knew her fingers had moved! Janessa had to be waking up, didn't she? I refused to believe that she'd never open her eyes again.

"You let me know when you're ready to let other people in here," the nurse said.

Wait. What? "Other people?" I asked.

She nodded. "There's a room full of them. We only allow one or two people in at a time, and since you're her fiancé and were here first, we've let you have as much time with her as you want."

"Her parents... are they here?" I asked, almost dreading the answer.

"Yes, Mr. and Mrs. Rodriguez are among those waiting. There are some men out there with the same emblem on their vests as you, and the others match your fiancée's father. They've been patient, but I'm not sure how much longer I can hold them off."

Shit. If I had known they were out there, I'd have let them come see Janessa before now. I didn't have a clue about the rules at the hospital, much less in ICU. I hoped Tex wasn't ready to kick my ass.

"I'll step out and let someone else come visit with her," I said.

As I made a move to stand, the fingers in my hand twitched and then tightened as they held onto me. My breath stalled in my lungs as I stared at our joined hands, then lifted my gaze to Janessa's face. Her lids fluttered, but she seemed to have trouble opening them all the way.

"Janessa?" I held her hand a little tighter. "Come back to me, sweetheart. Open your eyes."

It felt like it took forever, but eventually her eyes opened and locked with mine. My heart felt like it would pound out of my chest as I stared down at her.

She lifted her other hand and touched the ventilator that was over her mouth.

"Don't, baby. It's been helping you breathe," I said, moving her hand away from the apparatus.

"I'll get someone to come in and remove it," the nurse said. "Her doctor will probably stop in shortly. Now that she's awake, there will be some questions we need answered."

"Janessa, there are other people who want to see you. Your parents are here," I said.

She shook her head and held onto my hand, refusing to let go. More medical staff came in and they managed to remove the tube from her throat. She coughed and gasped, even gagged. Someone gave her some ice chips to soothe the ache.

"Seamus," she said, her voice croaking.

"I'm right here," I assured her.

"Don't leave," she said.

I wouldn't, not if she didn't want me to. I'd sit here and hold her hand all day and all night. If only two people were permitted in the room at a time, they'd just have to deal with me remaining in this chair. Whatever Janessa wanted I'd give to her.

"Well, there's our miracle," a doctor said as he came in and approached the bed. "We lost you for a moment there. Guess this guy gave you a good reason to come back."

Janessa smiled at me, then winced as her lip cracked and started bleeding. I didn't know who had hurt her like this, but if I ever found them, I'd make them pay. How anyone could beat the hell out of someone so sweet was unfathomable. I gave her hand another squeeze, then moved out of the way so the doctor could check her over.

"We're going to leave the monitors in place for now, but we'll lower the dosage on the pain medication you've been receiving," the doctor said. "We don't want you to become addicted, but if you can't handle the pain, let us know and we'll adjust it. The other bag has nutrients that you're going to need if you're going to properly heal."

"She has family in the waiting room," I said. "She doesn't want me to leave, but I was told there's a two-person limit for visitors in the ICU. Is there any way you'd let both her parents come in at the same time?"

"Of course," the doctor said. "I'll make sure the nurses' station is aware of the allowance. There's two small boys out there, though, and I'm sorry but I can't permit them in here. Ages fourteen and up only in the ICU. It's a hospital rule that I can't break."

"Noah and Clayton," Janessa said in her croaky voice.

"Maybe you can make a video on your mom's phone. You can say hi to your brothers and they'll see that you're all right." I winced. "Or maybe it would be better if you just talked to them. The bruising on your face might frighten them."

She reached up to touch her cheek, but I pulled her hand away.

"How bad do I look?" she asked, a tear slipping down her cheek.

"You're beautiful," I assured her.

The medical staff left us alone and I sat in the chair by the bed again. I knew I needed to talk to her, to apologize and find out what the hell had happened on that road. Why had she been heading south and not back home to Alabama? They'd said the doctor needed information, yet he hadn't asked any questions. I wondered why, until a Florida Highway Patrol officer stepped into the room, the doctor right on his heels.

"Miss Rodriguez, I'd like to ask you a few questions," the officer said. "My name is Sanchez. I'm a Florida State Trooper, and I'm the one who found you."

"Thank you," she said.

"Can you tell us why you were on that road by yourself?" he asked.

Janessa looked at me and I gave her a tight smile.

"It's my fault," I said. "I tried to do the right thing, and it backfired in a big way. I know I'm not good enough for Janessa, and I never will be. I thought she'd be better off back home, so I did something to chase her off."

"And what's that?" Sanchez asked.

"I kissed another woman," I admitted, feeling like shit just thinking about the look on Janessa's face yesterday.

Sanchez snorted and muttered something that sounded like "dumbass" before pulling out his pad and pen. I wasn't going to argue with him, not when he was right. I really had been a dumbass, and my stupid move had pushed Janessa to take off on her own, where she'd been ambushed in the dark. If I had just grown some balls and talked to her, then maybe she wouldn't be lying in the ICU right now.

"Miss Rodriguez, do you remember why you ran off the road?" the trooper asked.

"Gator," she said, her voice still raspy. "Saw a gator in the road. Then it was gone."

Sanchez made a note, but there was something in his eyes. He knew something about that gator, and I wanted to know what it was. Had there been a real gator on the road, or a decoy that someone had used to cause Janessa's accident? And why had they done it? If there had been other instances like what happened to Janessa, I wasn't aware of it, which meant it hadn't been leaked to the news channels yet.

"And after that?" he asked.

"Three men. They beat me until I passed out. I woke with my clothes torn, and..." Another tear slipped down her cheek.

"You weren't sexually assaulted," I told her, knowing exactly what she'd been worried about. At least there was one bit of good news I could give her. "The doctors checked."

She took a shaky breath and nodded. The tension in her shoulders eased a bit, and I hated that she'd been scared she'd been violated. They may have kicked the shit out of her and pissed on her, but they hadn't raped her. For that, I would always be grateful. Wouldn't stop me from putting the fuckers six feet under if I ever found them.

"Can you describe the men?" Sanchez asked.

"No. But... they were bikers. I think. They had leather cuts but I couldn't see a club name, or their road names. Just a skull on fire," she said, her voice gaining strength the more she spoke.

My back went ramrod straight at the description of the cuts and I looked at Sanchez. Yeah, he knew what that meant too. It seemed the local clubs weren't the only ones on alert about those assholes. But if law enforcement was watching for them too, that meant the rest of us needed to be careful how we handled the situation. I gave Janessa some more ice chips while the officer scribbled some notes.

"Your truck was off the road. You were found next to it, but there was blood on the roadway. Did they attack you, then drag you into the grass?" Sanchez asked.

"No. They came at me on the street, started hitting me and kicking me, tore my clothes and cut me. I blacked out at some point and woke up long enough to see them walking away. I don't know how long I was unconscious. When I came to, I started dragging myself to the truck, but one of them came back. He hit me in the head and a little bit later I heard some motorcycles start, from the rumble I'd say at least one was a Harley. I managed to drag myself the rest of the way to my truck and got my phone. I dialed 9-1-1 and that's the last thing I remember," Janessa said.

"Thank you for your time, Miss Rodriguez," Sanchez said. "I'll be in touch if we get any leads on the men who attacked you. Until then, please stay in the area in case we have more questions. Your truck was taken to the impound lot, but you can pick it up whenever you leave the hospital. There was some damage, but it should be drivable."

After he walked out, I tried to soothe Janessa the best I could, and I knew I needed to talk to her about what happened at the clubhouse. Preferably before her parents came in, and before a nurse said something about us being engaged. The last thing I needed was her losing her shit in the ICU and getting me kicked out, and her possibly flatlining again. It was the last part that had me the most worried. I'd already lost her once, even if only for a brief moment, but it would haunt me forever.

"Can I talk to you about something before any other visitors come in?" I asked.

"Guess it depends on what you want to say," she said.

"About last night, at the clubhouse. It was an asshole thing to do, and I'm sorry. You have no idea how fucking sorry I am. I thought I was doing the right thing," I said.

She blinked at me, then just stared. It was when her cheeks started to flush that I got a clue she was about to erupt. Maybe I should have held off on the conversation after all. I'd thought apologizing might help, but apparently it was the wrong damn thing to do.

"Kissing some whore was the right thing to do?" she demanded. "If you didn't want to see me, you could have told me to fuck off, Seamus. And yes, I used your fucking name. You might have earned the name Irish with your club, but you haven't earned shit with me."

I shifted on the chair, suddenly uncomfortable that I was getting hard while she was in a hospital bed and slinging curses at my head. Despite everything, seeing that fire inside her did something to me. I liked this version much better than the meek woman who had run off after I'd kissed the blonde, even if I was worried she might get too stressed. If she flatlined again, I didn't think I could handle it. I wished she'd called me on my shit at the clubhouse. I likely would have hauled her off to the nearest empty room and kissed the hell out of her, and she definitely wouldn't have been on that fucking road. Not that what happened to her was her fault, not in the least. If that blame lay anywhere, it was at my feet.

"Your dad will never let us be together, Nessa. You know it and I damn well know it."

"My dad doesn't get a say in my life, Seamus. I'm a grown woman and I can date whoever I want to.

If I want to fuck every guy in your club, then that's my choice."

I stood so fast the chair went flying. "Like fucking hell! Did someone come on to you while you were there last night?"

She squared her jaw and didn't answer, which told me plenty. I didn't know who had talked to her, but I'd find out, then I'd put my fist through their damn face. Brother or not, every last fucker in my club had better stay away from Janessa. Just because I couldn't have her -- *shouldn't* have her -- didn't mean she wasn't mine. Whether I'd wanted to admit it or not, she'd been mine from the day I'd met her.

A nurse came into the room, her lips thinned and her eyes flashing. "If you're going to upset the patient, and the rest of the ICU, I'm going to have to ask you to leave. We let you stay since you're her fiancé, but no more special treatment. Quiet down or leave."

She left as quickly as she'd arrived and I turned to find Janessa gaping at me.

"You're my what?" she asked.

I reached over and shut the sliding door, hoping to give us a little privacy for whatever Janessa was about to say. The last thing I needed was for the hospital to find out I'd lied this entire time. If Janessa threw me out, it was one thing, but I wasn't about to go just because a nurse was in a snit. The rule about only family seeing her was bullshit. No way I would have left her in this place all alone, not with her family two hours away.

"Fiancé," I said.

"They must have beat me worse than I thought. I seem to have forgotten your proposal, unless it was your tongue down the blonde's throat. In which case, I don't accept."

I tipped my head back and stared at the ceiling. I should have known she wouldn't make this easy on me. Not that I deserved any leniency from her. If I'd just admitted how I felt, that I'd loved her all these years even though that was completely insane, then she wouldn't have been hurt. I'd known all this time that screwing around was the wrong thing to do. I knew that plenty of my brothers did the same thing, but I'd taken it to a new level, and I wasn't the least bit proud of myself right now. My past was going to hurt Janessa. Probably made me the biggest asshole in the state, possibly the region. No. There was no contest. I was definitely the biggest asshole in the region.

"What do you want to hear? That I puked like a pussy when I heard you'd been hurt and were in the hospital? That I blame myself for what happened? Or do you want to know that I've thought about you every fucking day for five years, even when it made me a sick fuck because you were just a kid?" I asked. "And no, I didn't think about fucking you back then, but you stayed on my mind just the same. Couldn't escape you no matter how hard I tried. So, yeah, I've screwed around with the club sluts. They've just been a quick release and a distraction. I wanted to go after you when you turned eighteen, but I didn't. I knew Tex would kick my ass if I showed up on his doorstep."

Janessa was quiet as she looked up at me. I didn't see anger etched on her features like I'd expected. Instead, there was a cautious kind of hope. I didn't know which part of my speech had done that, but at least she wasn't screaming at me anymore. I wasn't entirely sure that hope was a good thing, though. I still had to deal with her dad, and he was going to be pissed, especially since he'd been cooling his heels in the waiting room while I was back here with his daughter.

"I'm sorry," I said again. "I never wanted to hurt you, Nessa. I just didn't see a way for us to be together. I thought if I pushed you away, then you'd be mad enough you'd find someone else."

"What about you?" she asked. "Would you find someone else?"

I shrugged. "Honestly? I probably would have continued on the way I have the last five years. But if you're asking if I'd have ever taken an old lady or gotten married? Probably not."

"I don't want anyone else, Seamus. I never have. I waited for you, and when you never came for me, I decided I was going to come to you. I just didn't expect…" She bit her lip. "My mom tried to warn me. She told me that you weren't the same guy I'd met before. She said you were wild now, but I didn't listen. If I'd just stayed home…"

"Hey," I said, reaching for her hand again. "None of this is your fault, baby. Not even a little. You want to blame someone, you blame me. I was an asshole and you ran from me. If I'd handled things differently, then you never would have been on that road."

"Seamus, I…"

"You're grounded until you're ninety," growled a voice behind me. I looked over my shoulder and saw Tex and Kalani.

"Daddy, I'm sorry," Janessa said. "I just wanted to come see Seamus, and I knew you wouldn't let me."

"So, you convinced your mom to let you go," Tex said as he came farther into the room. "Do you have any idea what it did to her knowing that you were hurt? She'd let you leave, and then we get a call that you're in the hospital."

Kalani placed a hand on his arm. "You're going to upset her."

"We should keep her calm," I said. "She already flatlined once."

Janessa gasped. "I did?"

Tex glared at me and I winced. Probably shouldn't have said that, at least not where Janessa could hear me. I had a feeling her daddy-dearest would be having a conversation with me soon, and might possibly use his fists to drive home his point. I didn't think he'd care that I hadn't made him cool his heels in the waiting room on purpose.

"I died?" Janessa asked softly.

"Yeah, sweetheart. You did," I said, taking her hand. "Scared the shit out of me. I was talking to you, trying to get you to wake up, and the next minute you flatlined and a siren went off. When they kicked me out of here, I was scared you weren't coming back."

I felt a hand on my arm and turned to see Kalani standing next to me.

"Thank you for being here for our daughter," she said. "The nurses said you refused to leave her side."

"They also said you're her fucking fiancé," Tex said. "And I know that can't be true, so what the hell is going on? How is it Janessa is lying here if she was with you?"

I knew I had to tell them, that they would find out sooner or later. I only hoped it didn't cause a problem between our clubs. With Tank's sister married to Jackal, and my VP's daughter married to Bull, the last thing we needed was a war starting between us, all because I fucked up. It was my fault, though. I'd almost lost Janessa because I was an idiot. Tex wouldn't care that I was sorry.

"I fucked up," I said.

"Seamus, I told you it wasn't your fault," Janessa said, sounding tired.

I focused on her, giving her hand a slight squeeze. She gave me a small smile, and then her eyes started to close. I felt my heart stop for a second as my gaze jerked to the monitors, scared shitless that I was about to lose her again, but it seemed she was only sleeping.

"You let her call you that?" Tex asked. "You earned the name Irish."

My lips twitched in amusement. "As your daughter pointed out, I may have earned the name Irish with my club, but I haven't earned shit with her and she'll call me whatever the hell she wants. I'm paraphrasing, mostly."

Kalani moved to Janessa's other side and smoothed her hair back. "She never did pull any punches. Once she was secure with the Dixie Reapers, and the threat of the asylum was gone, Janessa got stronger and sassier. I sometimes wish I was half as strong as she is."

Tex went to his wife, pulling her against his side. "You are one of the strongest women I know. Our daughter wouldn't be half as amazing as she is if it weren't for you. And if you hadn't sacrificed yourself, she might not be here at all. I love you and so does Janessa."

Kalani nodded but didn't take her gaze off her daughter.

"Janessa came to see me, but I wasn't expecting her," I said. "I didn't react well, so she ran. If I had handled things differently, she wouldn't have been on that road."

"It's not your fault she showed up out of the blue," Tex said. "As often as she's talked about you, asked if you were coming to the compound, I should have known she would eventually come to the Devils' territory."

"None of us is to blame," Kalani said. "The men who did this to her, that's who we blame. I want them found, and I want them to pay."

"Your wife is right," I said. "Janessa said the men who beat her wore cuts, but she didn't see a name. Only a skull with flames."

Tex started swearing and pacing the small space. Good to know I wasn't the only one alarmed. If the Dixie Reapers and Devil's Boneyard came together, then maybe this could be handled before the Highway Patrol got close enough to ask more questions. Although, the look on the officer's face told me that they might already know quite a bit.

Chapter Three

Janessa

It took three days before they moved me from ICU to a regular hospital room, but I still felt like I wasn't any closer to going home. I'd been here another two days since then, but the doctor wanted to keep me a little longer. Not that the police wanted me to leave the area even when I was released from this horrid place.

That wasn't entirely fair. The nurses and doctors had been great, but I was a lousy patient. Ever since the asylum, I hadn't done well being in places like this. I wasn't chained to the bed, and no one was hurting me, but it didn't stop me from remembering. Every time I drifted to sleep and woke up alone, my heart raced and I had this sudden fear that I was locked away again. My mom had been diagnosed with PTSD after we'd been rescued, but times like this made me wonder if I didn't have it too.

My parents had been taking turns sitting with me until I'd chased them both off. I loved them, but they were driving me crazy. I hadn't had any alone time with Seamus since being moved from the ICU. As soon as my parents left the room together, Seamus claimed the chair next to my bed. He didn't say anything yet, and the contemplative look on his face didn't tell me much. I reached for him and he grasped my hand, but there was a distance in his eyes that hadn't been there when I'd first woken in the ICU. It was like the Seamus who had poured his heart out to me had vanished once my parents entered the room. I wanted him back, but I didn't know how to make that happen.

"Seamus, what's wrong?" I asked, unable to take the pensive silence another moment.

"I'm surprised your parents left you alone with me. I don't think your dad is too happy right now. I'd go so far as to say that if we weren't in this hospital, he'd have tried to remove my balls already for daring to hurt his baby girl. Can't say that I blame him."

"Would you stop blaming yourself?" I asked.

"You can do so much better than me, Nessa. Why didn't you go to college? You could have met some nice guy, someone educated. I've fought hard to get where I am, but there's blood on my hands, baby."

"Do you think my dad's hands are any cleaner, Seamus? Or anyone else with the Dixie Reapers? They're my family, and I know they keep me safe. Just like you would keep me safe."

He smiled faintly. "I'm glad you have that much faith in me."

"Seamus, I… I know you think I'm too young, but I've known for five years you were the one I wanted. That hasn't changed. It hurt, seeing you with that blonde, and it hurts even more knowing there were others. A lot of others. I won't lie and say it doesn't bother me because it does."

"I know, and I'm so damn sorry, Nessa. If I could take it all back, I would. I didn't think I ever had a shot with you."

"So, what happens now?" I asked.

He laced his fingers with mine, then leaned over and gently kissed me. His lips were soft, yet firm as they brushed against mine, and I heard the heart monitor go crazy as my heart started racing. He chuckled softly and pulled back.

"Guess I shouldn't do that again until you're out of the hospital," he said.

"But you do want to do it again?"

"Oh, yeah. I could kiss you all day long."

I bit my lip, wondering if he'd think I was a bitch for saying what was about to come out of my mouth, but all things considered… "Seamus, I don't want you to be offended, but considering your past, if we're going to explore this more, I'd really like for you to get tested."

He sat back, the smile wiped from his face. "That's a fair enough thing to ask. I only wish you didn't feel it was necessary, but I understand. For the record, I've never been with a woman without a condom."

"I'm sorry for asking you to get tested, but I'd feel better if you did. I think we all know that condoms aren't foolproof. Neither is the pill from what I've heard. There's no guaranteed way to prevent pregnancy except not having sex. And while I'm sure the condoms kept you safe enough, what if they didn't? Are you willing to chance it?"

What I was really asking was if he was willing to risk him carrying something and passing it to me, but I didn't want to put it quite that way. I didn't want to be a complete bitch about it, but I seriously was concerned. If he'd been with that many women, and they looked as skanky as the ones at the clubhouse the night I'd gotten in town, then I definitely wanted to make sure he hadn't contracted something. I wanted to be with Seamus, but I also wanted to know for certain that it was safe for us to be together. If that made me mean, then so be it.

"If that's what you want, then I'll run over to the clinic after your parents get back. I'm sure those tests take a few days or more to get results back."

"You don't hate me for asking?"

He leaned over and kissed me again, briefly. "No, I don't hate you, Nessa. It's smart for me to get tested. I know a lot of the guys make it a regular thing every six months."

"Maybe I should have one done too," I said.

"You're a virgin, aren't you?" he asked.

"Yes, but…" I looked at the healing wounds on my arms and thought about those men and what they'd done to me. "What if they infected me with something? They urinated on me, and who knows how clean their knives were?"

"I'll ask your doctor if he already ran some tests. Try not to worry about it, baby. You're already stressed enough without adding more to it."

"You're going to come back, aren't you?" I asked.

"Your parents would probably like some alone time with you. There are some things I should take care of, but I'll come back tomorrow morning. I also want to check in with Cinder and Scratch, see if they have any leads on who did this to you. The police don't seem to have anything concrete and I want these bastards caught and punished. You know how the law works. They need hard evidence to make a move, and right now it's just your word against theirs."

"Be safe, Seamus. I don't want to lose you," I said.

"Baby, I'm not going anywhere. If you're sure I'm who you want, then not even your daddy will get in my way. I won't let him, or anyone else. You're the only woman I want, Nessa. I should have come to you sooner, and I'm damn sorry I didn't."

I reached up and placed my hand on his cheek. He didn't have a full beard, but his whiskers scraped my palm. I had to admit I kind of liked him looking all rough and rumpled. He'd run his hand through his hair a million times, and it stuck out here and there. But it was his eyes that drew me in the most. Those eyes had haunted me for years, and they were no less potent now.

I wanted to tell him that I loved him, that he was the only man I'd ever wanted. I wanted to beg him to let me stay, to make me his in every way that mattered. Instead, I just looked into those mesmerizing eyes and smiled softly at him. If he said he'd come back, then I'd have to trust he'd be back. Yes, he'd hurt me, but part of loving someone was forgiving them. Although, if we were truly going to be together, the next time one of those sluts dared to touch him, I might have to kick a little ass and show those bitches they shouldn't mess with the daughter of a Reaper and the old lady of a Devil.

I could hear my mom and dad coming down the hall and I tugged Seamus closer, pressing my lips to his again. "Come back to me," I said.

"You're going to have a hard time getting rid of me." He smiled and stood as my parents walked in.

Dad gave him the death stare, but Seamus just gave my parents a wave and stepped out into the hall. After the door shut behind him, my dad approached the bed. The harsh look he'd given Seamus melted away as he came closer. Dad might not have been part of my life until I was fourteen, but he'd made up for lost time, and I had no doubt that he loved me. Unfortunately, he sometimes showed that love by being overprotective.

"Daddy, you know I love you, right?" I asked.

"Yeah, baby girl. I know you love me."

"Then remember that I say this with love. Back off! You know how I feel about Seamus and all the dark looks you're throwing his way aren't going to do anything but make my life more difficult."

Kalani patted his arm. "She's all grown up, Houston. We can't keep her locked away forever. You knew that sooner or later she'd want to live her own life."

I wasn't sure what surprised me more. My mom using my dad's real name, since she usually called him Tex like everyone else, or the fact she was agreeing with me. I'd had to fight her just to get this far, and now she was siding with me? After the incident on the road, I'd thought they'd both try to put me on lockdown for the next twenty years.

"I was hoping she'd be more like twenty-five when she decided to go after a guy," my dad said.

"I love you, Daddy, but since when has a Reaper or a Devil ever settled with a woman that old? Face it. You bikers like the young ones, which means I'm at the perfect age for Seamus."

He snorted, but I noticed he didn't argue with me. He couldn't because he knew I was telling the truth. Even Mom hadn't been much older than I was now when Dad had married her. Didn't mean he had to like that I was right, but the sooner he realized I was all grown up and not just his little girl, the better. At least, it was better for me. I would always be a daddy's girl, but I was ready to start my life, have a home of my own, and a man I could love -- and I knew the guy I wanted was Seamus. It had always been Seamus. "When they release me from the hospital, I'm not going home with you," I said.

"Now wait one damn minute --" Dad was about to really get wound up, but Mom made him shut up.

"Let her speak," Mom said. "And for once, actually listen to what she has to say instead of trying to steamroll her."

"Fine," Dad muttered.

"I've known for five years that Seamus was the only guy I wanted. I want to see if we can make things work, and for that to happen, I need to be here. Besides, the police would like me to stay nearby in case they think of more questions or need to me to identify any suspects." I reached out and took my dad's hand. "I love you, Daddy. You and Mom, but I'm suffocating at the compound. Please understand that it's time for me to leave the nest."

"If he hurts you, I'll tear him to pieces," my dad said.

"And he's well aware of that," I said. "The only reason he didn't come for me sooner is because of you, Daddy. He was worried you wouldn't approve of him, that you didn't think he was worthy of me."

"He's not," Dad said.

"And who is?" I asked.

My dad just shrugged, which told me enough. My mom sighed and hip-checked him so he'd move out of the way, then she leaned over and kissed my forehead.

"You will always be our baby girl," she said. "But I understand that you're ready to grow up. We love you, and you will always have a place in our home. If things don't work out with Seamus, then you come back to us. We'll leave your room just the way it is for right now."

"Love you too. Both of you."

A nurse poked her head through the doorway and smiled brightly. "Miss Rodriguez, your fiancé said you had some questions. I thought I'd see if I could answer them, and if not, I'll page your doctor."

I glanced at my parents before facing the nurse again. They might not want to hear what I was about to ask, but I couldn't wait around for them to leave the room again. Besides, knowing my dad, it had already crossed his mind.

"I know what happened to me, and I was wondering if the doctors ran any tests to see if those men passed any diseases along to me? I mean, their knives could have been dirty, and I was told they urinated on me after I'd been cut. I can only imagine what types of things they could have given me."

The nurse gave me a sympathetic smile. "Of course, you'd be worried about something like that. The doctors did request some tests, and they've all come back negative. You're a very lucky young lady, even if you don't feel like it right now."

"Thank you," I said.

My dad stomped out of the room and Mom just shook her head as she watched him. I had a feeling if we'd been at home, he'd have put his fist through a wall. Dad didn't lose his temper often, and when he did, he never took it out on us, but he'd been known to put a hole or two in the sheetrock. He always patched it the next day and apologized to Mom. I think he worried about scaring her, even though he'd treated her like a queen since the day he'd found her.

"So you're going to stay here," Mom said after we were alone again. "Does that mean you're going to stay with Irish?"

"Yes. I think we've come to an understanding of sorts. It doesn't mean he's claiming me right now, even though I'd agree if that's what he wanted to do. I'm hoping we'll get some alone time so we have a chance to figure out whether or not there's an us. Like everyone keeps pointing out, it's been five years, and we didn't know each other all that well back then. We need the time and space to explore things a little and see if we're a good fit."

Mom smiled faintly. "That's a very adult thing to say. I'm proud of you, Janessa. I know I was against you running off and coming here, and it hurts knowing you were attacked, but maybe this is what you need right now. Best case, you discover that he's everything you've dreamed about and the two of you become a couple. Worst case, you find out you aren't well-matched and you come home, and this time you can look at the guys around you with open eyes."

"You just want me to hook up with a Dixie Reaper so I'll be close to home. The only one I don't consider an uncle is Saint, and he's more like a brother than a boyfriend. Sorry, Mom. You're just going to have to deal with the fact I won't be living at the compound all my life."

"You know I love you and just want what's best for you. If you think that's Irish, then I hope you're right. Your happiness means a lot to me," Mom said.

"You're the best mom ever, you know that, right? You didn't have to protect me at the asylum, you didn't have to treat me like your daughter when you married my dad, but you've always made sure I was cared for and loved. I don't care if we don't share the same blood. You're the only mother I remember, and the only one I want."

My mom sniffled, and I saw her eyes start to fill with tears. She gave me a smile and squeezed my hand. "I couldn't love you more if I'd given birth to you, Janessa. You're a gift that I'm thankful for every day. I'll miss you if you decide not to come home."

I gave her a sly look. "You know, you're not that old. At twenty-seven, you could easily have another baby. Maybe two. I don't think Dad would argue if you said you wanted more kids. The two of you are awesome parents, even if Dad can be overbearing at times. Besides, Noah and Clayton could use a little brother or sister."

"Noah was a miracle. Your dad and I discussed it and decided that it would be better if we didn't have more kids, then Clayton came along as a complete surprise. Your dad hasn't advertised it, but he had a vasectomy after Clayton. He'd talked about getting one after Noah, but he missed his appointment. My pregnancy with Clayton was rough, and the doctor said it would be best if we didn't have more babies."

"I'm sorry, Mom. I had no idea. I'd thought you just didn't want more right now."

She sat in the chair next to the bed and reached for my hand again. "The three of you are a blessing to me. As much as I would love a houseful of kids, it just wasn't meant to be. Besides, keeping up with Noah and Clayton is a full-time job."

"Speaking of... where are they? You and Dad have been here almost twenty-four hours a day since I woke up in ICU. Who's taking care of my brothers?" I asked.

"Scratch and Clarity offered. The boys have been having fun with their two sons. Noah is thrilled someone else has his name."

"How weird is that?" I asked. "It's not like Scratch didn't know about Noah. Did he just like the name or something?"

"From what Clarity said, they had planned to call him Nolen but somewhere between the labor and delivery, when the forms were filled out, Noah was put on his birth certificate so they just went with it. He's a cutie," Kalani said.

"Hard to believe that it wasn't all that long ago none of the bikers we know had kids, and now it seems they're popping up everywhere."

Mom arched a brow at me. "And if you and Irish hit it off, you'd better use double protection or you'll be next on the list of mommies. If the Devil's Boneyard men are half as potent as the Reapers, you'll be knocked up if he just gives you a certain look."

I snickered but knew she wasn't wrong. At nineteen, I wasn't ready for kids yet. I loved my brothers, and I'd babysat them plenty, and it had proven to me that I needed a little more time before I had one of my own. But I definitely wanted children someday. I figured Seamus would prefer not to use condoms -- didn't most guys? -- but we hadn't discussed whether or not I'd be on birth control. Even though I was a virgin, I'd been on the pill for four years. When I'd turned fifteen, my periods had been so heavy and painful, Mom had asked Dr. Myron if there was something that could help.

My brow furrowed as I realized I hadn't been taking them since I'd been in the hospital. I'd packed them, but they were probably in my bag, wherever that was. I knew my truck had been impounded so it was possible my bag was still in the truck. I didn't know what length of recovery I would have before Seamus and I could be intimate, but I should probably talk to the doctor before I was checked out, whenever that would be. The last thing I needed was a surprise pregnancy.

I didn't think Seamus would be too thrilled over having a baby right away either. We hadn't really discussed children, but after he'd been kicking up his heels the last five years, I didn't think he wanted diaper duty our first year together. If we even decided we had a future. As much as I thought I loved the man, maybe living with him would make me change my mind. Maybe I'd built him up in my head to be something he wasn't, or maybe we just wouldn't mesh well at all and would fight constantly.

I was trying to look at this logically, even though I wanted to throw myself into his arms and beg him to never let me go. I hadn't done a single impulsive thing in my life, until I'd come here uninvited, and look how that had turned out. No, I needed to keep my head on straight and not rush into something. If life had taught me anything, it was that making a rash decision could have bad consequences. Not that I was sorry my dad had knocked up my mom, because I was really grateful to be alive, but my grandparents had tried to ruin my dad's life and had damn near ruined mine, all because of two impetuous kids rushing into something.

Whenever I got out of this hospital, I'd go with Seamus and we'd talk and get to know one another, as adults this time. I'd just have to remind my surging hormones that I needed to go slow. It wouldn't be easy, especially since his kisses were so damn addictive. Already, I was looking forward to the next time I could feel his lips on mine. And if that felt sinful, I could only imagine how wonderful the rest would be. I had a feeling it wasn't going to be easy moving slowly with Seamus. If I fucked this up, my parents would never let me hear the end of it.

Chapter Four

Irish

The last few days, I'd rushed to get things ready for Janessa to come home with me. The hospital was finally releasing her. She'd been in ICU for several days, then in a regular room another four. Her bruises were starting to fade, and her cuts were scabbed over and nearly healed, except the few that had required stitches, but even the sutures had been removed from those. The doctor had cautioned me about her bruised ribs, but had said that intimacy wasn't out of the question if we were careful. My heart had started racing at the thought of having Janessa in my bed. I didn't want her to feel rushed, though, not after we'd been apart for the past five years. We were pretty much strangers, even if she had starred in my dreams for so damn long. Innocent ones at first, then after I'd realized she was legal, the dreams had shifted and I'd stopped thinking about her as a kid.

Which was probably why I found myself in the shower, the hot water beating down on me as I gripped my cock. Just thinking about Janessa made me hard. I braced a hand against the tiled wall and closed my eyes, wishing it was her hand on me. I stroked the shaft, long hard pulls, and imagine what she'd look like on her knees, her big eyes staring up at me. I groaned as I pictured her with pre-cum painting her lips before she sucked me. It only took a few more tugs before I was coming, jets of cum painting the shower wall, and even then I wasn't satisfied.

My breathing was labored and I stared at my cock in frustration, since I was still mostly hard. It wasn't the first time I'd jerked off since reconnecting with Janessa, and I doubted it would be the last. I didn't kid myself and knew that she would need time to recover. The last thing she needed was me bending her over every surface in the house the second we walked through the door, even if that thought had been fueling my fantasies the last few days.

I got out and dried off, wiping the steam from the mirror. I hoped she'd be happy here, that she'd like our new home. When the new compound had opened and everyone had moved from our previous location, Cinder had given each patched member the option to have a house inside the gates. Scratch still kept his Victorian in town, and Jackal seemed content with the home he shared with his family. Everyone else had opted to have a house built, including me.

I hadn't seen myself settling down at the time, and now I regretted it. I'd asked for a small two-bedroom, but if things worked with Janessa and we had kids someday, then we might need more room. Which was part of what I'd been working on while she was waiting to be released. I knew we'd want more space, something that we could make into a real home. A house that Janessa would be proud to call her own.

Cinder and Scratch had agreed that if I was seriously thinking about taking an old lady that I would need something bigger. They'd offered me a different home and said they'd have my current one remodeled for someone else to use later, unless anyone wanted to claim it as is. I knew there were a few brothers who swore they'd never have kids. I'd had the Prospects move my shit from my house over to a new location. There had been a vacant four-bedroom farther down the road from the clubhouse, but now I had a lot of empty rooms. I'd wanted everything to be perfect when I brought Janessa home, but it wasn't meant to be. At least I had my bedroom and living room furnished, and I'd already put all my bathroom shit in here.

I glanced at the counter and saw the razor I seldom used, my comb, and the few other products I used. Janessa had liked the cologne I'd worn back when we'd met, and I'd never been able to change after that. I'd kept wearing it, if only because I knew she'd liked it. I'd caught her sniffing me a few times since we'd reconnected, so it seemed she still liked the scent.

I had a true bachelor pad before this house. I didn't even own fucking plates, or I hadn't until now. Not only had my furniture and few possessions been moved to the new house, but I'd also gone shopping and bought the essentials, like cookware, plates, and other kitchen shit. I'd also picked up some new towels and bought some girly scented crap for Janessa. I'd remembered she smelled like cherry blossoms before and picked a few things in that scent, hoping she still liked it.

Clarity and Josie had made some suggestions on stocking my fridge and pantry. I probably should have just asked Kalani, but I wasn't sure how she and Tex felt about their daughter staying with me. Well, I knew how Tex felt. He was fucking pissed about it, but by some miracle, Kalani had convinced him to let Janessa live her own life.

There was no way in fucking hell I was putting Janessa on the back of my bike, not right now. I'd already arranged to use one of the club vehicles until we had her truck out of the impound. Tex hadn't been able to pull the truck, something about Janessa having to sign off since her name was on the registration, which meant they hadn't allowed anything to be removed from the vehicle either. I'd need to make room in the dresser for when she did have her things.

Just the thought of whether or not she wore cotton or lace had me groaning and looking down at my wayward cock. Fuck if the thought of her wearing barely there scraps of cloth didn't make me hard as a fucking post again. I glanced at my phone on the counter and saw that I was about ten minutes ahead of schedule, which meant I had just enough time to attempt exorcising the demons before I saw Janessa.

I dropped my towel and reached for the lube I kept in the bathroom, then slicked my shaft with the cool gel. My hand didn't feel anywhere near as good as I imagined Janessa's would, or her mouth. I stroked faster, my grip a little harder as I chased another orgasm, but I knew it probably wouldn't be enough. Since seeing her again, nothing was as good as the real thing would be. I groaned as I came, my dick twitching in my hand. It took me a few minutes to clean up myself and the bathroom, then I finished getting ready and left to get my woman.

The black SUV was comfortable enough, but I hated riding around inside a vehicle. I much preferred the wind in my hair and the thrum of my bike between my legs. But for Janessa, I'd suffer through the torture of being in a metal box on wheels. When I got to the hospital, I parked at the curb near the door and waited. Tex had assured me he'd get Janessa down to the car. He'd convinced Kalani to hang out with Clarity and the kids. I hoped like hell he didn't plan to follow me home. I didn't want him hanging over us like a dark cloud when Janessa saw the house for the first time.

Tex wheeled Janessa out of the hospital, and I jumped out of the SUV. I pulled open the passenger door, then stood back as Tex lifted his daughter into the vehicle. He buckled her in like she was still a little girl, then gave her a kiss on the forehead. When he backed away and shut the door, he turned to face me. I could see the uncertainty in his eyes, as well as the promise he'd fucking kill me if I hurt his daughter. I could respect that. He stared at me a moment, but didn't say a word, then he turned and walked off.

I blew out a breath and got behind the wheel of the SUV. Janessa gazed at me with a smile curving her lips. I reached over and took her hand, then lifted it to kiss the backs of her fingers.

"Alone at last," I said.

"I love my parents, but I'm glad they're giving us some space."

"How much space, exactly?" I asked.

She shrugged. "I think they're staying in town for at least a few days. Noah and Clayton were having fun playing with Scratch's kids. Honestly, I think this is the first time Mom and Dad have been away from the compound overnight since Clayton was born."

"About my house…"

"What about it?" she asked.

"I just moved so I don't have all my rooms furnished yet. It's kind of bare. Didn't want you to be disappointed when you see it. I have all the important shit like towels and kitchen stuff."

"Seamus, I don't care about that stuff. I just want to be with you."

"I, um, only have one bedroom set up. You can take the bed and I'll sleep on the couch."

I could feel her staring at me as I drove toward the compound. I didn't know if she was pissed that I said I would sleep on the couch, or if she just didn't know what to make of the entire situation. The quiet was a little disconcerting, but I was clueless as to what to fucking say. I wasn't used to driving around with a woman. I'd never allowed one on the back of my bike, and I'd sure as hell not been in a closed vehicle with one. Not in a long-ass time anyway.

At the compound, Killian opened the gates and waved us through. I'd have to talk to Cinder about tightening security with Janessa at my place. Jordan lived here with Havoc, but she could also take care of herself pretty damn well. It wasn't often that Clarity or Josie stopped by, but I knew they got together around town all the time. We hadn't had a woman visit the new compound before, especially an unclaimed one, except the club sluts. If the assholes who hurt my woman found out she was still alive and might be able to ID them, I had no doubt they'd come for her. I didn't like the thought of the Prospects not checking to see who they were letting into the compound. Yeah, I was in a vehicle owned by the club, but it wasn't unique. What if someone driving an SUV just like it had pulled through the gates instead of me?

I didn't kid myself. I was low on the totem pole, but I was sure that Cinder would agree that Janessa needed to be protected at all costs. I hadn't made her my old lady yet, but it was a possibility, and she was a Reaper's daughter. We had a truce with that club, along with a few others, and if Janessa got injured on our watch there would be hell to pay. Even if I never made anything official, she was mine. Would always be mine. Whether she agreed to be mine permanently or not, she was the only woman I'd ever consider my property.

I pulled to a stop in front of my new house and tried to judge Janessa's expression to see what she thought. The woman wasn't easy to read at all. She got out of the car, whimpering a little and clutching her ribs. I cursed and went after her.

"You couldn't wait for me to help you out of the car?" I asked.

"I'm not an invalid, Seamus."

"You have bruised ribs and you're still healing. You aren't an invalid, but you also aren't at full strength. Everyone needs help sometimes, Nessa."

She sighed and looked from me to the house again. Without waiting for help, because she was apparently a stubborn-ass mule, she let herself inside, then wandered from room to room. I shut the front door and twisted the lock, not wanting any surprises. I waited in the front entry, thinking Janessa would come back this way when she'd finished looking around. I was wrong. I heaved a sigh and went in search of her, smiling a little when I saw her stretched out on the bed. She'd obviously found my clothes since she'd pulled on a T-shirt and didn't seem to have anything under it. She was more beautiful than I'd imagined, and I'd imagined plenty over the past year.

"I see you found something to wear," I said.

She cracked an eye open and looked at me. "After wearing that horrid hospital gown for so long, I was ready for something comfortable. It was nice of the hospital to let me have a pair of scrubs since the police kept my clothes as evidence, but they felt weird."

"I'm surprised you didn't go straight for the shower."

"Are you saying I smell?"

I opened and shut my mouth. Well, I'd stepped in it that time.

"No, you don't stink, Nessa. I just figured you'd want to relax and maybe smell like something other than antibacterial soap."

"I think I want a nap," she said. "Are you okay with that?"

I eased onto the edge of the bed and smoothed her hair back from her face. "Baby, you can do whatever you want. As far as I'm concerned, this is just as much your home as it is mine."

"Really?" she asked, rolling onto her side.

My gaze dropped to her breasts, and maybe I was an asshole for noticing the way they moved under her shirt. I tried not to be a complete dick and stare, but my cock was already getting hard. Jesus Christ. It was going to kill me, knowing she was here in my bed and I would be out on the couch.

"Seamus," she said softly.

"Sorry." My voice didn't sound quite right and I forced myself to stand up, then immediately wished I hadn't. It was difficult to hide how hard I'd gotten and the last thing I wanted to do was scare Nessa.

"Wait." She reached out and wrapped her fingers around my wrist.

"I can't be here right now, Nessa. You haven't been in my house for even an hour and already I'm…" I stopped and took a breath. "You need to heal, sweetheart. The last thing you need is me getting hard every time I look your way."

"Do you know how flattering it is that you want me that much?" she asked. "Maybe some women would be offended, and if it were any other guy I'd probably feel the same, but I want you, Seamus, just as much as you want me."

I closed my eyes, trying to get my dick under control. Then I heard the bed creak as she got up and felt her fingers slide against my cheek. I felt like I was in high school. My cock got so fucking hard it was painful. She slid her hand down my neck and kept going until she reached my belt buckle. I sucked in a breath and my heart started pounding. I'd always thought if this moment happened, I would be the one seducing her, not the other way around.

"Nessa, what are you doing?"

"I think we should get it out of the way," she said.

"Get what out of the way?"

"Seeing each other naked."

I blinked and stared down at her. Did she just... "Nessa, did they give you pain medication before you left the hospital?"

"I have to be drugged to want to see you naked?"

"Um... babe... I don't want you to take this the wrong way, but you stripping me naked right now seems out of character. I know we haven't seen each other in five years, but Scratch is always telling me how sweet you are. Sweet and innocent were, I believe, his exact words. So, no, I don't think you have to be drugged to want to see me sans apparel, but the timing is a little strange."

She reached down and grabbed the hem of her top and yanked it over her head. Her breasts bounced free and I swallowed so damn hard it echoed in the room. My gaze scanned the rest of her body and my brain short-circuited. It wasn't like I'd never seen a naked woman before. Hell, I'd probably seen a hundred or more of them in my lifetime, but none of them were Nessa. She was perfection, and *mine!*

With a wink and a flirty smile, she turned and walked off, straight into the bathroom. I'd only taken two steps when she slammed the door shut, and I heard the lock click. Mother. Fucker. That little tease had wound me up, then shut me down. I grinned as I stared at the closed door and shook my head. Yeah, little Janessa Rodriguez was going to keep me on my damn toes, and I had a feeling I'd love every second of it.

I chuckled as I left the bedroom, pulling the door mostly shut behind me. If she needed something and called out, I wanted to hear her, but I also wanted to give her some semblance of privacy when she came out of the bathroom. Even if she'd stripped in front of me, I didn't think she normally would parade around naked in front of a guy. It didn't mesh with what little Scratch had told me over the years.

While she showered, I went to the kitchen and pulled out a box of macaroni from the pantry and some ground beef from the fridge. I set the noodles to boiling as I browned the meat, adding some salt and pepper. After I'd drained the meat and noodles, I turned on the oven and let it warm. Then I grabbed one of the foiled baking dishes I'd picked up, and mixed the noodles and ground beef before tossing in three different shredded cheeses and some Velveeta. I let the dish bake and prowled the house, making a mental note of the things I still needed to buy before this place would even somewhat resemble a home and not an empty house.

It really did look rather pathetic. I wondered what Janessa had thought when she'd walked through all the empty rooms. Did she see the potential in this big house, or was she disappointed in how little I owned? I'd never given a shit what a woman thought, and maybe it made me a pussy to worry about it now, but Janessa wasn't just any woman. She was the one I wanted next to me the rest of my life, if I could get over the hurdle of her dad.

By the time Janessa appeared again -- wearing a different one of my shirts and hopefully some panties -- I was pulling the dish from the oven and plating our food. Steam rose from the gooey goodness and the kitchen smelled pretty awesome. I'd run across some simple recipes online one night when I was bored as shit, and I'd actually pulled off a few. Like this one. I set the plates on the table, then grabbed some forks and got two sodas out of the fridge.

"Hope you're hungry," I said.

"For food that didn't come from a hospital cafeteria? I'm starved!"

"It's one of the few things I know how to make. Mostly I just microwave shit when I get hungry, or I eat at the clubhouse or the diner in town."

"How old are you, Seamus?"

"Thirty-two." I stopped and stared at her. "Why?"

She snickered a little. "You made it to the age of thirty-two, and you can only cook a few things? Do you have no survival skills?"

"Are you laughing at me?" I asked with some amusement.

"Maybe a little," she said, holding her thumb and forefinger a few centimeters apart. "I don't mind cooking. I sometimes even enjoy it."

"Your mom teach you to cook?" I asked.

She set her fork down, her gaze dropping to the table. What the fuck did I say wrong? I'd always thought moms taught their kids to cook. My mother hadn't bothered with that sort of thing, and the last time I'd seen her was a long fucking time ago, but surely some moms did that shit.

"Mom was in the asylum the first twenty-two years of her life. Dad did most of the cooking, even though Mom started to learn after a while. She still doesn't cook as much as Dad does, but I think he likes taking care of her."

"Fuck. I'm sorry, Nessa. I wasn't thinking. I sometimes forget that psycho doctor was after her when we first met. She doing okay now? She seemed happy. I know she was worried about you, but I could still tell that she seemed content with her life."

"She's good." Nessa smiled. "Dad dotes on her. I found out recently that the reason they've only had the two boys is that she can't have more kids. The doctor said it would be dangerous for her, so Dad got snipped. I can't help but think they'd have had a houseful. Mom's the best mother I could have ever asked for."

"Well… that's more than I needed to know about Tex, but I'm glad you had an awesome mother."

Nessa laughed and started eating again.

"When we're done here, maybe we can watch a movie. I'm sure you're supposed to take it easy for a while," I said.

"My doctor said you spoke to him." She gave me a coy smile. "Something about whether or not it was all right to be intimate?"

Shit. "Um, I wasn't expecting anything to happen, but if things progressed that far I wanted to make sure it was safe. And my tests came back fine, so I'm clean."

I tried not to wince at how ridiculous that sounded. With my reputation, which was definitely deserved, I wouldn't blame her if she got up and walked the fuck out. If she'd known all this time I spoke to her doctor about that, I wasn't entirely certain why she was even here. Shouldn't she have told her dad? I knew she hadn't, or Tex would have cut off my balls by now. Yeah, we'd talked about being intimate, but I hadn't expected her to just walk into the house and strip.

I wasn't scared of much, and honestly the Reaper didn't frighten me. He wasn't that much older than me, which was probably part of his problem with me being with Janessa. That and the fact I'd screwed anyone in a skirt for the last five years. I was lucky Janessa was willing to give me a chance, and I really didn't want to fuck it up.

"I'm fucking with you, Seamus," she said.

I wasn't sure what to make of her. She was so different from the girl I'd met before, and yet when I looked into her eyes, I still saw that young Nessa who had been cute and flirty despite the big age gap between us. The grown-up version was saucy and sexy as hell. If I hadn't been captivated by her before, I sure as fuck was now.

"We can watch a movie," she said. "I'll even let you pick, seeing as it's your TV and all."

"Very considerate of you."

"I'm thoughtful like that."

I just shook my head and cleared the table. I cleaned up the kitchen and led Nessa into the living room. She cuddled against my side on the couch, and I flipped through the channels until I found something I thought we might both like. At first I thought it was an accident when she brushed against my thigh, but then it happened again. When her fingers slipped dangerously close to my cock, I glanced her way. She was staring at the TV, but the look in her eyes said the movie wasn't on her mind, unless it had switched to a porno without me noticing.

I let her play her games, trying to act like I didn't notice. Another twenty minutes passed when her head rested against my shoulder and the hand on my thigh went lax. Her breathing was deep and even, and her eyes had closed. I contemplated moving her to the bed or leaving her alone. As she shifted against me, I realized she wasn't comfortable, so I shut off the movie and carried Janessa to the bedroom. The temptation of lying down with her was too great.

I toed off my boots, removed my belt and my cut, then stared at my jeans and hesitated. After a moment of arguing with myself, I kicked them off and slid into bed with just my boxer briefs on. I lay down next to her, trying to relax. She immediately curled against me, and I held her close. In all the years I'd been fucking women, I couldn't remember a single damn time I'd just held one all night and slept beside her. It seemed right that my first time should be with Janessa.

I breathed in her scent and closed my eyes, feeling content and happy for the first time I could ever remember. Other than my brothers, I hadn't trusted anyone in a long time. Maybe not ever. Well, not since I discovered that even parents would screw their kid over if it benefited them in some way. All little kids were trusting, until you gave them a reason not to be. The grown-up me, however, hadn't trusted anyone but the men I knew had my back. And now Janessa.

I only hoped it didn't all blow up in my face.

Chapter Five

Janessa

Waking up with Seamus wrapped around me was a pleasant surprise. The feel of his hard cock brought heat to my cheeks, but it also made me wetter than I'd ever been before. I'd never seen a naked man in person, not even living at the compound. With so many of the Reapers settling down and becoming family men, things had been curtailed from what I'd gathered. I once overheard a conversation between Flicker and Tempest, talking about the good ol' days when nudity was more the norm than family barbeques. I'd mentioned it to my dad and he said they were just jealous they didn't have beautiful wives like my mom, or awesome kids like me and my brothers. With Flicker, I could see that as being true, not so much for Tempest. He was as wild as they came.

It made me think of what my mom had said about Seamus, that he'd gone wild. He'd admitted to having been with a lot of women, and I wasn't sure how I felt about that. It wasn't like we'd had an agreement of any sort, and I'd been a kid until the past year. Didn't make it hurt any less, though. In my mind and in my heart, I'd been his and he'd been mine.

Seamus had said a lot of things during my hospital stay, made me believe he was ready for a commitment. What if he'd just felt guilty, though? It would explain why he hadn't touched me. Other than a few kisses while I was bedridden, he hadn't made a move. I suppose he could just be giving me time to heal, like he'd claimed, but part of me had to wonder if that's all it was. I wanted him, wanted to know what it felt like to be well and truly loved by someone. Was he running scared? Or had he changed his mind about us now that I was under his roof?

I tried to roll over and faced Seamus, but he had an iron grip on me. I felt him nuzzle my neck and I wiggled against him. He pressed his cock tighter against me, and I wondered for a moment if he was awake and just fucking with me. When he mumbled something and ground against me, I decided he was still sleeping. The way he'd acted yesterday, I had no doubt that if he were awake, he'd have put some distance between us by now. It was fun to tease him and get him wound up, but what I really wanted was for him to take charge and tell me what he wanted. I didn't much care for the Seamus who seemed afraid he would hurt me. Yes, I'd had the hell beat out of me and had been hospitalized for about a week, but I was home and I was healthy. My ribs were still bruised and tender, but my cuts were nearly healed. The areas that had been a nasty black and blue had faded to a yellowish green and would probably be gone completely in another few days.

"Seamus," I said softly, wondering if I should wake him.

He kissed the back of my neck and tightened his hold on me.

"Seamus, are you awake?" I asked.

"Morning," he said, his voice still rough from sleeping.

"Not that I mind the fact you're turned-on this morning, but I was kind of wondering if you were going to do something about it."

His body tensed, and then he groaned before putting some space between us. I hated that fucking space. Turning to face him, I cuddled close again. His gaze fastened on me, and I had to admit he looked pretty cute first thing in the morning. His hair was sticking up and the growth on his jaw was thicker.

"I'm not a baby," I said.

"I noticed."

"It's obvious you want me. I just don't understand why you won't act on it. I thought I was coming here to get claimed by a big, bad biker. Instead, I get a guy who doesn't want to touch me and seems worried about hurting my feelings or some shit. What the hell, Seamus?"

"You're still healing, Nessa. Besides, we don't know a damn thing about each other. I'm trying to do things the right way. You're not some club slut I'm going to screw and then forget."

I chewed the inside of my cheek and contemplated how I wanted to handle it. "No, I'm not a club slut, but I'm still a woman. I'm not someone who's going to run scared because you have morning wood. I'm a woman who happens to be really damn wet and turned on."

"You're not playing fair," he said, narrowing his eyes.

"Never said I would. Five years, Seamus. Five fucking years. Do you think I honestly want to wait a second more?"

"I want your first time to be special."

I snorted.

"What?" he asked. "I can't want to make it memorable? You only get one first time, Janessa. I'm trying to do the right thing for the first time in my fucking life."

"I'm a biker's daughter. I lived in an asylum for a while where the staff raped the inmates and tortured them. Mom protected me from that shit, but I wasn't stupid. I knew what was going on. I don't need you to handle me like I'm spun glass and will shatter at any moment. I'm tougher than you seem to think."

"Your dad entrusted you into my care," he said. "If he thought for one second that I fucked you, he'd cut off my balls."

"No, he wouldn't," I said, even though I wasn't entirely sure about that. "Mom wouldn't let him. She knows how I feel about you."

He reached up and ran his fingers through my hair. "I think it's pretty evident that I want you. I just don't want to fuck this up, whatever it is we have between us. I've never cared about a woman before, and I..."

"You what?" I asked when it seemed like he wouldn't finish his sentence.

He shook his head, apparently thinking better of whatever he'd been about to say.

"Seamus, I'm nineteen and until you kissed me the day I woke up in ICU, I'd never been kissed. I've never had an orgasm. Never seen a naked man. I wanted all those firsts to be with you, and now that I'm here, I can't seem to get you to make a move. So, I'm going to make this easy on you."

Sitting up, I tugged my shirt over my head and tossed it onto the floor. I hadn't bothered with panties last night, hoping Seamus might take advantage of me. He audibly gulped as he stared at me, then I settled back down on the bed next to him. When he didn't make a move, and I honestly couldn't even tell if he was still breathing, I reached out and grabbed his hand, then placed it on my naked hip. I could feel a shudder go through him and it made me feel powerful to have that kind of effect on him.

"You seem to be overdressed," I said, tugging on the waistband of his underwear.

"Are you sure about this? One hundred percent certain you want to do this?" he asked.

"I'm positive, Seamus."

"If you change your mind or want to stop at any time…"

"I won't," I assured him. "Now show me what I've been missing. Just watch the ribs."

He hesitated only a moment before he stripped off his boxer briefs and threw them over the edge of the bed. I sucked in a breath, then regretted it. Pain shot through my ribs, but I was too fascinated with Seamus' cock to pay them much mind. I didn't have anyone to compare him with, but he seemed rather… big. It didn't scare me, though. If anything, it just made me hotter.

I sat up on my knees and reached out to run my hand over his chest, down his abs, then paused before running my fingers along the length of his cock. It twitched and I saw a bead of pre-cum gather on the tip. His shaft was silkier than I'd expected, and he was really damn hard. I wrapped my fingers around him and stroked, marveling at how he felt. His breathing changed and his eyes darkened, but Seamus didn't utter a word of complaint or tell me to stop as I explored his body. His hands were fisted at his sides and I appreciated the restraint he was showing.

I eyed his cock and wondered what he'd taste like. Licking my lips, I leaned over and ran my tongue along his shaft. Seamus groaned and I glanced up to see his eyes close and his jaw tighten. His cock twitched again and I took it as a sign that he liked what I was doing. I hadn't known it was possible for that part of him to do something like that and found it rather fascinating. Truthfully, I just found *him* fascinating. Getting a little braver, I flicked my tongue against the head and was surprised the pre-cum I lapped up didn't taste as icky as I'd thought it would. Some of the girls in high school had claimed it was nasty, but I didn't find the taste repugnant. It wasn't as good as a candy apple that made me want to gulp it down, but I wasn't going to gag from the taste either. After teasing him with my tongue another minute, I fitted my lips around his cock and took as much of him as I could.

Seamus made a choking sound and I looked up, his cock still in my mouth, and saw that he was watching me. My pussy clenched at the need I saw in his eyes. I licked and sucked a few more minutes, more pre-cum coating my tongue, before he gave a growl and pulled me off.

"You keep that up and I'll come in your mouth."

"You make it sound like that would be a bad thing. I don't mind the way you taste. I'd thought I would, but… it's not horrible. Maybe I'd like for you to come in my mouth."

His eyes shut a moment and a shudder ran through him. "Nessa, you're going to be the death of me. Lie back, baby. It's my turn to play and see what you like and what you don't."

I was pretty sure I'd like anything he wanted to do to me. I'd been sneaking romances since I was sixteen, the naughtier the better, and had a fair idea of what I could expect. Or at least, I felt like I was prepared for whatever Seamus would come up with. I might be a virgin, but I wasn't completely ignorant of what happened between a man and woman. Not unless those books I'd been reading were complete bullshit. I knew they were fiction, but surely some of that stuff really happened.

Seamus spread my legs and knelt between them, then just sat there, staring at my body. I wanted to cover up the pudge around my middle, something I would never lose if I kept eating cookies and cake all the time. My hips were rather wide too, and my ass... well, someone had once told me it needed its own zip code. I'd punched that guy in the nose and been suspended by the school. My dad had bought me ice cream. But the way Seamus eyed me, he didn't seem to mind all my little imperfections. I hadn't thought it was possible, but his cock seemed to get even harder, bigger, and excitement thrummed in my veins as I waited to see what he'd do.

He reached out a hand and trailed it from my neck, down the center of my chest, down my belly, and didn't stop until his fingers brushed over the curls between my legs. I'd heard some of the women whispering at the compound about shaving everything off down there, but I hadn't had the guts to try it. Seamus didn't seem to mind. My body twitched when he ran his fingers up and down my slit. It felt good, but I wanted more. Seamus leaned over me, then took my nipple in his mouth. He sucked and tugged on the tip until pleasure rolled over me. I widened my legs, my body seeming to have a mind of its own, begging for more from the man I loved.

Seamus took his time, paying a lot of attention to my nipples as his fingers barely grazed my pussy, light strokes that just made me want to plead with him to do more. He lightly bit my nipples and I cried out. I could feel moisture slipping down the crack of my ass, and my cheeks warmed as embarrassment filled me over how wet I was. I didn't know if it was normal or not.

He slowly slid a finger inside me, and I couldn't hold back the whimper that rose to my lips. It burned a little, and felt strange, and yet oddly good at the same time. Seamus used his thumb to stroke my clit and it felt like sparks were shooting through me.

"So fucking beautiful," he said. "And so damn responsive. You want to come, baby?"

"Y-yes. Please, Seamus."

"Pinch those pretty nipples for me."

My hands trembled as I reached for my breasts, cupping the mounds, then pinching down on my nipples. His finger slid in and out of me in a steady rhythm as his thumb kept swiping over my clit. Something was building inside me, my body shaking, and I wanted to cry I felt so desperate.

"Seamus," I said, my tone pleading.

"Let go, babe. Let go and show me just how wet you can get."

He put a little more pressure on my clit and I came. I damn near saw stars and it felt like I was going to come forever. I kept murmuring his name, my head tossing side to side, and still he kept flicking my clit. I'd never felt anything so intense before, or so amazing. Little aftershocks rocked me, leaving me a mess and feeling completely wrecked. If I'd had that big a reaction to just coming on his hand, what would it be like when he was inside me?

"I could watch you come apart like that every day for the rest of my life and it wouldn't be enough." He smirked. "You soaked the bed."

"S-sorry."

"That's a good thing, Nessa. It means I did my job right and made you come really fucking hard. We can stop now, if you want."

I shook my head emphatically. No way I was backing down now. I wanted to know what it would feel like to have him inside me, wanted to come as his cock filled me. Seamus lowered his body over mine and kissed me. It was the sweetest, gentlest kiss.

"You're sure?" he asked again.

"I'm more than sure. Please, Seamus. Make me yours."

He hesitated. "I've never gone bareback with anyone, always used a condom. Do you want me to get one?"

I swallowed hard, knowing this was a huge decision. I wasn't ready for kids, or at least I didn't think I was. At the same time, I didn't want any barriers between us our first time together. I wanted to feel all of him, wanted the full experience.

"You don't need one," I said.

"Are you on the pill?" he asked.

I opened my mouth to respond, then remembered I hadn't been taking my pills for the last week, and I'd forgotten to talk to the doctor like I'd planned.

"I was, but then the accident happened and…"

"I want to be inside you without anything between us, but I'm not going to make that decision for you. If you haven't been taking your pills and you don't want kids, I should probably get a condom."

"You keep some here?" I asked, hating how vulnerable I felt in that moment. I hadn't wanted a reminder that he'd been sleeping with women, probably up to the day I'd shown up here.

"I keep a box in the bathroom, but if you're asking if I've had another woman in this bed, the answer would be no. I've never brought someone home with me, Nessa. They were meaningless fucks in a hall, a bathroom, or wherever was handy. You're the only woman I've had in my bed. Ever."

I nodded and chewed on my lip. How likely was it I'd get pregnant right away? I knew a lot of the Reapers ladies had gotten pregnant early in their relationships with their men, but surely it hadn't happened the first time. That kind of thing didn't really happen in real life, did it? I knew Mom was worried I'd do something reckless, but I figured she was being overprotective. It was what she and my dad did best.

"I don't want anything between us either," I said, making a decision I hoped I wouldn't regret later. Not that I would ever regret a child Seamus and I created together, but the timing could definitely be better.

"Nessa, this isn't something we can undo later. I don't mind using condoms until your birth control is back on track."

"They aren't foolproof, right? I could get pregnant even if you use one."

He shrugged. "Hasn't ever happened to me."

"But it has happened to other people we know. Please, Seamus. I just want you, all of you, and I want to feel everything without anything between us. It's my first time and I want to experience it fully. We can use a condom next time if you want."

He kissed me softly at first, then harder. There was an urgency to his kiss that made my body heat. Seamus pulled back and stared down at me, his eyes turbulent with emotion.

"If you want all of me, that's what you'll get. I'll go slow. Tell me if I need to stop." His gaze held mine. "I meant it, Nessa. You say the word and I stop, no matter what."

I gave him a slight nod and tried to mentally and emotionally prepare myself. The girls I'd attended high school with who had lost their virginity before senior year had made it seem like no big deal, but this was Seamus, and the fact he was my first was a *very* big deal. At least to me.

I felt his cock nudge against my pussy, and he slowly sank into me. I bit my lip, fighting back the urge to make any sort of sound that might make him stop, but it hurt more than I'd anticipated. Then again, Seamus didn't seem like a small guy down there, or anywhere. I tensed and he froze, his gaze locked on mine.

"You okay, baby?" he asked.

"I just... maybe need a second."

He nodded and the muscles in his body strained. I could tell it cost him, holding still like he was, but he hadn't complained or given me some excuse that he couldn't. I'd asked him to hold on and he had. It gave me the courage to give him a nod. Seamus entered me another inch and stopped again.

"Maybe we just treat this like a Band-Aid? Just get it over with?" I asked, not sure if this slow and steady method was any better than if he'd just do it already.

"I'm already hurting you, Nessa. I don't want to make it worse."

"I want this, Seamus. Want you. I know it's going to hurt, but I'm going to feel the pain either way, right?"

He closed his eyes a moment, then his gaze fastened on mine again. Before I could say anything else, he entered me hard and fast. I gasped and my body locked up from the shock and pain of both my lungs and him being inside me. No one had said anything about it hurting like this. I couldn't stop the tears that leaked from the corners of my eyes. Seamus held still, even though I could tell it was costing him, his control seeming thin at best. The pain slowly began to ebb and I took a breath, then let it out slowly.

"It's not so bad now," I said. "Maybe try moving?"

Seamus took his time, withdrawing, then sliding inside me again, every stroke slow as he watched me. It wasn't pleasant, not at first, but after a few thrusts I actually started to enjoy it. I was still sore as hell, but pleasure was seeping into me the more my body adjusted to the intrusion and his size.

"I won't break," I told him.

"It's not a race, Nessa." He smiled faintly. "You only have one first time. Want to make it memorable for you."

I reached up and cupped his cheek. "It's with you; of course it will be memorable."

Seamus leaned down and claimed my lips in a searing kiss. When he pulled away, he rolled us so that he lay on his back. I sat awkwardly, not knowing what to do. In the books, it always seemed so easy, but being on top my first time ever made me a bit unsure.

"Ride me, baby. Move however brings you the most pleasure."

I experimentally shifted my hips until I found a rhythm. Seamus reached down and rubbed his thumb across my clit and I gasped, then moaned. My eyes slid shut as instinct took over, every move of my hips more bold and sure than the one before. Soon I was riding him, just like he'd said to, and I could feel an orgasm building. I braced my hands on his abs to give me better leverage, and his thumb stroked me again. I came.

"Seamus! Oh, God! Oh, God! So good."

It felt like I was going to come forever, but eventually the intense feeling started to fade. There was a wildness in Seamus' eyes as I opened mine and looked down at him. He gripped my hips, then thrust upward. He took what he wanted, what he needed, and soon I felt the hot splash of his cum inside me. My thighs shook and my hands trembled. Seamus tugged me down onto his chest and he wrapped his arms around me, his cock still buried inside me.

"That was…" I didn't even have words. Yeah, it had hurt like a bitch at first, but then I'd started to enjoy it. Now that it was over, I felt emotionally raw and wrung out.

"Still glad you waited?" he asked, running a hand down my hair.

"Yes. I can't imagine sharing something like this with anyone other than you."

He pressed a kiss to the top of my head. "Thank you, Nessa. You've given me an incredible gift. You didn't have to wait for me, but I'm glad you did."

"I love you, Seamus. I think I always have," I said softly. "There was never anyone for me but you. Even when I was too young to even think about dating I was drawn to you."

"I love you too, Nessa. I'm sorry I've been such an ass. I shouldn't have made you wait, should have come and claimed you when you turned eighteen and graduated high school. I thought I was doing the right thing by staying away."

"Us being apart is never the right thing," I said.

Seamus tightened his hold on me. "Stay with me. Not just right now while the police want you in town. I want you to move in, to be mine."

I lifted my head and looked at him. "Are you asking me to be your old lady?"

He hesitated a moment, but it made me wonder if he'd ever be ready for a true commitment. Yeah, he'd called me his fiancé at the hospital, but it hadn't been a true engagement. If I stayed with Seamus, there was a chance he'd never give me everything I wanted.

"Is that what you want?" he asked after a few minutes.

"It doesn't matter what I want," I said. "If you don't want the same thing, then what's the point?"

"I want you, Nessa. Not just temporarily. I want to wake up next to you every day, want to have a family with you when we're ready. I love you, but I want more than just to make you my old lady. Doesn't seem right to ask you to marry me without a ring, though."

"You want to marry me?" I asked softly.

"We should do this the right way," he said. "Go all out. Marry you, give you a property cut, let the entire world know you're mine in all ways."

"I'd like that."

"Then we'll plan on that. But for now, I think we should just get used to being with each other, and maybe ease your dad into the idea of you remaining here with me. Tex doesn't scare me, but I have no doubt he'll try to castrate me when he finds out I took your virginity and don't plan to let you leave."

I smiled. He wasn't wrong about that. My dad was extremely overprotective, but I loved him and I loved Seamus. Eventually, my dad would come to realize that the biker wasn't just who I wanted, but who I needed. Mom would talk him into it at some point.

I just needed to convince the woman who guarded me as fiercely as a momma bear with her cub that the man lying underneath me was exactly what had been missing from my life. If I could win Mom over, then anything was possible.

Chapter Six

Irish

I'd looked online for ways to soothe any aches Janessa might have, so I had her soak in a hot steamy bath. I'd read that adding lube after her bath could help, and if all else failed, either a heating pad or ice pack. Thankfully, I had all those things and would be able to make her more comfortable. I hated that she was sore and hurting.

I decided to keep busy while she soaked in the tub and pulled out ingredients for breakfast. Even I could scramble eggs and make bacon without fucking it up. I added a little milk and cheese to the eggs, hoping Janessa would like them. I'd just plated our food, and removed the extra helpings from the burners, when there was a knock at the front door. I wiped my hands on a kitchen towel and went to answer it.

Tex and Kalani stood on the doorstep with their two boys. I stepped back and motioned for them to enter.

"Janessa's taking a bath and I just fixed breakfast," I said. "You can eat with us if you're hungry. Should be enough."

"We already had something," Kalani said. "But thank you for the offer."

Tex held up two plastic sacks. "Kalani went and bought a few things for Janessa. We didn't know if she had her overnight bag or if it was still with her truck. They wouldn't let me anywhere near it."

I took the bags from him. "Why don't you have a seat in the living room, and I'll give these to Nessa."

He glanced at the living room and snorted. Couldn't blame him. It was mostly bare, with just a couch and entertainment center. My other place hadn't been big enough for much more, and I hadn't exactly had time to go furniture shopping. Besides, if Nessa was going to make this her home, then she should help me furnish the place.

Despite the lack of furniture, the two boys made themselves at home. I noticed Clayton never seemed to look directly at anyone, and I made a mental note to ask Janessa about it later. The last thing I wanted to do was attract attention to the kid if he didn't want any. The other one, Noah, looked around in curiosity. I stepped into the room, set the bags down, and reached for the remote. I didn't know much about kids, but I found a cartoon channel in hopes it would occupy them.

Kalani sat on the couch and Tex stared at me, his arms folded over his chest. His gaze scanned over me and I waited for the questions I knew would come. Especially since I was shirtless and barefoot. I hadn't even brushed my hair or showered since sleeping with Janessa. It was quite apparent I'd just come from bed, and her daddy was clearly wondering if his darling girl had been in that bed with me.

"I should take those clothes to Nessa," I said. I picked up the two sacks and without another glance in Tex's direction, I headed to the master bedroom.

Nessa was standing near the window, wrapped in a towel with her wet hair hanging down her back. She was stunning with the morning light caressing her honey-colored skin. I didn't know anything about her birth mother, but she had her dad's coloring and could easily pass for Kalani's true daughter. She glanced my way and gave me a smile, one of those soft, sweet ones.

"Your family is here," I said, moving closer and setting the bags on the bed. "Your mom picked up some clothes for you. Guess she had good timing. Or not, depending on how you look at it."

"You just wanted an excuse for me to run around naked," she said, humor glinting in her eyes.

"Pretty sure I can think of some good reasons."

She reached out and whacked me on the arm before digging through the sacks her mom had brought. I couldn't help myself and moved in closer, wrapping my arms around her and pulling her tight against me. I loved the scent of her, the way she felt. Despite the fact her family was in the house, I was growing hard just being this close to her.

"Didn't you say my parents were here?" she asked, looking at me over her shoulder, a coy smile on her lips.

"Yep. The brain in my head doesn't seem to be communicating that very well to other parts of my body."

She giggled and rubbed her ass against me.

"Nessa." I growled at her in warning. "If you don't stop, then I'll forget you're sore and I'll take you right here and now."

"And that would be bad because why?"

She tugged the towel free and tossed it aside. With my arms full of naked woman -- *my woman* -- I knew I was lost. She reached back and wedged her hand between our bodies, rubbing my cock through my jeans.

"We can be quick," she said.

"Nessa, we shouldn't."

She rubbed a little harder and my eyes closed. Damn but she wasn't playing fair. I slid my hand down and noticed that she was already incredibly wet. I tried to pull away. I didn't know if I was trying to get some distance and clear my head, or go get a condom. Nessa seemed to be a few steps ahead of me, though. She reached over to the nightstand and slid open the drawer. I saw she'd shoved a bunch of condoms in there, as well as the lube I kept in the bathroom.

"Baby, are you sure?" I asked.

"Positive. If you don't take care of the ache that's building inside me, then I'll have to do it myself."

Fuck if that didn't make my cock jerk, the thought of her fingers sliding in and out of her pussy, bringing herself pleasure. I put just enough space between us to unzip my pants and shove them down. Reaching for a condom and the lube, I sheathed my cock, then squirted some of the gel onto my fingers. Even if she said she wanted me again, I knew she had to be sore from before.

I slowly eased my fingers inside her, feeling her stretch around them. When I hoped she was slick enough I wouldn't hurt her, I pressed a hand to the center of her back and bent her over the bed. I placed my lips near her ear and teased the shell with the tip of my tongue.

"Do you want me like this?" I asked softly.

"Yes, please! Seamus, I need… I want to experience everything with you. Every position, every…" She gasped as I slid in deep. "Oh, God!"

I leaned back and placed my hand on her smooth skin again, holding her down as I fucked her with slow strokes. I wanted to make it last, to make it good, but I knew her family was waiting.

"I'll make it better next time," I promised.

She gave a squeak of surprise when I slammed into her harder and faster. I angled my hips so that I'd stroke her just the right way. Leaning over her, I reached between her and the bed, rubbing her clit. She buried her face in the bed to muffle her cries and as she came, I let go. My hips slapped against her in jerky thrusts as I chased my orgasm. When I came, I had to bite my lip so I didn't make any noise. My chest heaved as I tried to catch my breath. I slipped from her body and grabbed the condom to keep it from slipping off.

"Damn," I said, then leaned over and trailed kisses across her shoulders.

Nessa sighed and had a dreamy look on her face. I gave her a swat on her ass, making her yelp and jolt upright.

"I have breakfast ready. It's on the kitchen table," I said.

"I'll be there in a minute."

I got rid of the condom and cleaned up, then went into the bedroom and kissed my woman. Nessa pulled away and dug through the sack of clothes, taking out a bra and panties that were probably meant to preserve her innocence. Plain cotton in bland colors with no embellishments. Unfortunately for her parents, that was long gone now, and I'd honestly find her sexy in anything. I grabbed a T-shirt out of the dresser and pulled it on, then ran a brush through my hair before going back out to her family. I didn't know how long it would take her to get ready, and I didn't want to leave them out there alone for too long. When a woman said she'd just be a minute, I'd learned it sometimes meant more like a half hour or longer.

Kalani was in the living room with the two boys. They seemed to be occupied so I kept moving and found Tex in the kitchen. He'd poured himself a cup of coffee and was leaning against the counter, his gaze locked on the doorway. He didn't say anything as I stepped into the room, just watched and waited. If he thought he would make me nervous, he was wrong. I didn't plan on letting Janessa walk out of my life, which meant Tex and I were going to be family. I had a feeling we might have to come to an understanding at some point.

He turned and got a cup from the cabinet behind him, poured another mug of coffee, and handed it to me. I accepted it, then sat at the table in front of the plate I'd fixed myself, food that was quickly going cold. I wasn't eating until Janessa joined us. I'd just pop the plates into the microwave whenever she was ready.

"So. You're sleeping with my daughter," Tex said, then took another swallow of coffee, his gaze locked on me. As calm as he looked, it was almost as if he were just discussing the weather and not his daughter's virginity. I wasn't fooled. The man was anything but calm and cool.

I rubbed at the scruff along my jaw. I could deny it, but what would be the point? Tex wasn't stupid. The second he saw me with Janessa, he'd know something had happened between us. And I'd taken longer than I should have when I'd gone to the bedroom.

"I'm claiming her," I said. "I should have done it a year ago."

He stayed silent for a moment, contemplating me. The man looked like a coiled snake, ready to strike at a moment's provocation and I knew I would have to word everything carefully or risk setting him off. The last thing my club needed was an issue with the Dixie Reapers.

"Why didn't you?" Tex finally asked.

"Didn't think you'd like it too much."

Tex smiled a little. "You're not wrong. What's changed? Because I still don't like it, but something tells me you don't care what I think anymore."

"After watching her flatline, I decided I didn't give a shit. She wants me. I want her. I don't really see how that's any of your business. She may be your daughter, but she's an adult and you don't fucking own her."

Tex arched his eyebrows and tried to stare me down. I wasn't flinching, though, and I wasn't backing off. The man might be older than me, but he didn't hold any higher rank in his club than I did in mine. It would take much more than that to scare me off. Janessa was mine. Tex would have to get used to it sooner or later. Something told me Kalani would be more accepting. Of course, she wasn't in here to back me up. If she was all right with Janessa being with me, then I knew Tex would be as well. Or maybe he'd at least stop glaring at me.

"You think you deserve my little girl?" he asked after a few minutes.

"No," I answered without hesitation. "I'm nowhere near good enough for her. She deserves some college graduate with an office job, a house in the suburbs, and a flashy car. What she's got is a biker with not-so-clean hands who will treat her right and will do anything possible to make her happy. I also plan to take care of the men who hurt her, and any others who come along and think they can put hands on her."

"Fair enough."

"I know I haven't made the best impression, haven't earned the right to be with someone like her, but I want to be the reason she smiles when she wakes up. I want to hold her hand through the tough times, and laugh with her during the best of times. I love her, whether you want to hear that or not."

I heard footsteps come up behind me.

"Houston, leave him alone. Stop doing the papa bear thing. Janessa knows what she wants, and I think she made that abundantly clear when she came here," Kalani said. She went to her husband and hugged him. "Let her be happy."

"You know better than to use my name outside the house," he told her gruffly, but I could see there was no bite to his words. It was clear he adored his wife.

Kalani waved a hand at me. "He's as good as family. Doesn't count."

I hid my smile behind my coffee cup.

"You left the boys unattended in a strange house," Tex said. "You know how Clayton gets."

I cleared my throat. "I noticed he seemed… different from his brother. Wouldn't look directly at me. If he's uncomfortable here, I can bring Janessa to you after we've eaten."

"It's just how Clayton is," Kalani said. "Janessa thinks we should have him tested, that he could be on the autism spectrum, but I still can't stand psychiatrists. I'm better when it comes to regular doctors, thanks largely in part to Dr. Myron."

Janessa had reminded me about enough of Kalani's past not to dig any deeper on the subject. The woman would likely never trust someone in a white lab coat, and I couldn't blame her. I could tell by looking at Tex and the way he held his wife that he wouldn't take the kid behind her back. At one point, I'd have laughed and said the man was whipped, but

I'd have been wrong. It was clear that Kalani was his entire world.

Tex pressed a kiss to the top of her head. "Better get back in there with them. I promise not to shoot Irish in your absence."

"Probably a good idea," Kalani said. "Our daughter would probably kill you in your sleep if you did."

Speaking of their darling daughter, I'd been correct in assuming her few minutes would be quite a bit longer. Unless her mom had also bought bathroom products, I didn't have a clue what could be taking her so long. I was about to get up and go check on her when Janessa walked into the room, but she looked a little pale. I got up and went to her, wrapping an arm around her waist.

"Everything okay?" I asked.

"I turned on the bedroom TV while I was getting ready. It was already on a news station so I just left it there, and now I wish I hadn't. There was another woman attacked, but she didn't make it. I think it was the same men who attacked me. They said a little about what happened to her and it sounded too familiar. What if they find me, Seamus? What if they come back for me?"

"I'm not going to let anything happen to you." I tipped her chin up. "You have an entire club standing behind you, more than one. They have to get through a lot of men to get anywhere near you."

"But it can happen. Rin thought she was safe, so did my mom, and Delphine, and…" She bit her lip. "The bad guys always seem to find a way, Seamus. I can't stick my head in the sand and pretend everything is fine, that they can't reach me, because club history tells me that they can and they will."

"I'll meet with Scratch and Cinder today," Tex said. "Then I'll call Torch and Venom, see if we can spare any guys. If we need to, we can always call in the other clubs. Seamus is right, sweetheart. We're going to do everything we can to keep you safe, but that means you have to do your part too."

Janessa took a breath and let it out, then nodded. "I know. I can't leave the compound without protection, if I can leave at all. Make sure I'm armed if I'm alone, and don't trust anyone I don't know."

"Your daddy taught you well," I said. "What exactly do you mean by armed?"

"My dad taught me to shoot and throw knives," Janessa said. "I've never used anything but paper targets or tree trunks, but I think I could hit someone if I needed to. Honestly, I'm glad I don't know for sure because it means I've been safe."

"Until you weren't," Tex pointed out. "And if you'd been carrying, then you might have had a better chance at getting away. Even if you'd just fired in their general direction, they may have decided you weren't worth the effort."

"You have a carry permit?" I asked, my brow furrowed. What else did I not know about her? Obviously, a lot. I'd never have imagined my sweet Janessa knowing a damn thing about weapons. I was glad to hear that she could take care of herself, though. Those assholes on the highway might have gotten the drop on her, but I'd make sure she had whatever weapons she wanted or needed to ensure it didn't happen again.

"Yeah. Dad made sure I got one when I turned eighteen," she said. "When I turned nineteen, I got a conceal and carry permit, but I left my gun at home when I came here."

Tex growled.

"I know, Daddy. You don't have to say it. It was stupid and it could have cost me my life. I couldn't remember if Florida was a reciprocity state with Alabama and I didn't want to take a chance on getting arrested or something."

"What kind of gun did you have?" I asked.

"Bought her a Ruger LC9s, but it works better when she has it on her," Tex said, obviously still pissed she hadn't packed her gun. Couldn't blame him. I wasn't too happy that she knew how to defend herself but had left her weapon at home, a weapon she could legally carry in her purse or on her body. It wouldn't have taken her but a few minutes on a phone or at a computer to find out she could bring it with her across the state line.

"Let it go, Daddy," Janessa said. "I can't change the past."

"I don't have anything that small," I said, "but I might be able to get my hands on a Kahr CW9 rather quick. Not quite the same, but they'll be similar in size and power. Close enough anyway without getting the exact same gun."

"Where can she practice with it?" Tex asked. "She'll need to get comfortable, since she's only ever used the Ruger."

"There's a shooting range in town that we typically use. If we go, I think we need to make sure we have at least a half dozen guys with us just to make sure Janessa stays protected the entire time," I said.

"Don't I get any say in any of this?" Janessa asked.

"No," I said. "Not when it comes to your safety. I will ask your opinion on a lot of things, Nessa, but not when it could mean the difference between you breathing or lying in a coffin."

She nodded and clung to me a little more. I hated to scare her, and I still didn't have all the facts, but I knew we weren't dealing with random events. The guys who had attacked her had things too well planned. The gator across the road had obviously been a decoy to ensure someone ran off the road. And the emblem she'd described was enough to confirm my thoughts that shit was about to get bad. Well, worse than it already was. I hadn't had a chance to discuss it with anyone yet, but I knew Cinder and Scratch were aware of the club that used a flaming skull for their colors. I'd been too preoccupied with Janessa and making sure she was healthy to follow up on the lead. New players in our state who were spreading like locusts across the south, and I wasn't happy about it. No one was.

"You know something," Janessa said. "About the men who attacked me."

"Nothing one hundred percent, but yeah. You were right when you said they were bikers, and their club is bad news. They're starting to infiltrate the south, or they're attempting to. If they didn't have road names or even the word Prospect on their cuts, then I think the attacks are part of an initiation of sorts," I said. "The plain cut with just the club colors is probably their way of making sure The Inferno gets credit for the crimes. They're a bunch of sadistic bastards."

"Originally out of California, they've recently been trying to claim territory in other areas, especially in the southern part of the country. I think they want a foothold in the coastal states because of easy access to traffic in drugs and women. Torch has called a few meetings about them, but I didn't realize they'd gotten so close to the Devil's Boneyard territory," Tex said.

He cast an accusing glare my way, like I had any say in the matter.

"We knew they were in Florida, but we hadn't realized they were pretty much at our back door until the incident with Janessa. Scratch and Jackal keep their families in town, outside the compound. If those assholes are this close, then security will need to be increased at their homes and here," I said.

"Call Scratch," Janessa said. "You get me a handgun and some ammo and I can handle myself. The clubs need to take care of this before it gets even worse. What if they start attacking children next? Killing women is bad enough, but what if they decide to start selling kids?"

She wasn't wrong, and the thought had crossed my mind. I just didn't like the thought of leaving her alone, even behind a locked gate.

"I'll stay here with them," Tex said. "Do whatever you need to. I'll contact Torch and Venom, see if we can get things moving. Havoc's woman is related to Devil's Fury, right?"

"Yep. Her brother was a prospect for them. He just patched in a month or two ago. He goes by Dingo now because I've heard he's a crazy motherfucker, just like those wild Aussie dogs," I said. "I've only met him a few times, and he's on his best behavior when he's in our territory, but if he thinks his baby sister could be in danger? All bets are probably off on him behaving."

"Sounds like the kind of guy we need in on this," Tex said.

"I'll bring it up."

Despite our audience, I gave Janessa a kiss, though not nearly as hot of one as I'd have liked, then I pulled on my boots and left to find her a gun so she could defend herself if necessary. I'd drop by Scratch's place on the way. I hated to go, even though I knew her dad wouldn't let anything bad happen. After watching her die, I didn't think I'd be able to leave her for any length of time without my chest feeling tight.

I'd done my best to not think about Janessa for years, especially the last year, but I'd failed miserably. It had been hard enough to keep her out of my thoughts when we'd been miles apart, and now she was here and I didn't want to leave her side. I only hoped I hadn't lied to her, that I would be able to protect her and keep her safe from The Inferno. If I lost her, I didn't know what I'd do. Whatever it took, I'd keep her safe.

Chapter Seven

Janessa

"Do I need to ask if you're practicing safe sex?" Mom asked.

I stared at her and gaped a moment before snapping my jaw shut. I couldn't believe she'd just asked me that. Although, technically, we hadn't. Not my birth control pills, since I'd have to start over now, and not even a condom that first time, even though Seamus had offered. I still needed to get my pills from my purse, which was in my truck. Or I hoped it was since I didn't have it. I didn't have much in there -- a handful of cash and the emergency Visa gift card my dad made me carry -- but I hoped no one had taken it.

"I'm going to take that as a no," Mom said, then sighed. "You're not ready for kids, Janessa. They're a lot of work. Exhausting! And they constantly need things, and they whine or cry. Not to mention the expense! I love all three of you, but there have been a lot of sleepless nights, and plenty of times when all three of you needed new clothes and shoes at the same time. Thankfully, your dad seems to always have enough money to cover what we need, and I'm not going to ask where it comes from. I don't think you're at the point yet that you could handle something like that."

"Guess we'll find out," I said, secretly hoping we *wouldn't* find out. I'd have to ask Seamus to use condoms from here on out until my pills were back in my system. I knew Mom was right. I wasn't ready for kids, but if I ended up pregnant, I knew I'd love our baby whether I was ready to be a mom or not.

"I know what it's like to want to be with someone so much you throw caution to the wind," Mom said. "With your dad…"

"*Ew*! Mom, just no. No! Any sentence that has anything to do with you, Dad, and sex should never be uttered in my presence."

Mom smiled a little. I had to admit, I was thrilled that she and Dad were so in love and completely into each other. After everything she'd been through, it surprised me that she'd ever let him get that close. I was glad. Really glad. Kalani had been my protector, and now she had my dad to keep her safe.

"Just be careful, sweetheart," she said. "Seamus has been with more than just a few women. I don't want you to get hurt."

"If you're talking about him giving me something other than a baby, then we're good. He said he got tested while I was in the hospital and that he's clean. I believe him."

She nodded. "All right. I won't meddle, but if you ever need to talk, I'm always here for you. Even if I'm back home in Alabama, I'm just a phone call away."

"I know." I leaned over and hugged her. "Love you, Mom. If I ever do have kids, I hope that I can be just as awesome a mother as you are."

When I pulled back, I saw a sheen of tears in her eyes. My mother had to be the most tenderhearted person I'd ever known. Her life should have hardened her, but it hadn't. And maybe the love of my dad had something to do with it. Whatever the case, the day she came into my life, I was blessed. Yes, my birth grandparents had dumped me in an asylum when my birth mother had died, but it had brought me Kalani, and had put her directly into my dad's path. Things couldn't have worked out better. I just wished that everything she'd endured at the hands of the doctors and staff could have been avoided.

Mom reached up and cupped my cheek. "I love you too. So much."

"I know." I smiled.

"Maybe we should check on your dad? He's been outside with the boys for at least a half hour."

"Afraid he's lost one?" I asked.

She blinked at me. "I would never..."

I snickered because yeah, she would. Dad had lost Noah once. Maybe not lost, per se, but Noah had run off to Flicker's house when Dad had his back turned for just a minute. Mom had freaked out, Dad was in a panic because of Mom losing her mind, and the entire club had been searching for my brother. Then Flicker had wandered over with Noah in his arms and told them what happened. Ever since, Mom didn't trust him with the kids for very long. I didn't think either of my brothers would get hurt inside the Devil's Boneyard compound, but anything was possible. Especially with two small rambunctious boys, and Noah had recently discovered a love of climbing trees.

Mom got up and made her way outside. I channel surfed while I waited on them to come back inside. I knew my dad had already made sure the back of the house was locked up tight before he'd taken the boys out front, and he'd make sure the front door was within his sight at all times. It was just how he was wired, being ex-military.

I found a marathon of one of my favorite shows and settled in to watch it. I didn't know how long

Seamus would be gone, and as much as I loved my family, there was nothing here to occupy the boys. They had the attention span of a gnat, if even that much of one, and anything Mom would have brought with her was over at Scratch's place. I wasn't technically Irish's old lady, or anything to him really, but I reached for the cordless phone on the table. When I'd walked in the kitchen earlier, I'd noticed a note taped to the fridge with a few numbers on it. I'd assumed Seamus had put that there for me at some point.

"CJ" was on the list, along with some men who had road names. I figured this CJ person was likely a Prospect and would be perfect for running an errand. I dialed his number and waited for him to answer.

"What can I do for you, Irish?" a man asked with an accent I couldn't quite place.

"Um, it's actually not Irish. I'm Janessa."

The line was quiet.

"Hello? Are you still there?" I asked.

"Why are you calling from Irish's phone?" he asked.

"Well, he went to talk to Scratch about something and said he had an errand to run, but my little brothers are here right now with nothing to do. I was hoping you, or maybe someone who isn't busy, could run and pick up a few things like some cars or a ball? If they get bored, there's no telling what they'll do," I said.

"And are you paying for this?" CJ asked. "Because I don't see the club letting me use club funds for some chick at Irish's house just on her say-so."

I clenched my hand and tried to control my temper. I wasn't just *some chick*, and even though Seamus said he was claiming me, I didn't think he'd done anything official yet. I wanted to tell this guy off, but I was trying not to make waves. The last thing I wanted to do was blow up at someone and have Seamus get into trouble for it.

"Does this mean you don't want me to go buy toys?" he asked.

"My purse is missing," I said. "Or at least it's not here with me. I know Irish would pay for it if he were here."

I'd assumed everyone knew I was here and who I was, but the attitude I was getting from this guy suggested otherwise. If a Prospect with the Reapers had talked to any of the old ladies, or even potential ones, the way this guy was speaking to me, I knew Torch would knock them down a few pegs and stomp their ass in the dirt.

"Right. I'll just get right on that, then."

The line went dead and I stared at it a moment. The longer I looked at the phone, realizing a dipshit Prospect had hung up on me, the angrier I got. I put the phone down, put on some shoes, and stormed out of the house. Mom and Dad stopped mid-conversation as I stalked past them and started down the road through the compound.

"Where you going?" my dad called out.

"To put some asshole named CJ in his fucking place," I said, and kept walking.

I heard footsteps behind me and could tell they were both following, probably carrying the boys. I didn't think I was going to get kidnapped or assaulted inside the gates, but anything was possible. The clubhouse came into view and I saw some men standing outside smoking. They eyed me, but didn't say anything as I approached. One had *Renegade* on his cut, another said *Shade*. One more member was lounging against the build with *Shadow* stitched on his cut. There was another that said Prospect and I paused.

"You CJ?" I asked the Prospect.

"Nope. I'm Killian."

I nodded and continued into the clubhouse. I heard Dad murmur something to Mom, then he followed me inside, along with the guys I'd just passed outside. I scanned the interior and saw two more prospects at the bar. My hands fisted at my sides as I got even angrier, listening to them laugh as they downed beers.

"Which one of you assholes is CJ?" I asked.

The both turned to me, and one immediately dismissed me. My money was on him being CJ. The other guy raised his eyebrows, then pointed to his drinking partner, ratting him out. I walked over and stared at the dickhead, but he refused to look at me.

"Do not ever fucking hang up on me," I said.

CJ continued to ignore me. It seemed like everyone in the clubhouse got eerily silent and I heard booted steps come closer. Even if meant getting in trouble, I wasn't going to let this guy get away with treating me like garbage. I hauled back my hand and punched him in the arm.

He growled and shot off the stool. "Fucking bitch!"

"You never call me a bitch, and sure as hell never hang up on me."

"You're just some two-bit whore Irish gave a pity fuck. Look at you." He sneered as his gaze went from my head to my toes. "Like a man like him would ever stoop so low."

Oh no he didn't! I was preparing to launch myself at him when an arm came around my waist. I recognized my dad's scent, but it didn't stop me from going into honey badger mode and trying to get the little shit in front of me.

"Nessa!" My dad used that commanding tone I knew meant I needed to stop and listen.

"Did you hear what he called me?" I asked. "Never mind that when I called and said I needed him to get a few things for the boys, he hung up on me."

"That true, boy?" a deep voice asked from nearby.

I turned my head and saw Cinder. I'd met him once before when he'd visited the Dixie Reapers. He'd seemed nice, if a bit intimidating. Scratch was like a big teddy bear around the women and kids at the compound. But this guy? There was just something about him that screamed *don't fuck with me*.

"Come on, Cinder. Like I need to be an errand boy for some slut Irish brought home?" CJ asked.

"I want you to think really fucking hard. You're already on thin ice for that shit you pulled with your sister. I warned you that one more incident and your ass was out of here."

CJ's brow furrowed and he glanced at me, confusion evident in his gaze. I could tell he truly had no idea who I was, or what I was doing at the Devil's Boneyard. Did these guys never say a damn word to each other? Christ! The Dixie Reapers were like a bunch of old women, sitting around gossiping. Everyone knew everyone else's business back home.

"She's the daughter of a Reaper, jackass," the man called Shadow said.

"And the only woman Irish has ever wanted," said a familiar voice. I looked over and smiled at Scratch. "I have no doubt he'll be asking for a property cut."

Cinder crossed his arms and stared at the Prospect. CJ shifted in place and swallowed hard enough I heard it.

"Sorry. I didn't know who she was. I thought she was just some slut Irish had taken home for the night," CJ said. "I heard he'd changed houses, but I didn't know why. I wasn't part of that since I was handling an errand for Phantom."

"Since when has he ever taken a woman home?" Scratch said. "Only woman he was ever going to allow into his house was this one here."

"I didn't know," CJ said. "Irish doesn't talk to me much unless it's club business."

"You apologize, and both she and her daddy accept, then I might let you stay," Cinder said. "Or maybe I should let Havoc and Jordan decide."

CJ paled. "Don't ask my sister. She hates me."

"Can you blame her?" Shadow asked. "You left her to die on the side of the road. I'm surprised Cinder didn't kick your ass out of here right then and there. I know I would have."

"It shouldn't matter whether Irish and I are together are not. You disrespected me and called me names. I asked you nicely to do something for my brothers and you hung up on me," I said.

"And don't think for a second she wouldn't have done some damage if I hadn't grabbed her," my dad said. "The Inferno might have put her in the hospital, but if the odds had been one on one, they would have had a harder time taking her down. She might not be as hardcore as Jordan, but she can defend herself."

"So what do you think, Tex?" Cinder asked.

"I think if you decide to keep him, he needs extra time before he can be patched in, but it's your call. You're the Pres. I'm just visiting," my dad said.

Cinder focused his gaze on me. "And you? You're not just visiting. You have more right to here than CJ does."

I glanced at CJ, who was starting to look a little green. I didn't understand why he was so horrible to me, and apparently his sister at some point, but I could tell the thought of not being part of this club really bothered him. Whatever his reason for being here, I didn't want to take that from him. Maybe he needed the support the club offered, a place to call home.

"I don't care if he stays, but if he talks to me like that again…"

"Then Irish will kick his ass," Cinder said. "And he'll be tossed out. One last chance, CJ. You blow this one, and that's it. I'm out of patience and don't want to deal with your shit anymore."

CJ nodded and hurried out of the room, going to the back hall. My dad released me, and I gave a sheepish look to all the club brothers staring at me. I hoped they'd enjoyed the show, and that I never put on another one again. Thankfully, Seamus hadn't been around to witness me lose my shit. It didn't happen often, but I'd been told I had a wicked temper when someone pissed me off.

"Sorry, guys," I said.

"You kidding?" Renegade asked. "Best entertainment I've had all month."

"Hell, if Irish doesn't step up, maybe I should claim you," Shadow said with a wink.

I shook my head, knowing he was kidding. At least, I was pretty sure he was kidding. I started to leave the clubhouse, but a hand on my arm drew me to a halt.

"Name's Killian," the guy said. "You needed something for your brothers?"

"Just a few cars and maybe a ball. They're bored and I want to have a few things at the house to keep them occupied. Not just for today, but if they visit again it would be nice to have some stuff."

He nodded. "I'll get it handled and drop it by your place in a bit. You need anything else, you let me know."

"Thanks." I smiled and then left the clubhouse. Dad didn't follow and Mom was waiting for me out front. She didn't ask what happened, but I took Noah's hand and we started walking back to the house.

"Everything all right?" Mom asked as we walked through the front door.

"Yeah. Just dealing with a stupid Prospect who thought I was a one-night stand trying to make demands."

My mom coughed to cover a laugh. Yeah, she knew exactly how well something like that would go over with me, especially where Seamus was concerned. We let the boys pick a cartoon and I collapsed on the couch. I didn't know what was taking Seamus so long, or when to even expect him back. Did I need to start checking out the kitchen to figure out a plan for lunch? Or maybe ask that Killian guy to pick up something?

"We lost our babysitter," Mom said.

"I'm sure someone is lurking somewhere. Cinder and Scratch were at the clubhouse, so Dad probably wanted to talk to them about The Inferno. Or maybe he was just needing some guy time and a beer."

Mom stretched and yawned. "He can have all the guy time he wants, but I want a nap."

"I don't think Seamus has a guest room set-up yet. The house is barely furnished. I wanted to talk to him about it, but there really hasn't been time."

"Your dad and I can't keep crashing with Scratch. We'll either look at the local hotels, or see if there's a furnished empty house inside the compound we could use. I know he won't leave until the issue with The Inferno is settled. He'll want to know you're safe."

"Until the club has to deal with another threat anyway. There always seems to be something going on."

Mom smacked my arm. "Hush. You'll jinx everyone. There's hardly any trouble these days. Although, it seems all the guys pick women who need help getting away from something bad. Aside from that, things are usually quiet. It's not like the old days, or so I've been told. Drug deals or arms deals going wrong, getting busted for chopping cars. At least everyone is home and safe."

"Almost everyone," I said, remembering something Venom told me once. A few of their brothers were doing time, guys we'd never met because they'd been locked up for so long. And one who had hit the road when things went bad. Venom had mentioned guys named Hammer, Cowboy, and Joker. Two were supposedly in prison and the other had left for some reason. He'd possibly had a bit too much to drink that night and was rambling about times past, before anyone had an old lady or kids.

Mom yawned again and curled into the corner of the couch. Not five minutes later, she was asleep. I noticed there were shadows under her eyes and she seemed thinner than I remembered. I didn't know if it was the stress of my incident, or something else. The boys were good and stayed occupied with the TV for the most part. Killian eventually arrived with a few bags of toys.

Noah wanted to go out and play with the ball, I didn't want to leave Clayton in the house while Mom was sleeping. I convinced him to play with the cars, and Clayton reached for a set of blocks. Killian had gone above and beyond. There were also puzzles, some crayons and coloring books, and a small train set.

"Cinder said all this is on the club," Killian said. "Renegade sometimes does woodwork to de-stress. He said he'd make a chest to keep everything in, then you'll have this stuff the next time the kids come visit."

"Thanks. Um, my mom mentioned that she didn't want to stay with Scratch indefinitely, and she didn't think my dad was budging until The Inferno was handled. Do you know of any place they might be able to stay?"

Killian scratched at the stubble on his chin. "Maybe. They're not very big, but Cinder had a strip of four studio-sized suites put in. They're pretty bare. Bed, couch, TV, and appliances. I'll ask him about getting a few things for one of them so your parents can stay there. Maybe pick up some cots for the kids or something."

"Thanks, Killian."

He nodded and then held out his hand. "Give me your phone and I'll program my number into it."

"I don't have it right now. It's with my purse, probably still in my truck. At least, I hope no one stole it. Or maybe the police have it. I honestly have no idea where it is right now." I pointed to the cordless phone on the coffee table. "I used that to call CJ earlier. Irish had his number and a few others on the fridge."

Killian walked out of the room and I followed him to the kitchen. He added his name and number to the list, then gave me a wink on his way out. I heard the front door open and shut, and went back to the living room to keep an eye on the boys. Another cartoon was playing, but neither of them was watching. I changed the channel and hoped that my dad and Seamus would be back soon. I didn't do well with boredom, and other than the TV and my family, I had nothing to occupy my time.

Chapter Eight

Irish

I'd stopped to talk to Scratch, picked up Janessa's purse from the police, and arranged for her truck to be released from the impound lot, then ran a few other errands. Tex might not have been able to get very far, but this was Devil's Boneyard territory and I knew which palms to grease to get what I wanted. By the time I got back to the compound nearly five hours later, Cinder was calling a meeting and a few more Reapers and some Devil's Fury were in town. I didn't even want to know how fast they'd ridden to get here so quick, but I was thankful for the extra hands and eyes. I'd do anything to keep Janessa safe.

My brothers sat around the table with the other clubs leaning against the walls. Tex had taken up a spot near the head of the table, his arms folded and ankles crossed, but I knew he wasn't nearly as relaxed as he appeared. Flicker, Wraith, Grimm, and Zipper had made the trip from the Dixie Reapers, and Dingo, Dagger, Outlaw, and Demon were present from Devil's Fury.

"What? No Hades Abyss?" I asked jokingly.

"They'll be here later tonight," Havoc said.

My eyebrows rose. I hadn't actually expected them to show, but I shouldn't be all that surprised. When one club needed help, the others seemed to appear almost instantly. Hades Abyss had ties to the Dixie Reapers, and Janessa was technically a Reaper's property since she was Tex's daughter. Until I officially claimed her, which I'd do at the end of this meeting.

Devil's Fury was tied to both the Devil's Boneyard and the Dixie Reapers by blood. One big happy family.

"And we have some new faces heading here too," Demon said.

"New faces?" Ashes asked.

Demon nodded. "I called in a favor. My cousin used to date a guy in the Reckless Kings."

I let out a whistle. The Reckless Kings MC had a foothold in just about every state in the country, and even had some chapters in Ireland, Scotland, and Russia. Word on the street was they were involved with the Bratva as well as the Irish Mafia. I didn't know how they walked that slippery slope, but every club I knew spoke about them with reverence. I'd never had a chance to meet any of the Kings before, but I was grateful for their assistance.

"Your cousin must be something if they're willing to help just because she dated one of them," Gator said. "Does she have a magic pussy?"

Demon smirked. "More like a magic dick. My cousin is a dude, and as gay as they come. Snake is bisexual and isn't ashamed to tell the world, so his entire club knows he was with my cousin. If asked, he'll say it wouldn't be fair to deny anyone the pleasure of his... touch."

A few of my brothers snickered. Some clubs had a big issue with anyone not straight, or white for that matter, but the guys in this room were open-minded. A lot of the brothers in all three clubs had served in the military at some point and had learned that we all bleed the same color, that it's what a man does when shit hits the fan that really matters, not who he's fucking or what he looks like.

"Is this Snake person coming?" Dagger asked, a gleam in his eye that told me he might be just as open sexually as Snake.

"Far as I know," Demon said. "They're also sending Copper and Prospero."

"Like that dude from the Shakespeare play?" Tex asked.

"Uh, no. More like the guy from one of Poe's twisted tales," Demon said. "He can be an arrogant ass, and comes from a family who has a shit ton of money and influence. Guy's pretty much untouchable."

"What chapter are these guys from? If they're in every state…" I let the thought trail off. Demon said they were sending help, but how long would we be waiting?

"They're in Tennessee, not far from Blackwood Falls," Demon said. "Far enough that we aren't stepping on each other, but close enough they'll get here pretty quick."

"All right," Cinder said. "Now that social time is over, everyone ready to tackle this issue with The Inferno? They're pissing off clubs nationwide, and now those fuckers are in our town and hurting our women."

"Not that I don't want to help Janessa, but isn't she technically a Reaper's family?" Shade asked. "Unless Irish has something to add?"

The fucker. I could tell by his smirk that he wanted to put me in the hot seat. Little did he know, I'd planned to address the situation with Janessa before we adjourned. She was mine, even if I hadn't made it a formal announcement.

"The VP gave me permission to claim her, and I am," I said. "I was going to request a property cut at the end of Church, but since you brought it up now…

Janessa is mine. I'm making her my old lady, and I plan to ask her to marry me."

Cinder rubbed his beard and looked at Tex. "You okay with that?"

Tex shrugged. "As my wife and daughter have both pointed out, Janessa is an adult now. If she wants Irish, I won't stand in her way. But if he fucks up, I'll make sure he doesn't look so pretty anymore."

Cinder chuckled. "Fair enough. All right, we'll order a property cut for her today."

"The Inferno has been causing problems in damn near every state," Scratch said. "Each club in this room has a vested interest in handling the problem here in Florida. If we can take down one chapter, then it will weaken the others and means they might fall too. The police are looking at this pretty close, and from what I've heard, they know about The Inferno and have eyes on them."

"You have police connections now?" Demon asked.

"Irish gave us the first heads-up when he heard Janessa's description to the police." Scratch shrugged. "But what can I say? My wife has gotten pulled over a few times. Officer Thomas fell under her spell just like most men do. He knows she's mine and not going anywhere, so if there's someone gunning for the club, he's going to give me a heads-up. Not because he gives a shit about us, but because he wants Clarity and the kids safe."

"You okay with that?" Zipper asked.

"Clarity isn't going to stray. She compared him to a puppy that followed her and the kids home a few months ago."

"Yeah, but the puppy is still there and isn't so small anymore," Shadow pointed out.

"It's not an issue," Scratch said. "Besides, it's good to have someone willing to give us info from the police department."

"The Inferno is not just accepting prospects at random. The guys who want to patch in have to first prove themselves worthy to be an Inferno member before they even receive a Prospect cut. Janessa saw The Inferno's colors on the cuts the men wore but no writing. They're committing their crimes in the name of the club in hopes of prospecting. Here's where things get even better." Cinder flipped open a file folder in front of him. "From what Wire and Shade have determined, once they're permitted to prospect, the crimes have to be even more violent in order to patch in. The assault on Janessa was bad, and they've killed some people already. If they're willing to go that far just be a prospect, can you imagine what they'll do to be a patched member?"

"Jesus," Tex muttered. His face turned a little green. "The increase of rapes and murders are in all the cities near The Inferno chapters. It's been all over the news and some of the clubs have been talking, but I hadn't realized it's Prospects trying to patch in."

Cinder nodded. "That's what we're thinking. And it's going to get worse. School shootings, bombings, nothing is out of the realm of possibility with that crew. We need to end it, even if it means calling in every club we can. The Reckless Kings have some pretty big reach, but we may need to call in some others too. We can't just take down the Florida Infernos. That club needs to be dismantled nationwide. Taking down one chapter will weaken them, but it won't stop them."

"Agreed," Zipper murmured.

"So what do we do right now?" I asked. "Is it safe for Janessa to be out around town? Or will they come after her again if they see her?"

"I wouldn't leave her unprotected," Cinder said. "Not even inside the compound. I'm adding some new Prospects, guys I know we can trust. They'll patrol the fence for now. When she's out, make sure patched members are with her. I trust our prospects, but I want more experienced brothers watching her. Scratch and Jackal are also going to have added protection at home for their families."

"Who are we adding?" Shadow asked.

"Malcolm is friends with Cobra; Dixon is friends with Renegade; and Jin is related to Phantom. They'll be joining us by tomorrow morning. Right now, they're meeting with Killian to go over a few things, then I'll talk to them when Church is over," Cinder said.

"Are we just in a holding pattern until everyone else gets here?" I asked.

"Other than increasing security, I also have Havoc checking into a few things. Maybe he can flush them out, or find out where they're hiding. Shade is also attempting to hack into The Inferno accounts, with help from Wire and Outlaw," Cinder said.

"Wire has his eye on some fresh hacking talent up around Hades Abyss territory. He's going to reach out and see if the guy would be willing to help," Flicker said. "That club doesn't have a hacker yet, and we can always use another tech guru on our side."

"Then, if that's all…" I said, looking around the room.

"Go to your woman," Cinder said. "Keep her in the compound if you can, but I know tying her down won't be easy. She has to be bored already."

Shit. I hadn't even thought of that.

Cinder looked over at Tex. "Killian called me. He's setting up one of the small suites for your family. It already has a couch and a queen-size bed in there, but he was going to get some cots for the kids and make sure the kitchen was fully functional."

"Appreciate it," Tex said.

"Clarity was happy to have y'all stay longer," Scratch said. "But I understand about wanting your own space, especially with two boys."

"I think my Noah was getting confused with a second Noah in the same room," Tex said with a smile.

Scratch ran a hand down his beard. "Yeah, he wasn't supposed to have the name Noah, but someone couldn't read my handwriting. It was too much of a hassle to fix it, so Clarity said to leave it be."

"Bet Wire could handle it," Outlaw said. "He's always hacking into the government sites."

Scratch nodded. "Maybe, but he already knows his name. No need to confuse the kid."

I stood and pushed my chair under the table. Cinder gave me a nod and I made my escape before they went off on another tangent. I loved my club, but a few had trouble staying on task, even in Church. Janessa's purse was in my saddlebag on my bike, and I knew she was anxious to have it back. When I got home, I found her mom asleep on the couch, and looking completely exhausted. The two boys were playing with some toys, and Janessa looked like she was bored to death.

"Sorry I was gone so long," I said, carrying her purse over to her. "One of the guys will bring your truck here, probably tomorrow. I grabbed this for you, though."

She snatched her purse and started digging through it. "Thank God! I was worried my wallet and phone would be gone, but they're both here, and it looks like nothing was removed from the wallet."

"Cinder said your parents and brothers are going to have a place to stay here at the compound. Maybe your mom will get more sleep behind the gate. I'm sure she's used to that extra security."

Janessa gave me a deer in the headlights look. "I hadn't thought of that. Do you think that's why she hasn't been sleeping? She looks exhausted, and she looks thinner to me."

"I can't say as to whether or not she's thinner, but she does have some dark circles under her eyes. I'm sure she's been worried about you."

She nodded.

"Do your brothers like pizza?" I asked.

"They're boys. Of course they like pizza."

"Right. I'll place an order for a few. What do they like on theirs?"

"The boys like cheese, but my dad will eat anything, and Mom just picks off stuff if she doesn't want it on hers. You can order whatever you like," she said.

I leaned down, caging her between my arms, and kissed her softly. When I pulled back, she had a dreamy expression on her face and sighed. I wanted to do so much more, but not with her mom and little brothers sitting here. Once they were gone, I would remind her just how much I needed her, wanted her. And then I'd tell her that she was officially mine, even if she didn't have a property cut just yet.

"I'm going to place the order; then we're going to talk. You had that glazed look people have when they're bored out of their minds. We'll have to come up with some ways to keep you occupied while we handle the current situation," I said.

She smiled. "I can think of something."

I chuckled and kissed her again. "Behave. Your mom is right there and so are your brothers. But keep that thought in mind for later."

I pulled my cell phone from my pocket and scrolled for my favorite pizza place, then ordered four different types of pizza, breadsticks, and some drinks. I didn't know how long her family would stay before checking out their temporary lodgings, but I wanted to make sure there was plenty to eat. Cranky little kids or a cranky Tex didn't sound like much fun.

While we waited, I sat next to Nessa and pulled her against my side. It was nice, just sitting and watching TV. I'd never really done the snuggling thing, but I liked it with her. Then again, I'd never permitted a woman to sleep next to me either. I was tackling a lot of firsts with the woman beside me. First time meeting the parents, though I had technically already known hers, first time doing stuff as a family -- if eating pizza counted, first time just holding a woman all night. And I was loving every second.

I eyed the boys who were still quietly playing. I'd always thought having kids in my house would be like something out of a horror movie. But if they were anything like Noah and Clayton, then I might actually like it. I wouldn't rush Nessa. She was still young, really damn young. We'd been careless once, but I'd make sure it didn't happen again. The last thing I wanted to do was give her a baby she wasn't ready for, and honestly, I didn't know if I was prepared either. Being around Jackal's or Scratch's kids in small doses was one thing, but having to take care of a kid twenty-four hours a day every day of the year? That was one hell of a commitment.

I wanted that one day. A family with the woman curled against me. Maybe not a ton of kids, but one or two wouldn't be so bad. Well, unless they were like Havoc's daughter, Lanie. That kid was a menace and she was only a year old. If you didn't give in to her demands, she'd bite the fuck out of you, and was known for throwing herself on the floor and screaming. Havoc would just growl at her and tell her to stop being a brat. It usually worked, until she gave him that teary-eyed look, and then he'd turn to mush. My brothers and I tried like hell not laugh when our big, scary Sergeant at Arms turned into a teddy bear around his kid. Only Lanie could get that reaction from him. Even his woman, Jordan, didn't get him to go quite that soft. Then again, Jordan was something of a badass herself.

Nessa sighed again and I looked down to see her eyes sliding shut. It seemed her mom wasn't the only one who was tired. She was still healing, and I knew sleep was good for her. I'd let her rest until the food arrived. A Prospect would get it at the gate and bring it by the house. I'd just have to put the money back into the funds the club kept for that kind of thing, but it wasn't a big deal. I ordered out rather frequently and always dropped some money into the cash box twice a week to cover my expenses.

The front door opened and shut, then Tex walked in. He looked every bit as worn out as his wife and he leaned against the wall.

"Did I miss anything?" I asked.

"Nope. I see Kalani didn't make it long, and neither did Nessa."

"Your wife was asleep when I got here, and Nessa just passed out a few minutes ago. I ordered some pizza so I was planning to wake them when it got here."

He nodded. "I stopped by the suite Cinder is letting us use. Your Prospect even put some toys and books in there for the boys and grabbed some blankets with cars on them."

"Sorry I don't have the extra bedrooms set up here," I said.

He waved me off. "It's fine. I'm sure Janessa would like to furnish her own home. Besides, you might need those rooms for people other than us. Might need a crib and not a regular bed in there."

"Uh no. Janessa isn't ready for that, and I'm not sure I am either."

"Then I'd suggest you be extra careful," Tex said. He nodded toward Kalani. "We didn't plan for Noah or Clayton. Wraith sure as hell didn't plan to knock up Rin. That's my baby girl over there. I don't really want any details of your sex life, or to even think about the fact she's having sex at all, but be careful. If the two of you really aren't ready for kids, don't take any chances."

I tried not to give anything away, but I must not have succeeded. He shook his head and looked away a moment, then sighed heavily.

"Dammit, Irish."

"I asked if she was sure. I offered to..." I slammed my mouth shut as he looked at me. "Right, so..."

"I'd suggest you find out as soon as you can. If she's pregnant, you'll need as much time as you can to prepare. Janessa hasn't led an easy life. I've tried to make up for it the past five years, but I can't undo the time she spent with her mother's family or at the asylum. She's known love and compassion since I came back into her life, but I sometimes worry that the first fourteen years may have scarred her. Watch her carefully. She's yours to protect now."

I looked at the woman cuddled against me. The things Tex said made me wonder what her life had been like before. We hadn't really talked much, and in a lot of ways we were strangers. I didn't regret claiming her. We would have the rest of our lives to learn everything about each other.

Assuming we could stop The Inferno before they came for her again.

Chapter Nine

Janessa

The morning light was barely coming through the window when I woke. Seamus was still asleep, one arm across my waist and the other shoved under his pillow. It took some skill, but I managed to slip from the bed without him noticing. I'd been trapped in the house for three days, and I needed some fresh air. I knew if he was awake, he'd find a way to keep me inside. My family had come to visit every day, but it wasn't the same. If I left the house, it felt like I had two dozen sets of eyes on me at any given time. I hated that feeling and it just seemed better to stay in the house.

I quickly dressed, ran a brush through my hair, cleaned my face and teeth, then crept from the room. At the front door, I put on my shoes and then left the house as quietly as I could. I took in a deep breath when I got outside and started toward the front of the compound. Even I just walked along the roadway for a bit, the fact I was blissfully alone was enough to make me happy.

As I neared the front gate, the frantic voice of a girl caught my attention. I hurried along the road and didn't stop until I'd reached the Prospect keeping a girl and a toddler out. The older one couldn't have been more than fourteen or fifteen, and tears were streaming down her cheeks.

"Please," the girl begged. "I have to see Seamus. It's really important. My mom told me if anything ever happened to her, that I had to come ask for Seamus."

I eyed the girl, knowing she was way too old to be his daughter. What connection to Seamus have with her mother? I placed a hand on Killian's shoulder.

"Let me talk to her," I said.

Killian shook his head. "Irish would have my ass if I let you talk to her, especially if you step outside this gate. And I'm not about to let her in here."

I studied the girl, then the smaller one in her arms. When the toddler looked at me, it felt like I'd been punched in the chest. She couldn't be more than two or three. I knew those eyes. I'd been dreaming about them the last five years. The little toddler had Seamus' eyes, which meant…

"Who are you?" I asked.

"Shella Murphy," the girl said. "And this is Payson."

"Why did your mom tell you to come find Seamus? And where is your mother?" I asked.

"She had a one-night stand with him." Shella looked at the girl in her arms. "Payson was the result, but she never wanted to tell Seamus. She said he was too wild to ever take care of a kid and she didn't want him to feel trapped. But my mom died this week. Payson's three and I don't want her going into the foster care system."

My heart ached, both over the fact I wasn't going to be the woman to give Seamus his first child, and also at the loss these two had experienced. I smacked Killian on the arm.

"Either let them in or I'm going out," I said.

"You're just going to take her word for it?" he asked.

"Did you see Payson's eyes? Because I look at those eyes every morning. I don't need a DNA test to prove that kid belongs to Seamus, which means she's mine too."

"Yours?" the girl asked, her brow furrowed.

"Janessa and Irish are together," Killian said. "She's going to be his wife. If what you're saying is true and Payson is Irish's kid, then that makes Janessa her stepmom."

Shella blinked rapidly and nodded, but not before I noticed the tears in her eyes. She handed Payson to me, and the little girl grabbed onto my shirt. She was unusually quiet for someone so small.

"I see my truck is over in front of the clubhouse. Any idea where the keys are?" I asked Killian.

"In the driver's seat." He hesitated. "Janessa, you shouldn't leave the compound. You know it's not safe. You should at least take some men with you."

I ignored Killian, knowing that taking care of these kids was more important. Besides, we were just going to pick up their things and come straight back. We'd hardly be gone anytime. I tipped my head toward the truck. "Come on, Shella. Let's go to your place and see what Payson needs to bring with her, and you can tell me where you plan to stay."

Shella nodded but nibbled at her lip as we walked over to my truck. I had a car seat in the back that I'd put in for Clayton and I used it to buckle Payson and keep her safe. Shella got into the front and buckled as I started the engine. She gave me instructions to a side of town with small, older homes. They weren't rundown, and it wasn't the worst area I'd ever seen, but the people here were obviously struggling to make ends meet. She pointed to a white clapboard home and I pulled into the driveway. There was an older car parked in the carport, but no signs of life other than that.

"Who's staying with you?" I asked.

"My mom's friend. She's only here until arrangements can be made. That's her car," Shella said, pointing to the carport.

"Why didn't she bring you to the compound?" I asked.

Shella shrugged and looked away. I had a feeling there was a story there. I got out, unbuckled Payson, and followed Shella into the house. The place was moderately clean, and very sparsely furnished. If Seamus knew his daughter had been living like this, he'd blow a gasket. Well, after he had a coronary from the shock of having a kid he knew nothing about.

I paused at a picture of the two girls with a woman I assumed was their mom, and the blood in my veins froze. I knew that face, had seen it not too long ago on the news. Their mom was the woman who had been attacked by The Inferno and had died from her injuries. Had she been picked on purpose? Did they know of her connection with Seamus somehow?

"That's my mom. Irina Murphy," Shella said.

The woman didn't look old enough to have a daughter Shella's age, and I could see why Seamus had been taken with her. She was beautiful, with long blonde hair and big blue eyes. I envied her a little. Even though Seamus was mine and she'd never truly had him, she'd had his daughter and it hurt. Little Payson was adorable, though, with her daddy's eyes and her momma's hair.

As I followed Shella through the house, I noticed a woman passed out on a bed, fully dressed and snoring. Bottles littered the floor and the stench of alcohol made my nose wrinkle. I could now understand why Shella had walked to the compound and not asked her mother's friend for a lift. I hoped the only reason she'd been drinking so heavily was the loss of her friend, but that much alcohol would likely kill someone, especially a person not used to consuming large amounts.

Shella led me into a small room with a twin bed and a much smaller, toddler bed. There was one dresser that looked like it had seen better days, and I didn't see a single toy or book in sight. Shella opened the closet and pulled out a pair of dress shoes that had to belong to Payson they were so tiny, then she opened one of the dresser drawers and pulled out all the clothes.

"We don't have a suitcase, but I can put everything into a plastic sack," Shella said.

"Where are Payson's toys?" I asked.

Shella pressed her lips tightly together and didn't say anything, which was answer enough. This little family had struggled so much that the little girl in my arms didn't have a single toy or book.

"Shella, if Seamus is taking Payson, who are you going to stay with?" I asked. "Is your father going to take you in?"

"My mom said my dad was a deadbeat loser. One night when she'd had too much to drink, she admitted that she's gotten knocked up after a concert in high school. She never even knew the guy's name. I'll probably end up in the foster system."

"How old are you?" I asked.

"Sixteen," she said. "I'll be seventeen in a few months."

Holy shit! She was almost as old as me! I'd pegged her for quite a bit younger, and I wondered if a lack of nutritious meals had kept her from filling out. I looked around and knew I needed to make a decision and make it quick. The woman in the other room could wake up, and I knew drunk women could be highly unpleasant. Not that my mom was a drinker, but I'd seen others, when I was younger and still lived with my mom and grandparents.

"Pack your things, Shella. You're coming with us," I said.

Her eyes went wide and she hesitated only a moment before pulling her clothes out of the dresser and closet too. Everything looked a little too worn and threadbare in spots. I knew they were going to need new clothes and shoes but had to have something to wear until we could take them shopping. After Shella had stuffed all their belongings into a garbage bag, we went back out to my truck. I was driving through the middle of town when I heard it… the unmistakable sound of motorcycle engines. I thought Seamus had woken and realized I'd slipped out of the compound, but when I saw the men coming up on my bumper way too fast, I knew they weren't Devil's Boneyard, or anyone else I called family.

My heart started to pound harder, and I gripped the steering wheel. I glanced at Shella and Payson, making sure they were secure, then pressed the pedal harder hoping we could outrun them. I'd have gladly welcome a police officer pulling me over right then, but none seemed to be in sight. We were nearing the outskirts of town, getting closer to the compound, when two of them veered off, then swerved toward the side of my truck.

I panicked and jerked the wheel, nearly going off the road. The second time they did it, I plowed my truck into a light post. My chest ached from the seatbelt restraining me and Payson was crying and screaming in the backseat. I glanced at Shella, noticing that she was pale and looked scared as hell, but she was still breathing and didn't look hurt. I unbuckled and climbed over the back of the seat to reach Payson. I'd no sooner unfastened the car seat buckle and pulled her into my arms than the rear door of my truck was jerked open and one of the men reached for me.

I kicked at him and thrust Payson toward Shella. My purse was at home, and I was cursing myself for being an idiot and leaving it behind, especially since it had my new gun inside. A flash of silver caught my eye and I saw one of the sets of throwing knives my dad had given me. I hadn't even realized they were in my truck until now. I wrapped my fingers around the sheath as they pulled me from the truck.

I gripped one of the blades tight and slashed at the wannabe biker who was manhandling me. I didn't know who this fucker was, but the fact he didn't have any so much as the word Prospect on his cut meant he was a great big nobody. The guy laughed and released me, but I had nowhere to run. Not that I would ever leave the girls behind. I looked at the four men, taking note of as much about them as possible this time. They'd attacked during the day and couldn't hide in the darkness.

The one who had grabbed me might wear a cut with The Inferno colors, but he didn't have any other patches or titles on his cut, which meant he was a lowly pissant. Every club in the country had some sort of text boasting of the man's rank. Same for the other three. They may have caught me by surprise before, but not this time.

"Lock the doors," I screamed at Shella as I slammed shut the one I'd just been pulled from. I heard the locks engage and the men around me snickered.

"You think that's going to keep us out? Once we're done with you, we'll take care of them." There was a gleam in his eyes that I didn't much like. I'd die before I let them get their hands on those sweet girls. Payson belonged to Seamus, and Shella belonged to Payson. As far as I was concerned, that meant they were both mine to protect right now.

"Your funeral," I said. "I'm a Devil's Boneyard old lady, and those kids belong to me and Irish. You hurt any of us and you're going to die a slow and painful death."

"I'm shaking in my boots," one of them said.

"You should be."

The younger of the four waved a hand at the knife I still clutched. "You aren't going to do anything with that. Might as well drop it and accept your fate. Need to send a message to the local club, and you seem like the perfect way to do it. The two young ones will make a nice profit when we sell them."

Bile rose in my throat, and I knew that I couldn't go down this time. I couldn't let them take me, not when Shella and Payson needed me. I drew back my arm and let my knife fly. It sank into the side of the youngest one, right between the ribs if I had to guess. He clutched at it, his eyes wide with shock, as he sank to his knees. When he started having blood bubbles come out of his mouth, I knew I'd hit his lung.

The other men didn't seem impressed as they moved in closer. I reached for another knife, but before I could react, I heard the most beautiful sound ever. At least a half dozen Harleys were heading toward me from the general direction of the compound, and while I had no way of knowing for sure they were Devil's Boneyard, I had to hope that help was on the way.

The man closest to me reached out and wrapped his hand around my wrist, jerking my body toward him. I lost my balance and dropped my knives. My heart pounded as I glanced at the girls in the truck, hoping they would be safe. The guy dragging me along shoved me toward his bike.

"You get on and come with us, we'll think about leaving those girls alone," he said.

I swallowed hard and nodded. Without another glance, I climbed onto the back of his bike. I had no doubt that I'd pay for it, but as long as Shella and Payson were safe that was all that mattered. As the biker climbed onto his motorcycle, revved the engine, then took off, I looked one last time toward the compound and saw Irish heading straight for me. I'd have recognized him no matter how far away he was. Tears slipped down my cheeks as I held out a hand to him, hoping that he would understand why I had to do this, and that someday he would forgive me.

The bike beneath me jerked and took off down the road. The other two men followed and I closed my eyes as I faced forward. After a moment, I tried to keep track of where we were going. If I had the chance, I would escape. I didn't think they'd give me the opportunity. They'd likely kill me once there was some distance between us and the Devils. Irish would need to take care of his daughter before he could even think of coming for me, and I wouldn't have it any other way.

It felt like we rode forever, but I knew it hadn't been that long. Probably a twenty-minute ride from town, if that. They pulled the bikes down a dirt path and didn't stop until a small house came into view. The porch sagged and the windows were covered in grime. Whoever owned it obviously hadn't cared much for upkeep. The bike came to a stop and I got off, my legs shaking and my body trembling as I wondered how much I would suffer before they ended my life.

I was hauled into the house and forced down onto a ratty couch with springs sticking up from the cushions in places. The men paced and kept looking out the windows, but no one touched me or said a word. I wasn't sure what it meant, that I was here and they looked almost... worried? That couldn't be right. They'd seemed to not fear the Devil's Boneyard when they'd hauled me from my truck. What had changed in such a short time?

"Did you see the way he looked at her?" one of the men asked the one who seemed to be in charge, the one who had forced me onto his bike.

"Yeah. He's not going to back down," the man agreed.

"So we kill the fucker if he shows up here," the third one said. "No big, right? It's not like we haven't killed before."

"That wasn't one club coming for her," the first guy said. "There were at least four, and who knows if there are others. Whoever she is, they're going to want her back. No one bands together like that. Not over a woman."

The guy who'd taken me turned a glare my way. "Who the fuck are you?"

"I told you. I'm an old lady for Devil's Boneyard."

"That ain't all you are. What else?" he asked.

I shrugged. "I'm a Dixie Reapers daughter."

"And the other clubs?" the other one asked. "How are you related to them?"

"I'm not. Not by blood anyway. My Uncle Tank has a brother who's in Devil's Fury. My Aunt Laken is married to someone from Hades Abyss. All our clubs are tied together in one way or another, so you fuck with one of us, you get all of them." Not that Tank and Laken were my blood relatives, but they were Reapers and that made them family just the same.

The one nearest the window paled and started cursing.

"I say we kill the bitch and dump her ass by the road," the second one said, glancing around as if he expected the Boogeyman to jump out at any moment.

"There's nowhere you can hide, no place you can run that will ever be far enough," I said. "Irish and my dad *will* find you, and they will make you pay."

"We're fucked," the one at the window muttered. "I'm sorry, but no club is fucking worth this shit. We're all dead men walking for taking this dumb bitch. You just had to take her, didn't you, Bud? Saw that truck and decided she needed to pay for surviving. Now we're all gonna pay for your mistake."

At least I had a name now. One of them anyway. Unless it was a term of endearment or a nickname, but I didn't think so. The asshole looked like a Bud.

"Shut up, Skeet. No one fucking asked you," Bud said. "No, when we kill her, we'll send a message. A loud and clear one that we're untouchable and don't give a fuck about the pansy ass clubs coming to save her."

"So if you're going to kill me, why take me? Why not just get it over with where they could see you do it?" I asked, then wished I'd kept my mouth shut. *Great, Janessa. That's it. Give them ideas and amp them up even more.*

"Because we want to take our time," Bud said, giving me a smile that chilled me.

Hurry, Seamus. I don't know how long I can hold out.

Chapter Ten

Irish

Seeing those bastards take off with Janessa, I'd felt a spike of fear, but not nearly as great as the terror I felt staring into eyes that looked exactly like my own, but on a much smaller, female person. Seeing the kids in her truck had drawn me to a halt, if only long enough to ensure they were safe. I'd heard a few bikes continue on and hoped they could keep up with the assholes who had Janessa. Then I'd seen the smallest girl. Even if the older girl in the truck hadn't said the little sprite was my daughter, I'd have known. I barely remembered her mom, wasn't even sure I'd ever known her name. The woman had been right to think I'd have run when faced with the prospect of being a dad. I hadn't been ready then, probably wasn't ready now, but I didn't have a choice.

I looked at Tex, who looked less than thrilled that my transgressions had caught up to me, and his daughter had discovered it first. The second most of the men with me had seen the children, they'd stopped pursuing The Inferno. For one, those were some crazy bastards and none of us were dumb enough to try and take them on without enough manpower. I didn't know why Tex had stopped as well, but I was wishing he hadn't found out this way that I had a kid. Hell, I was wishing I hadn't discovered it this way either.

"Nessa. I can't let them take her," I said.

"I think you have someone else right here who needs you," he said.

He wasn't wrong, but I couldn't leave Janessa with those men. I'd wasted enough time checking on the kids, then getting over the shock that I had a daughter. I had no doubt they intended to kill her this time. They had to have recognized her truck and targeted her on purpose. My gut clenched at the thought of losing her. She'd nearly died once already, and I knew if she didn't come back, I'd fall apart. She'd quickly become the center of my entire world.

Zipper held out his hands. "Give her to me and go after your woman. I'll make sure these girls get back to the compound in one piece."

"Take the truck," I said. "Have a Prospect come back for your bike."

He nodded. "They'll be cared for until you get back, but time's wasting. You're going to lose their trail if you don't hurry."

I got back on my bike and took off in the direction of The Inferno. I could hear my brothers and the other clubs at my back, but noticed one member was missing. Tex pulled alongside me and we led the way. I saw Stripes, Cobra, and Renegade near some tire marks that veered onto a dirt path and Stripes gave a nod toward the path. I was immediately grateful they'd thought to keep pursuing Janessa and The Inferno. I started down the bumpy road, hoping he wasn't wrong and they had really come this way. A little ways down the road, I stopped my bike and killed my engine. If they were down this way, the last thing I wanted was to give them a heads-up that we'd found them. The rumble of our bikes would be a dead giveaway.

"On foot from here," Tex said. "Everyone armed and ready? I don't care if you take down every one of these fuckers."

"But leaving one alive might give us some information," Cinder said.

I hadn't even realized he'd joined us, but I was grateful. He took charge, barking out orders, and putting everyone into place. If it had been left to me, we'd have charged the house, and I likely would have gotten Janessa killed. I wasn't thinking rationally, even I could admit as much. If Cinder got Janessa out of there, I'd do whatever he said without question. I should anyway, since he was my Pres, but my head wasn't in the right place at the moment.

Cinder speared me with his icy glare. "You stay at the back, Irish. I don't know what we'll find when we get in there. The last thing I need is you coming unglued and doing something stupid. You hear me?"

I nodded and swallowed hard, trying not to think of what he meant about what we might find when we reached Janessa. The thought of those monsters hurting her made my stomach churn and fury engulf me.

"Boy, I mean it," Cinder said. "You have a kid to think about now. Don't go in half-cocked and get yourself killed."

He was right. I couldn't shake the sight of those eyes staring at me, the ones just like my own. The other girl had said my daughter's name was Payson. Janessa's tender heart had led her outside the gates. She should have had protection, and the fact Killian let her leave without any would be addressed. He'd been a good Prospect, a good friend, but he'd fucked up and it might have cost me the woman I love.

We fanned out and crept closer to the rooftop we could see in the distance. The house that came into view looked about two seconds from falling down. That wasn't what made the blood in my veins turn to ice. It was the screams coming from inside. I tensed, ready to bolt into the house, but a hand gripped me tight.

"Steady, Irish," Grimm said. "We'll get her back, and we'll make them pay."

"I can't... I can't sit here and hear that, hear them tormenting her," I said.

"Stay out here," Grimm said. "Wait until we have them under control, then you can come inside for Janessa. She's family to me, and I swear that every Reaper here will make sure she's alive and those men pay for hurting her."

I nodded and watched as everyone converged on the house. I heard Janessa scream again and I wanted to roar out my anguish at being unable to stop them. I watched as Cinder kicked in the front door and heard the back door give way as well. The house was surrounded, and no one was getting away. Shots were fired and Janessa screamed again. I couldn't take it another moment and charged for the house, not stopping until I'd stormed inside and found her, cowering in the corner of a bedroom.

Blood dripped down her face and neck, and bruises were forming on her neck and arms. She sobbed when she saw me and started crawling in my direction. I rushed toward her and gathered her in my arms. I rocked her, my heart hammering in my chest as her tears soaked my shirt.

"I've got you, sweetheart." My throat was tight and my voice hoarse as I tried to comfort her. Gently, I lifted her into my arms. I didn't look around, just carried her out of the house.

Tex was outside and gave me a nod as I walked past. I carried Janessa to my bike, then worried whether she'd be able to stay on. I wasn't staying around, though, not long enough for someone to bring a vehicle. I helped her onto the back of my bike, then swung my leg over the seat. Her hands trembled as she placed them around my waist, and I covered them with one of my own. When I was certain that she would be able to hold on, I started the bike and headed for the compound. I stuck to the back roads, not wanting any attention.

Killian was at the gate and opened it. I pulled inside, then stopped my bike. Giving Janessa's hands a squeeze, I got off the bike and approached the man I'd thought of as a friend for so long, a soon-to-be brother, and I hauled my fist back and clocked him across the jaw. Killian stumbled, then spat some blood on the ground.

"I deserved that," he said. "I had every intention of sending someone after her, Irish. I called up to the clubhouse after she pulled out, and no one would answer the damn phone. I tried every number in my cell phone and couldn't get a single brother or Prospect to answer. I couldn't leave my post. Shade stopped by and found a device nearby that was making it seem like my calls were going through, but they weren't, despite the ringing I heard. I think they were watching and waiting, Irish. I don't know why they didn't take her right away, unless the girl in the truck with her threw them off balance. Maybe they were hoping Janessa would drop her somewhere, and then they could take your woman when she was alone."

"You left her unprotected! She could have died!" I was screaming and couldn't seem to stop myself. I went after him again, blow after bow, not caring that my knuckles split open or that Killian wasn't fighting back.

"Seamus."

Her voice was soft, nearly a whisper, but it broke through the haze of my rage. I stopped and turned toward her. She swayed a little and I lurched, wrapping my arms around her before she could fall.

"Call the doc," I told Killian.

I didn't stop to see if he was following my instructions. I left my bike and walked to my house, carrying Janessa. I carried her inside and took her to our room, easing her down on the bed. As much as I wanted to hold her hand and never leave her side, I couldn't leave her looking like this. I got a warm, wet cloth from the bathroom and cleaned the blood from her face and neck. There was a cut along her cheekbone, and it looked like finger marks darkening along her neck.

Dr. Chansy came into the room, a bag clutched in his hand, the kind doctors used to use in the movies. He took one look at Janessa and pierced me with his steely gaze.

"Out of the room, Irish. I need to be able to talk to her without the young lady worrying you might be upset by what she says," Dr. Chansy said.

I looked at Janessa and she gave me a slight nod, which wasn't encouraging. I stepped out, but left the door opened a little, and I waited right outside. As I listened to her talk to Dr. Chansy, I couldn't help but feel like I'd failed her. I hadn't kept her safe like I'd promised. They'd taken her, nearly killed her.

"Janessa, I need you to be honest with me," Dr. Chansy said. "Other than the bruising and cuts, did they do anything else to you? Did they rape you?"

"No," she said, her voice soft but sure. "They didn't seem interested in that. They liked to hit me, cut me, and make me scream."

"Any other cuts?" he asked.

I heard rustling, like she was removing her clothes. Their voices dropped to a murmur and I couldn't hear what was said next. After a few minutes of waiting, I couldn't take it anymore. I pushed back into the room and went to sit on the other side of the bed, reaching for her hand.

"Thought I told you to wait outside," the doc said.

"Decided I didn't want to listen."

"You need some antibiotics," Dr. Chansy said. "Any chance you might be pregnant?"

Janessa and I shared a look before she gave him a slight nod.

"It's been less than a week," I said.

"My period is due in another week," Janessa said. "Could we tell then?"

"We can discuss that more later. I'll prescribe something that wouldn't hurt a baby in case you are pregnant. You should also know that while you're taking these, birth control isn't going to work unless you use condoms."

I waved a hand at her, noting the cuts on her legs and along her side. "You think I'm going to do anything while she's hurting like this?"

"Seamus, it's not as bad as it looks," she said.

"It could be worse," the doc agreed, "but don't make light of what you've been through, Janessa. Try to take it easy and keep the wounds clean."

"I'll make sure she doesn't strain herself," I said.

"Call me if she gets worse or if you need anything," Dr. Chansy said.

"Thanks, Doc."

Dr. Chansy nodded and wrote out a prescription for Janessa before leaving. I ran my fingers through her hair, and noticed my hand wasn't that steady. It had scared the hell out of me, seeing them take off with her. Hearing her screams was something that would fuel my nightmares for years to come. I'd been through a lot of shit, both in the military and with the club, but I'd never been truly afraid of anything until the two times I'd nearly lost Janessa.

"I love you," I told her. "So damn much."

"Love you too, Seamus."

I leaned down and kissed her softly. "Rest a bit."

"The girls?" she asked. "Are they okay?"

"Zipper brought them back here to the compound."

"Seamus, they're all alone. Shella said she'd have to go into foster care, and Payson…"

I saw the flash of pain in her eyes and knew I'd put it there by having a kid with a woman I didn't even really remember.

"I'm sorry, baby. So damn sorry."

"She needs you," Janessa said. "They both do."

"We can talk about it later, sweetheart. I need to help you get clean and into your pajamas; then you're going to rest. I'll make something for us to eat in a little while."

"Bring the girls here, Seamus."

"I have nowhere for them to sleep," I reminded her.

"Then fix it. They shared a room. Your daughter didn't have any toys or books. They barely have clothes."

I could tell she was getting tired now that she was safe and at home where she belonged. I kissed her softly again, promising to take care of the girls. Anything to get her to rest and stop worrying. I helped her bathe and dress, then waited until she'd fallen asleep.

As much as I hated to admit it, Nessa was right. Those girls needed a place to stay. Since I hadn't known about Payson, there was no way I was listed on her birth certificate. I'd have to prove I was her father before I'd get custody of her, and I didn't have a clue what to do with the older one. Shella. She looked like a kid, even though I'd been told she was a teen.

I made arrangements for someone to get the appropriate furniture and toys for a girl Payson's age, then I called the clubhouse to see if anyone had made arrangements for Shella. I knew my tenderhearted Janessa would want to keep the girl here, but I wasn't sure how I felt about it. Yes, she was Payson's sister, but I didn't think Janessa would be up for a toddler and a teen, and I knew I damn sure wasn't. Cinder seemed glad that I was doing the right thing by Payson. It might have upset me that he'd had doubts, but I'd doubted myself. I felt like an asshole for not letting Shella stay, but I knew in the long run, she'd be better off elsewhere.

"Demon spoke to his Pres. Grizzly lost his wife to cancer a while back and his daughter is now married to Badger. There's another young girl living at his place, the one we rescued in Columbia. He's agreed to take in Shella, give her a home and a chance at a decent life. He thought maybe Shella and his other adopted daughter could become friends and give each other some much needed support. They're already working on the arrangements," Cinder said.

"I guess I need to arrange a paternity test for Payson," I said.

"We'll handle it. For now, we've notified the authorities that she's here and that you're her father. They may be sending someone from social services around to start the proper paperwork, but I got Judge

Thompson to name you as the girl's guardian for now."

"How did you…" Maybe I didn't want to know.

Cinder chuckled. "When you've been around as long as me, you gather some favors along the way. Don't worry about the how. I heard you have some prospects scrambling to get a room set up for your daughter. That's good. We've got her entertained at the clubhouse until you're ready for her. How's Janessa?"

"Doc says she'll be fine, but he left a prescription. If anyone's available, can you have them swing by and pick it up? She'll need to start taking it tonight."

"Consider it done," Cinder said. "I know I come across as a hard-ass sometimes, but I'm glad you have Nessa and Payson. Don't fuck it up."

"I won't," I said, hoping I wasn't lying.

"Jackal sent over some clothes for Payson, things Allegra has outgrown. They're in better shape than what the kid brought with her so they thought you could use them for now. I'm sure you'll want to take her shopping once Janessa is healed and things have settled a bit."

"Yeah, I'll be sure to thank him. Just give me some time to get a room set up, and then I'll come get Payson."

"I'll bring her by," Cinder said. "Shouldn't leave Janessa alone."

"I'm surprised her family hasn't already shown up on the doorstep," I said.

"I'm keeping them at bay until tomorrow. The doc spoke with them and let them know their daughter would be all right. If she's up to visitors later, then you can invite them over. Tex asked permission to stay another two days before they head home."

"Thank you, Pres. For everything."

"It's what I'm here for. Now take care of your girls."

The line went dead and I decided to pick a room for my daughter. The thought still staggered me, that I had a kid I'd never known about. And a girl at that. I didn't know a damn thing about raising a little girl, but if Jackal had managed it, then so could I. Hell, he'd been just as bad as me at one point, if not worse.

I chose a room down the hall from mine, not wanting her close enough that we'd keep her awake if we got a little loud at night, but near enough she hopefully wouldn't be scared. When the new stuff arrived, I put the little bed together and tried to make the room look inviting. The walls were a plain beige, but I didn't want to take the time to paint. It would take a day to paint the walls and possibly another before they were dry. I wanted my daughter to know this was her home now and that she was welcome here. Payson had been through enough already without staying with strangers, although I was honestly a stranger to her as well, even if I was her dad.

After I placed the call to Cinder, I went to the kitchen and made some tomato soup and grilled cheese sandwiches. I knew that he wasn't overly comfortable around kids, but I also knew that Meg would be at his place. Ever since she'd come here from Columbia, she'd gone out of her way to take care of the Pres. Cinder didn't bother ringing the bell and just came into the house, my little girl clutched in his arms. She looked around with wide eyes, then blinked as she stared at me.

"You remember me, Payson?" I asked. "I took you out of the truck earlier."

She nodded slowly.

"I'm... I'm your daddy," I said, my voice catching.

Cinder set her down and she slowly came toward me. She wrapped her fingers around the denim of my jeans, then held up her other hand. I glanced at Cinder and he motioned for me to pick her up. Once I had her in my arms, she placed her hands on my cheeks and stared really hard for what felt like forever.

"I'm sorry we didn't meet before now," I said.

Janessa stumbled into the kitchen and Cinder caught her before she tumbled to the floor. He eased her down onto a chair at the table and didn't let go until she remained upright.

"Nessa, you shouldn't be up," I said.

"I heard voices," she said, her gaze straying to Payson. "Hi, Payson."

I walked closer and knelt with Payson still in my arms. "Payson, this is Nessa. She's going to be my wife, which means she'll be your stepmom."

Nessa gave her a slight smile. "I promise, I won't ever try to replace your mom. But I'd like to be your friend."

Payson held her hands out to Nessa, and she took her, wincing a little. I tried to take Payson back, but Janessa waved me off. "I've got her."

I put the food on the table and noticed that Cinder had disappeared without a word. As we sat down and ate, I watched my two girls. I might not have planned any of this, but I was glad to have them here with me. Maybe one day, we'd be a proper family. I knew it wouldn't happen overnight, but I had hope that Payson would learn to love us the way she'd loved her mother, and that Janessa wouldn't hurt every time she saw my daughter, knowing I'd had a kid with someone else.

For now, I just needed to help my girls heal, in whatever capacity I was able.

Epilogue

Two months later
Janessa

I looked down at the rings on my finger. Seamus had officially proposed and given me an engagement ring the week after they'd handled The Inferno. The other club was still causing trouble in the southern states, but at least things were quiet here at the Devil's Boneyard. Maybe they'd learned their lesson and would give the club a wide berth. I could hope, anyway.

Seamus was out back chasing Payson around the yard. The little girl giggled and seemed so full of life. It was a big change from the girl I'd found that day. She'd settled in with us nicely, and seemed to be happy. I'd been a little concerned that she was behind a bit so we worked every day on recognizing her letters, shapes, and colors. We'd discussed putting her in a parent's day out program that helped prepare the kids for kindergarten, but we hadn't made a decision yet.

I placed a hand over my belly and wondered if my news would change anything. Seamus looked up and smiled when he saw me. "You going to come join us?" he asked.

"I actually wanted to talk to the two of you, if you think you can take a short break?"

He grabbed Payson's hand and led her over to the back steps. I looked at the man who had held my heart since the first moment I saw him, and the little girl who looked so much like him. I loved them both, and hoped they would be happy about the new addition to our family.

"I thought I'd let Payson know that she's going to be a big sister," I said, then waited for my words to sink in.

Seamus blinked at me a few times, then gave a *whoop* and caught me up in his arms, spinning me around.

"Easy!" I said, patting his shoulder. "You'll make me throw up with all that twirling."

When he stopped, I knelt in front of Payson. The little girl was quiet and seemed uncertain.

"Payson, I know having a baby in the house will be a big change, but I was hoping you might be able to help me. I don't know that I can handle it all on my own. Do you think could help me pick the right toys and blankets? Maybe help me pick a color for the room after we find out if we're having a boy or girl? Being a big sister is really important. The baby will copy what you do and will want to grow up just like you."

She glanced at her daddy, then at me again, and I could see that she looked a little scared.

"Honey," I said softly. "We're not going to love you any less. Your daddy is always going to love his first little girl. And you know I adore you."

"What will the baby call everyone?" she asked.

"Well." I looked up at Seamus. "I'm sure your sister or brother will call your daddy the same thing you do -- Daddy -- and call you sister."

"What will the baby call you?" she asked.

I cleared my throat. "Momma."

Payson looked from me to her dad, then back again. "Can I call you Momma too?"

Tears blurred my vision as I nodded. She wrapped her arms around my neck and hugged me tight. "I love you, sweet girl," I said. "I'm so glad you came to live with us."

"Me too," she said. "It's much nicer here."

I hated that she'd lost her mom, and that her mother had obviously struggled with taking care of her, but Payson had filled a spot in my life. A place I hadn't even realized was empty. I'd been scared about being a parent, step or otherwise, but she'd shown me that I was more than ready.

I looked up and noticed that Seamus seemed to have tears in his eyes, then he cleared his throat and knelt down with us. His arms came around both of us and he brushed a kiss against my temple. "Love you, Nessa. You have given me the greatest gift ever."

"I love you too," I said, then kissed him.

Payson giggled and squirmed away from us. She always thought it was funny when I kissed her dad, or vice versa. I heard her running around the yard as Seamus deepened the kiss and made my knees go weak. No matter how long we were together, I would never grow tired of his kisses.

"You are my entire world," he said. "You and my kids. And I will never let anything hurt any of you ever again."

I cupped his cheek. "Don't make promises you can't keep. Just love me, Seamus. That's all I need."

His kiss, his touch, the way he watched me... all those things told me enough. I knew he loved me every bit as much as I loved him, and that's all I would ever need.

"I think Payson might like a sleepover at Scratch's house," he said, then lowered his voice, "so we can properly celebrate."

My cheeks warmed and I gave him a smile. "I'm already one step ahead of you. Scratch is stopping by in a few minutes to pick up Payson before he heads home. I have a bag packed for her."

"Good thing she likes playing with Noah," Seamus said. "I wouldn't want her to feel like we were trying to get rid of her."

I kissed him softly. "She'll be fine, papa bear. She's become close with Noah and Caleb, even though Caleb does his best to act disinterested in a little girl. I've caught him watching her when he thinks no one is watching, and I've noticed he hands her things if she drops them."

Seamus groaned. "Great."

"What? I think it's sweet."

"Yeah, you think that now. Wait until our kids are teenagers. When Caleb is seventeen and our daughter is fifteen, you'll change your mind. Trust me, I know exactly what seventeen-year-old little boys think about," Seamus said.

"Do you honestly think any kid that belongs to Scratch and Clarity would be anything but a complete gentleman when it came to our daughter?" I asked.

He shrugged.

"Are you two marrying our kids off already?" Scratch asked as he came around the corner of the house. "Your daughter isn't even in school yet. Don't you think you're jumping the gun a bit?"

"Never too early to start preparing," Seamus said.

"Well, I'll try not to plant any ideas into their heads while Payson is at our house," Scratch said. He put his fingers to his mouth and let out a shrill whistle that had Payson running straight for him.

"Okay, then we can talk about the way you whistle for my daughter like she's a puppy?" Seamus asked. "Because it's a bit disturbing."

Scratch chuckled and scooped up Payson as she launched herself at him.

"You two stay out of trouble," Scratch said.

"Her bag is by the front door," I told him. "I haven't had a chance to tell her she's going with you."

"Spend the night?" Payson asked.

"Yes, baby. You're going to spend the night with Caleb and Noah."

She squealed and clapped her hands. Scratch smiled at her fondly, then gave me a wink as he headed inside to get her things. Seamus wrapped his arms around my waist and pulled me tight against him. He nuzzled the side of my neck, giving me goose bumps.

"So, we have the house all to ourselves," he said. "Whatever should we do to pass the time?"

"We could go mess up the bed," I suggested.

"Now that sounds like an amazing idea."

I laughed as he picked me up and headed into the house. He kicked the door shut and strode straight to the bedroom. As he set me on my feet, he turned to shut and lock the bedroom door. By the time he'd turned back around, I'd already started removing my clothes. The look he gave me was enough to make my nipples hard and had me shivering in anticipation.

Seamus took his time stripping off his clothes, and I licked my lips as his incredible body was uncovered a little at a time. I'd never get tired of looking at him. Despite the fact I'd been cooking homemade Mexican food and a ton of pasta, I didn't think he'd gained a pound, unlike me. My clothes were already getting tight and I knew it wasn't baby weight.

When he was naked, and I was still drooling over him, Seamus came closer and reached for me. With one jerk of his hand, he ripped my panties off, leaving me gasping in mock indignation. Honestly, I found it hot and sexy as hell when he did things like that. He always replaced any clothes he ruined, which was a good thing or I'd have run out of panties long before now.

"In a hurry?" I teased.

"Always. Seeing your curves on display always makes me hard as fucking steel. Hell, just watching you bend over when you're fully clothed makes me adjust my dick so Payson doesn't ask what's wrong with my pants."

I burst out laughing and clung to him. Only Seamus could make me laugh when we're about to have sex. And it was even funnier that I knew he was dead serious.

"I love you," I told him.

"Love you more."

I pulled away from him and sprawled across the bed. "Then I guess you'd better show me."

He smirked. "Challenge accepted."

Seamus crawled onto the bed and pressed his hands against my legs until my heels were on the bed and my thighs were spread wide. His heated gaze locked with mine as he lowered his face. The first drag of his tongue along the seam of my pussy had me biting my lip. Seamus thrust his tongue inside me, and I couldn't hold back the moan building in my throat.

"Oh, God. So good," I murmured.

He sucked my clit into his mouth and worked my pussy with his fingers. He tugged the bud with his teeth, lightly scraping it, and my hips bucked as pleasure washed over me in waves. I whimpered as he thrust his fingers harder in and out. It still didn't take much for me to come. Just the slightest touch was almost enough to set me off most days. I came, screaming his name, my body shuddering and my thighs shaking.

"One more," he said, before teasing me again.

His tongue circled my clit, then flicked against it before circling again. Seamus crooked his fingers inside me, rubbing against that magic spot that made me see stars. I felt the gush of my release and clutched the bedding as my heart raced.

As he crawled up the bed, I pushed at him until he rolled onto his back.

"Does my baby want to be in charge?" he asked, then his eyes darkened. "Or does my naughty woman want to suck my cock?"

I squirmed as his words made me tingle in all the right places. I straddled his thighs and then scooted farther down. My breasts pressed against his legs as I leaned over and took a long, slow lick of his cock. Seamus groaned and put his hands behind his head. I grinned, knowing it was the only way he wouldn't reach for me.

I sucked on the head before sliding my lips all the way down his length. He filled my mouth, brushing the back of my throat, before I pulled back, then swallowed him down again. I swirled my tongue around his shaft, then flicked the head. His body was tense, and I could feel him straining, fighting not to take control.

"Seamus," I said, licking my lips. "Remember that fantasy you told me about?"

He looked at me, heat blazing in his eyes. "The one with you on your knees?"

I nodded, then slid off the bed and knelt on the floor. I leaned in closer and wrapped my hand around his shaft. As he dragged me closer to his cock, I felt my pulse speed up.

"Open that gorgeous mouth," he said.

I parted my lips and he slid his cock inside. I placed my hands in my lap and let him control the movement. He tipped my head back a little more and he slid in deeper.

"That's it, baby. Take it all. Every Goddamn inch." He groaned and tightened his hold on me. "God, Nessa. You're so damn beautiful."

I moaned around his shaft.

"I'm gonna fuck your mouth, baby. You want that, don't you?"

I hummed my agreement and tried to relax my throat as he plunged deep. Seamus took what he wanted and I felt the swell of his cock moments before he came. Spurt after spurt of hot cum filled my mouth.

"Swallow," he commanded.

I managed to swallow all of it and he pulled free. He swiped his thumb across my bottom lip, then picked me up off the floor and tossed me onto the bed. I waited to see what he would do next, and he didn't disappoint me. Seamus reached into the bedside drawer and pulled out the handcuffs. We'd only used them once before, but it was one of my favorite memories.

I stretched my hands up to the headboard and he shackled me to it.

"Spread those legs, sweetheart. You do everything I say, then you'll get a nice big reward."

I parted my legs. When he reached into the drawer again, I didn't know what to expect. It certainly wasn't two vibrators and a bottle of lube. I stared at the items, not sure where this was going, but I trusted Seamus with my life.

"First, I'm going to get you nice and worked up," he said.

He picked up the smaller of the two vibrators and clicked it on. The soft whirring sound filled the room as he reached down and parted the lips of my pussy. He gently touched the toy to my clit and I bucked and cried out, nearly coming from that brief, quick contact. Seamus grinned and did it again. He toyed with me, giving me just enough pleasure that I would nearly come, and then he'd back off.

I was a squirming, frustrated mess by the time he finally let me come. My body twitched from the force of my release, but he didn't seem to be done with me yet. I heard the lid open on the lube, and I watched to see what he'd do next. He set the small toy aside long enough to lube the bigger one, then he turned it on.

"Just going to play a little, but I'm not going to do anything you don't want me to," he said.

His words alone sent a hint of apprehension through me and when he parted the cheeks of my ass and placed the toy against that forbidden spot, I gasped and my eyes went wide. He didn't try to put the toy inside me, just circled the spot and let it buzz against me. Once I relaxed, it started to feel really good.

Seamus picked up the smaller toy again and put it back on my clit. The two vibrators going at once nearly made my eyes roll back in my head, they felt so incredible. I went wild when I came again, my body seeming to have a mind of its own. I cried out and went still as I felt the vibrator enter my ass. Frozen in shock, I wasn't sure if I was hurting or if I liked it. My mind wouldn't work right.

"Um, Nessa. Just so we're clear, that was all you, babe. I didn't try to put that there, but you kind of impaled yourself on it during all that thrashing,"

Seamus said, watching me warily. "If you'll give me a second, I'll pull it out."

Did I want that?

"Wait," I said. I tried to calm myself and focus. It wasn't the most comfortable feeling in the world, but the vibrations actually felt nice. I burned some from being stretched open, and I had no doubt I'd be sore tomorrow, but I kind of liked it. I'd heard that anal hurt the first time, even the first several times. Maybe my endorphins were to blame, from coming so hard and so often, but it wasn't nearly as bad as I'd thought it would be.

Seamus teased my clit again and I moaned as my eyes slid shut in pleasure. He didn't do anything to the other toy except hold it. We seemed to have an unspoken agreement that I was in control when it came to that aspect of our play right now. I shifted a little, experimenting with how it felt, and soon I was begging Seamus for more.

"Fuck me," I begged. "Please."

"I need you to be really clear right now. Fuck you where?" he asked.

"My ass. Fuck me with the toy in my ass, and… and…" My brain felt like it was short circuiting as I felt another orgasm building. He slowly thrust the toy in and out of me while the other buzzed against my clit. In a matter of seconds, I was coming harder than I ever had before. I might have even blacked out for a second or two.

When I opened my eyes, Seamus was staring at me with a bemused expression.

"What?" I asked.

"I can't believe you did that and seemed to not only like it but want more. I fully expected to spend the next few weeks easing you into the idea."

"Seamus, I love you, but your cock is nowhere near as small as that vibrator. You try to stick your dick up my ass, and I may murder you in your sleep."

He snickered and turned off both toys, tossing them aside.

"All worn out?" he asked. "Or do you want more?"

I eyed his cock, which was fully erect again. "I want you."

He covered me with his body and entered me with one, hard thrust. My toes curled and I wrapped my legs around his waist. Seamus took me like a man possessed and the headboard crashed against the wall over and over. He brushed against my clit with every stroke and soon I was coming again. I felt his body tense and his thrusts became more erratic.

"Can't hold on," he muttered.

He groaned as he came inside me, the hot stickiness of his release filling me. When we both were breathing heavily and had nothing left to give, he unlocked the cuffs and cuddled me close.

"I think that was a new record for you," he said. "I lost count of how many times you came."

"What can I say? You touch me and I go up in flames."

He smoothed my hair back from my face and gave me a tender look. "You're the only woman I've ever wanted by my side, the only one I've ever loved. I would be completely lost without you, Nessa."

"I'm not going anywhere," I promised. "You're my one and only. Only death could keep me from your side."

He pressed a kiss to my lips. "Then I guess you better plan on living forever."

I smiled and curled against him, breathing in his musky scent, and feeling happier than ever before. I'd gotten the man of my dreams, a daughter who was a total sweetheart, and a baby I'd created with the love of my life. Everything had turned out absolutely perfect, and I couldn't wait to see what all our tomorrows would bring.

Tank (Dixie Reapers MC 9)
Harley Wylde

Emmie -- I overheard my father promise me to a man who is so cold I'm not sure he even has a heart. So I did what any woman would do. I ran. My sister, Federal Agent Lupita Montoya, gave me sanctuary in the US and helped me file the paperwork so I could stay. Now Lupita's in prison and my time is running out. My father and Ernesto will be coming for me. When Lupita sends me to the Dixie Reapers compound in Alabama, I know they're my last hope. I just didn't count on falling for one of them.

Tank -- The hot little Latina I've had my eye on for three weeks is in trouble, and the time for waiting is over. Emmie is really Emelda Montoya, sister to the woman I chased around Christmas, and someone my club owes a debt. It makes Emmie hands off, but I've never been good at backing down, especially when I see something I want. She's over a decade younger than me, but I'm not going to let something like age stand in my way, and I'm sure as hell not going to let her mobster father get between us. I'll bury him if I have to, along with that sick bastard, Ernesto.

But the more digging my club does, the more twisted the tale becomes. For the first time in my life, I'm not sure we can handle the trouble that's landed on our doorstep, but I will die trying to protect the woman I'm falling for, the woman I accidentally knocked up, the woman I call *wife*.

Prologue

Emelda

I pressed a hand to the glass separating me from my sister, the only person who had ever cared about me. I clutched the phone to my ear with my other hand. Lupita didn't deserve to be locked up, but I understood why she'd done it. It was wrong on so many levels, but she'd wanted the Dixie Reapers to owe her a favor, and she hoped by association that Casper VanHorne would as well if the Reapers couldn't protect me. The kind of trouble I was in wouldn't be solved easily, so my big sister had taken it upon herself to guarantee I'd have help when I needed it. And that time had come.

"Lupita, why couldn't you have just asked them for help?" I asked.

"I've told you before, I couldn't take a chance they would deny my request. You need protection, Emmie. Not even my connections could save you. Besides, it's more like a resort here. I get to watch TV, get free food, and there's a gym. What more could I want?"

Freedom? I eyed the glass separating us, and I wasn't convinced she was telling me the truth about the resort quality, but I knew Lupita was hard as nails and a complete badass. If anyone could handle themselves in prison, it would be her. I just hated it had come to this. She'd been locked up for too long already, and I worried she'd never get out.

"I'll be out of here before you know it."

"They think you killed all those men," I whispered. "You're never getting out of here. It's been two years already! Nearly two and a half!"

"Sure I am." She flashed her teeth in a smile that looked downright predatory. "Just have to have dirt on the right people and it's amazing what you can accomplish. I'm out of here in about three more years, maybe less. A lot less. In the meantime, go find Tank. The compound is in Alabama, a small town not too far from the Florida panhandle. I left the directions in our secret place. The man's a total man-whore, but I don't think you're his type. He seems to like tough women."

I looked around, making sure no one was listening.

"Lupita, what if they turn me away?"

"Then you come back here and tell me. I'll make their lives a living hell," she said, her voice flat and hard. I knew she meant it too. "One in particular would never see his woman and kid again, and I know they'll do whatever it takes to keep that from happening. When you leave here, don't stop until you're out of the state. Go straight to Tank, and only stop for short breaks. They'll be watching you, Emmie."

"I know." I pressed my lips together. "It's not fair, Lupita."

"Life never is," she said, "and as women, we're often dealt a shitty hand. Rise above, Emmie. Rise above. I'd tell you to stand and fight, but you've never been much of a fighter. I don't think I've even seen you kill a bug before."

I smiled faintly. My sister had always been fierce and I loved that about her, but it just wasn't who I was. She'd tried to train me to fight, but I'd never mastered the skills as well as she had. I could hold my own for a brief time, but Lupita could take a man down and keep him down. I'd barely give myself enough time to run away.

"Go, Emmie," she said, her voice hard again.

"I'm going. I love you, Lupita."

"This isn't goodbye forever," she said, smiling. "Just bye for now. Take care of yourself, kid. And whatever you do, don't fall for a Reaper's charm. They'd chew you up and spit you out."

I hung up the phone and pushed my chair back. The guards eyed me as I left, and I signed out of the prison that housed my sister for who knew how much longer. Just like her resort comment, I wasn't sure I believed her about the three years either.

It was a hot rainy day, spring having bled into summer. Two years and nearly six months. My sister had been in that place for too long already. She'd turned herself in right before Christmas two years ago, and it hadn't taken long before she transferred to this horrible place. Since she'd pled guilty, the trial had moved at a lightning pace. My gut clenched when I thought about her being stuck here. She'd never tell me if it was as bad as I imagined.

I got into my car and stared at the prison one last time before driving away. I checked my mirrors often, the way she'd trained me to do, and hoped no one was following me. I knew my life would be over if my father, or Ernesto Lopez, got their hands on me.

Growing up, I hadn't realized my father was a bad man. I knew he was busy and didn't have time for me, that our family was far from normal, but Lupita had always been there. At least, until she'd turned eighteen and moved to America. She'd attended college here and pushed herself, excelling at everything she tried, and eventually landed a job with the FBI. She was a lot older than me, and I'd always looked up to her, which is why I eagerly moved here to be with her after I overhead my father. Selling me.

Maybe "selling" was a bit harsh of a description. He'd actually been negotiating a marriage contract, to a man who was old enough to be my grandfather. I'd peeked into my father's office after hearing their discussion, and the man signing the papers had made my stomach turn. It wasn't that he was ugly, even though he was far older than I'd have preferred. No, it was the coldness that seemed to seep from him and permeate the surrounding space. His eyes were flat and dead, and I knew his soul was too. It hadn't taken much for me to learn who he was, or who my father was for that matter. Anyone with an Internet connection could read the articles on either man, and none were good. So, I'd run.

Lupita had kept me safe as long as possible, but with her locked up, no one would stop my father or my husband-to-be if they came for me. I didn't know how Lupita had kept them away for so long, but she'd managed it. Even while she'd been incarcerated, they'd kept their distance, but I knew they would come sooner or later. It was only a matter of time before my freedom was gone, and my life would be over. I'd read every article I could find on Ernesto Lopez, and what I'd found made me sick. He was a cruel, vicious man, and I knew I would only feel pain if I married him.

I didn't understand why Lupita had waited so long to send me to the Dixie Reapers. If she'd thought Tank could help, why hadn't she mentioned him sooner? All this time, and barely even a mention of the Reapers, other than how they pertained to her case and getting locked up. It made me wonder if she'd heard something, even in prison, and knew my father was closing in. Or maybe her connections who had kept me safe so far were backing off? I had so many questions I wanted to ask her, but with prison guards listening in, it hadn't seemed wise.

My sister's home office of the FBI hadn't been far from the Dixie Reapers, but they'd incarcerated her in a special federal women's prison up north. I had a long drive ahead of me, and I tried to hum along with the radio to pass the time. Lupita's words stayed fresh in my mind, and no matter how tired I became, I kept driving. I stopped long enough to retrieve the directions she'd left me at our secret place, and found an envelope with a little cash, then got back on the road. Ever vigilant about just how long a car remained behind me. It took me over twenty hours, having to stop for breaks to stretch my legs and chug enough caffeine to stay awake. Finally, I approached the Dixie Reapers compound, and I couldn't shake my fear. Whatever happened next would decide my fate.

And if they did turn me away, I knew I couldn't go back to Lupita. For one, I didn't have enough cash. For another, I was worried about the man who had the family, the Reaper my sister had mentioned. Lupita wouldn't hesitate to ruin him if she thought it would help me in some way, and that was the last thing I wanted.

I rolled down my window when I came to a stop, and a man wearing a leather vest that said *Prospect* came toward me.

"Are you lost?" he asked.

"Um, I don't think so? This is the Dixie Reapers compound, isn't it?" I asked.

His gaze narrowed. "You related to Diego?"

"No. I'm looking for Tank."

His eyebrows shot upward. "Tank? He expecting you?"

"Probably not," I said. "My sister sent me. She said Tank would protect me."

"And who's your sister?" he asked.

"Ex-Federal Agent Lupita Montoya. I'm Emelda Montoya. Emmie." My hands trembled where I gripped the steering wheel and I just knew he would send me away. Then I'd be left to fend for myself with no money, and no one to keep the monsters from taking me. Well, almost no money. I could probably get a room at some rundown motel, but how long would that last? There was very little left in the envelope.

"You can leave a name and number. I'll have Tank call you. He's not here right now," the man said.

My shoulders slumped and the fatigue of the last day pressed down on me. I knew the funds I had left wouldn't be enough for me to last very long. As much as I hated to do it, I needed that motel room I'd just been thinking about. No matter what happened from this moment forward, I would need rest to face whatever it was. I pulled a napkin from the glove compartment and a pen from my purse, then I scribbled my name and cell number down and handed it to the man. I didn't know if Tank, or anyone here, would remember my sister. She'd gone to jail for them, but that didn't mean anything. Maybe that happened in their world all the time.

"Please. It's really important that I see him," I said, pressing the napkin into his hand.

"Sure. I'll make sure he calls."

I knew my sister would have argued with him, insisted on being let inside the gates, but I'd never been a fighter like Lupita. Maybe the Tank person she'd said

I should see would have listened, but the one at the gate wasn't letting me get that close. I didn't know if I believed him when he said Tank wasn't available, but what good would it be to call him a liar?

I backed down the drive, and right before I turned onto the road, I saw him toss the napkin into the trash. If I couldn't even get past the guy at the gate, how did I have a prayer of getting to see Tank? As far as I knew, there was no other way inside. And if this guy, who had seemed friendly enough at first, wouldn't help me, why would Tank or any other Dixie Reaper? Tears blurred my vision as I pulled away. If the Dixie Reapers wouldn't help me, then I had no one. I couldn't use the money in my account, in the event my father had a way to trace it. I hoped it would take him a while to find me. Lupita had even asked me to buy a cheap pay-as-you-go phone when she'd been sent to prison, in hopes our father couldn't trace it. I wasn't as strong as her, and I didn't know how long I'd make it on my own, but it looked like I was about to find out.

Chapter One

Tank
Three weeks later

The new waitress at the diner was a cute thing, and familiar somehow. Her dark hair hung down her back in curls, nearly falling to her waist even with her hair pulled back in a ponytail. It was the first thing I'd noticed. The second had been the killer curves that would be more than a handful. I'd always had a thing for short, curvy women. Her skin was flawless, even though she looked overly tired with dark circles under her eyes. Fatigue seemed to be weighing her down, and I noticed she struggled to keep up. She'd popped up a few weeks ago, and I'd been here nearly every day since the first glimpse I'd had of her. It was her eyes that seemed so familiar.

"Isn't she a little young for you?" Wire asked, nodding toward my obsession.

I shrugged. It was true enough, she didn't look very old, and I preferred my women closer to thirty, if not older. Didn't mean I couldn't look. Woman with a body like that, it was really damn hard not to stare. I got hard just thinking about that perfect ass of hers, bent over as she begged to be fucked. I wondered if she was a screamer.

I wasn't the only one noticing her. Several of the male customers checked her out. I'd even seen one try to grab her ass, but she'd managed to twist away. I'd been about two seconds from getting up and handling the situation, but she'd kept going like it hadn't happened. Made me wonder if she dealt with that shit all the time, and it only pissed me off. I'd never condoned men taking what wasn't offered. There was a difference in fucking a willing woman and trying to grab someone who didn't want your attention. Some assholes learned that the hard way, usually after I'd put my fist through their face to teach them some manners.

My conscience pricked when I thought about Wraith's woman, Rin. I'd nearly tossed her out on her ass the first night she'd appeared at our gates. If I'd done that, she'd be dead right now. I'd been an asshole to her, and I wasn't proud of myself. At the time, I'd been hurting over a stupid cunt who had tried to trick me into staying with her, and I'd taken it out on poor Rin. Blair had been a complete bitch, but I hadn't gotten away soon enough. I'd apologized to Rin for my behavior since then, but I knew Wraith wouldn't forgive me anytime soon.

The petite waitress didn't seem like the kind of woman who would string men along, unlike the woman I'd been seeing up until two years ago. I'd found out Blair had several stallions in her stable, confronted her about, and then she'd tried to trick me into believing I'd gotten her pregnant. I'd strung her along a little longer, until I could prove her to be a liar. She hadn't soured me on women, though. Pissed me off good and proper, but I still got my dick wet at the clubhouse often enough. No, the woman who had fucked me over in my early twenties had soured me on relationships. Blair was my first attempt to be with a woman longer than a few days, and look how that had turned out.

The little Latina waitress had a name tag that said *Emmie* and the name was as cute as she was. My brothers had given me hell, telling me I should just ask her out. I was always careful not to sit in her section.

I'd noticed the first time we'd come in after she'd been hired she froze when she saw us enter the diner. The blood had drained from her face, and I'd thought she might faint. It wasn't the first time a woman had been afraid of us, and I doubted it would be the last. I knew I was more intimidating than most with my height and size. I wasn't the enforcer for my club without reason. Someone started a fight, I could finish it, usually with them requiring a coroner when I was done.

"Are we going to eat here all the damn time just because you want to bang the hot little Hispanic girl?" Tempest asked. "Because the food is decent enough, but I'm starting to get tired of it."

"No one said you had to come along," I told him, my gaze still locked on Emmie.

"And miss it when you finally find your balls and go talk to her?" he asked. "No, until you man the fuck up and ask her out, I'll just keep tagging along. Might be worth it if she shoots you down. I don't think I've ever seen a woman turn you away, except that federal agent. That one over there, she doesn't look like someone who would be interested in a guy like you."

"Why's that?" I asked.

"For one, she's what? Five feet nothing to your six feet five? How the hell would that even work?" Tempest asked.

I looked over at him and raised a brow. "Really? Do you need lessons? Is that why you're still single? Not keeping the ladies happy in the bedroom?"

Tempest flipped me off, and I went back to watching Emmie.

No one knew her story. I'd asked around, but she was a complete unknown. No family in the area, and I'd heard she was staying at some shit motel on the other end of town. It wasn't safe, and I'd taken to driving by there when I knew she was going home from work. Even though I made sure she got into her room without any problems, it was impossible to guarantee her safety past that. Not unless I camped out at her doorstep all night.

The bell over the door jingled, and Emmie went deathly pale, dropping the plate she'd been carrying. It shattered at her feet, but she was frozen in place. My gaze locked onto the men who had just entered the diner. It was obvious she recognized them, even though I didn't, and I made it my mission in life to know all the big players in town. These men with their expensive suits, three hundred dollar haircuts, and arrogance weren't small fish. They also didn't look all that young.

"Emelda, it's time to do your duty," one of them said.

"How did you find me?" she asked, her voice soft and shaky.

"That doesn't matter. Your fiancé is here, and he's willing to forgive this transgression," the man said, waving a hand at the guy standing next to him.

Fiancé? I hadn't noticed a ring on her finger in all the days I'd been here. And yeah, I'd looked. I might be an asshole at times, but I never poached. If I'd have thought she belonged to someone else, I'd have backed off. Not that I'd really made a move yet anyway.

"I'm not going with either of you," she said, tipping her jaw up.

The men advanced on her, and I knew I had a decision to make. Stand back and let things play out, or step in and extract the little angel from a situation she clearly wanted to avoid. I didn't know who these men were, but it didn't matter right then. They scared her, and that put them at the top of my list of assholes who needed to disappear.

I pushed my chair back and made my way over to her, but she didn't even look at me. Her hands were clenched at her sides, but I could see the fear in her eyes, and I was willing to bet these men could too. They came closer, pausing a moment as I stepped up behind Emmie. I wrapped an arm around her waist and hauled her back against my body.

"Everything all right, baby?" I asked. "These men bothering you?"

"Stay out of this," the supposed fiancé said. "Emelda is mine, and if you know what's good for you, you'll just walk away. This is family business."

"Family business?" I asked. "Then I guess I'll just have to stick around, seeing as how Emmie is my woman."

I could feel the shock coming off Emmie as her body slightly stiffened at my declaration, but she didn't pull away. If anything, she pressed closer to me and placed her hands over the arm banded around her waist. There was a tremor in her fingers as they pressed against my skin. Whoever these men were, they scared the shit out of her, and that was unacceptable.

"What is this nonsense?" the other man asked. If the first was her fiancé, I wasn't quite sure who this man was. He seemed a decade older than the other man. Older brother maybe?

"I told you, Father. I'm not going with you," she said.

Well, shit. I hadn't expected that, but I wasn't backing down. If she needed help, I was going to give it to her. If anyone knew calling a man "father" didn't mean anything, it was me. My dad had been a real jackass, and once I'd put him in my rearview, I'd never looked back. I had a feeling Emmie had tried to do the same thing, but he'd found her.

"You expect me to believe you'd be living in that shit motel if you were seeing someone?" the fiancé asked. "Or maybe he can't afford a place and lives in the gutter. You prefer this caveman over me?"

"Pretty sure she'd prefer dog shit over you," I said. "And not that it's any of your business, but I've been trying to get her to move in with me. You know how stubborn Emmie can be."

Her father sneered at me. "Emmie. Her name is Emelda, or did you not know that?"

The fiancé's face darkened and he took a step closer. "Did you sleep with him? Let him fuck you?"

I felt a tremor rake her small frame, and I decided I'd have enough of this shit. I turned and put Emmie behind me, then stepped up to the two assholes who were ruining my night. Without so much as a warning, I planted my fist in the fiancé's face and knocked him out cold before leveling a glare at her father.

"You want to be next? Or would you like to walk out of here?" I asked.

"You're nothing. Less than nothing." Her father sneered at me, then spat at my feet. "You think someone like you will stand in my way? You stay with my daughter, and I'll bury you."

I snorted as I let my gaze travel over him, not the least bit impressed. Yeah, he was used to having power and throwing his weight around, but this was Dixie Reapers' territory. I wasn't going to let him come into my town and pull this shit, especially not with the sweet woman I'd been fantasizing about for weeks.

"This isn't over," her father said.

"Oh, trust me. It is. Be sure to take this piece of trash with you on your way out."

Her father tried to intimidate her, but I made sure to block his view.

"Emelda, we'll discuss this another time when this brute isn't around. You have a duty to this family, and you *will* marry Ernesto."

I folded my arms over my chest. "You're wasting valuable time. If you're still here in another thirty seconds, I'll take it as an invitation to kick the shit out of you."

His jaw clenched, but he wisely didn't say anything. I tried not to laugh as he attempted to drag Ernesto out of the diner. The man didn't have much in the way of muscle. He might have power, but it wasn't the kind that came from using his fists, and I sure as fuck wasn't afraid of him.

I waited until they were both clear of the door and it had swung shut before I turned to face Emmie.

"You all right, sweetheart?"

She nodded and wiped at the tears streaking her cheeks. "I don't understand."

"What don't you understand?" I asked.

"The Dixie Reapers wouldn't help me before. Or at least the man I spoke to wouldn't. Why did you stand up for me now?" she asked.

Everything in me went still. What the fuck was she talking about? The first time I'd ever seen her was here at the diner. If she'd ever come to the compound, I sure as hell would have remembered. And I damn sure wouldn't have sent her away. "Before?" I asked.

She nodded. "I went straight to your compound like my sister told me to. The man at the gate took my name and number, said Tank wasn't available but he'd pass it along. I saw him throw it away as I drove off."

"I'm Tank," I said, tipping her chin up. "Who's your sister, sweetheart?"

"Lupita Montoya. She said you'd help me. Keep me safe."

My breath froze in my lungs for a moment and my heart gave a hard kick. Lupita Montoya? The sexy as fuck federal agent who had taken the fall when Wraith had massacred everyone at town hall? I'd tried to get into her pants, but she'd been a feisty one and always shot me down. It had been fun verbally sparring with her, even if she had given me blue balls. It figured the woman I'd been fascinated with the last few weeks was her sister.

"You're Emelda Montoya?" I asked.

"Yes."

I stroked her chin with my thumb. "You tell me what day you came to the gates and I'll find out who was working that night. Then I'm going to beat the shit out of him for turning you away."

She looked out the glass door of the diner and shivered. "They know where I've been staying."

"You're not staying at the motel anymore, Emmie. It's not safe."

"I can't afford anything else."

"Hey." She locked her gaze on mine again. "No one is going to hurt you, because I won't let them. You'll come to the compound with me and stay in my guest room."

I heard a cough-covered *bullshit* that sounded like it came from Tempest. I'd deal with that asshole later. Now that I knew who she was, it meant she was off-limits. I had no doubt if Lupita Montoya found out I'd slept with her baby sister, she'd find a way to take my balls, even while she was locked up in prison. That was one she-devil I'd never underestimate. We'd all either witnessed or heard about what she'd done at city hall when everyone had gone after Rin.

"My shift isn't over," Emmie said.

"Yes, it is." The diner manager came out, his arms folded. "You're done here. I told you I didn't want trouble. When you asked to be paid under the table, I knew something was wrong. I just thought you were some illegal cunt from south of the border."

Emmie's cheeks flushed and I growled at the manager, ready to take his head off for offending her.

"I'm from Spain, not Mexico," she said. "And all my documentation is in order. Not that it should matter. Calling any woman a cunt is inexcusable."

So not a Latina like I'd assumed, but a pretty Spanish rose.

"Pack your shit and leave," the manager said.

Emmie nodded and I could see the tears in her eyes again. She stepped around the manager and disappeared into the back. I leveled the man with a glare.

"We give this place a lot of business. Maybe we should rethink our choice of eating establishments," I said. "Wonder how much you'd lose if none of the Reapers ever came here again? Or our women. Don't Ridley and Isabella meet here at least twice a week for breakfast?"

The man audibly swallowed. "I can't have her here making trouble. She's always breaking stuff, and now this... It's not good for business."

"Right. And it has nothing to do with the names you called her just now?" I asked. "Are you a racist jackass? Perhaps the owner needs to be made aware of how you treat the women in your employ."

The man started sweating. "I'm sure we can work something out."

"You give Emmie her last check, and make sure you include a bonus for having to put up with your bullshit. Once I have things sorted out with her family, if she wants to work here again, you'll hire her back and treat her with some damn respect. Understood?" I asked.

He nodded and scurried into the back and out of my sight. Emmie passed him, a small bag clutched in her hand, along with a set of keys. She shifted from foot to foot when she stopped in front of me.

"You follow behind me to the compound," I said. "My brothers will be right behind you to make sure your dad doesn't try to fuck with you. You're safe now, Emmie. I won't let anything happen to you."

I waited until she was tucked into her car and the engine running before I went to my bike. I pulled out of the lot with Emmie right behind me, and my brothers trailing her. When we got to the compound and I saw Fenton flinch as his gaze locked on Emmie's car, I knew exactly who had turned her away, and I'd be getting to the bottom of it really fucking fast. He'd been a good Prospect, so I wasn't sure what had happened to make him toss Emmie's number. If those men had found her when I wasn't around, things could have gone badly for her. It pissed me off that he'd put her in danger.

I went straight to my house and when I parked my bike, Emmie pulled in next to me. I held her door open as she got out of the car and nervously looked around. I took the keys from her and tossed them to Tempest, who had stuck to us even inside the gates. "Get her shit out of the car, then stop by the motel and clean it out too. I don't want her going back to that place, even with an escort," I said.

"On it," Tempest said. He paused and glanced at me. "Sorry about the shit I said before. I didn't realize who she was."

Yeah, I hadn't either. I wasn't the only one who'd heard she was Lupita's sister. All my brothers had been listening closely to that exchange. I had no doubt they'd rally around her, make sure Emmie was taken care of at all times. Her sister had earned our respect, and we all damn well knew we owed her. At least those of us who had been around back then. The Prospects were newer and might not have heard about Lupita. If she hadn't taken the fall for the shit that went down right before Christmas two years ago, back when Rin was in trouble, then Wraith would probably be serving multiple life sentences right now, leaving Rin alone to raise their child, if the stress hadn't made her miscarry.

I led Emmie into the house and let her look around. It was relatively small. Even though it had three bedrooms and two bathrooms, the entire house was maybe twelve hundred square feet, if that. The master bedroom was a decent size, but the other two were tiny. It hadn't been an issue before, but now I wished I had a better room to offer Emmie. I'd put a full-size bed, nightstand, and five-drawer chest in the guest room. It was modest, but I'd never really had a use for it. Josie had stayed there for a while, and her daughter had used the third bedroom, but they'd moved out a few years ago and I'd changed the rooms. The third room was now empty of furniture and I had a tendency to shove stuff in there and use it for storage. If I wanted to see my sister and her kids, I went to her house. It was easier than asking her to travel with the rugrats.

I rubbed my beard and looked around my house, realizing I was maybe a bit messier than I'd ever realized. There were some empty beer bottles on the coffee table in the living room, my kitchen sink was full, and the hamper in my tiny-ass laundry room was overflowing. I didn't even want to think about the state of my bedroom. I never brought women here, so it hadn't been an issue. Emmie probably thought I was a slob, and was possibly wishing she'd run the other way when I'd said she was coming home with me.

"It's not much," I said, as she peered into the guest room, "but it's free and safe. You won't have to worry about some drunk or drugged out asshole breaking into your room, and I promise to keep my hands to myself. You have nothing to fear while you're here."

"Did you and my sister ever…" Her cheeks flushed and she looked away. "Never mind."

"Did we sleep together?" I asked.

She nodded. "You seem like her type, and I'm sure she's the type of woman you like."

I smiled a little. "No, we didn't sleep together. I did try to get in her pants, but she shut me down. Her fire did draw my attention, but I think while we could have burned up the sheets short-term, in the long run we'd have made each other crazy. Besides, she's all law-abiding and shit."

Emmie sighed and looked away. "Not anymore."

Fuck. *Way to put your foot in your mouth, asshole.*

"I'm sorry about what happened," I said. "None of us expected her to do that. I guess I can understand now why she did. She hoped we would protect you, didn't she?"

"Yeah. She saw an opportunity and dove in headfirst like she always does."

"You'll be safe, Emmie. I won't let your dad or that Ernesto dick get their hands on you. And once all this is over, maybe we can find a way to get Lupita out of prison. In a legal way."

"Don't make promises you can't keep," she said softly. "Tomorrow is never guaranteed for any of us."

She had a point, but what she didn't know was I planned to keep both promises. No matter what it took.

Chapter Two

Emmie

Tank had left me to get settled, even though I didn't really have much to put away. I'd left my clothes and shoes at the motel. I'd purchased a few necessities with my first two days of tips, and it was all I had at the moment. Since I'd left in such a hurry, I hadn't had a chance to pack anything. I hadn't even called the college I'd been attending for fear my father would track me there. I'd just disappeared mid-term and left all my belongings. I knew my dorm room was gone now, and my chance at getting a degree was momentarily flushed. Lupita had found a way for me to go for free and she'd paid for my dorm room, but now all that was gone. No way they'd let me return.

I didn't know what to make of Tank. He was far bigger than I'd anticipated. Lupita was a good six inches taller than me, and I was certain he'd tower over her too. When he'd wrapped his arm around me back at the diner, I'd been shocked and a bit scared at first, and then... it had felt oddly right. Which just scared me even more. I had no business being attracted to a man like him. Like he'd said, he didn't exactly walk on the right side of the law. I doubted I wanted to know the extent of his crimes, but if he could keep me away from my father and Ernesto, then I wasn't sure I cared if he'd murdered fifty people. Wrong? Sure. But I'd quickly learned I had to look out for myself, and not care quite so much what happened to other people. Except Lupita. I'd do anything for my sister.

I heard the front door open and shut, and then a deep male voice carried down the short hall.

"Tempest asked me to gather the woman's stuff when he got called out. She didn't have much, Tank. Just a few changes of clothes and two pair of shoes that look like they came from the discount store," the man said.

The rustle of a plastic sack carried over the short distance, and I winced when I realized everything I owned probably fit into a small shopping bag. I could hear someone rummaging through the sack and then a soft growl I recognized as Tank.

"Wait here."

I heard his booted steps, but they didn't come toward me. I inched closer to the door, but stayed hidden. What was he doing? I listened hard but couldn't hear anything else. When his steps came closer and then stopped again, I held my breath and strained to hear what he said.

"Take this and ask Janessa to go with you. She'll know what to get. I wrote the sizes down."

Wrote the sizes down? My curiosity got the better of me and I crept into the hall. Neither man noticed me, and I saw Tank hand the guy a piece of paper and a wad of cash. My sack of belongings lay on the floor, one of my shirts spilling out of it.

"I'll drop everything off in a bit," the man said.

"Send Fenton over. I need a word with him," Tank said.

"Sure. But if you're going to make him bleed, you might want to take it elsewhere. The girl might be squeamish."

When he turned, I saw the word *Prospect* across his back along with *Dixie Reapers MC* and a rather menacing image. What were those vest things called?

Oh yeah, a cut. I'd watched reruns of a show about bikers back at the motel and had tried to learn as much as I could, even though I doubted everything on TV was even close to factual.

Tank shut the door behind him, then turned and spotted me.

"How long you been there?" he asked.

"Long enough to wonder what you're doing."

"King is going to grab Tex's daughter and take her to the store. She's nearly eighteen and should be able to pick a few things you'll like. You need more clothes than what you have. Not to mention the shoes look like they'll fall apart if I look at them too hard."

"It was the best I could do with what little I had," I said, feeling a little defensive. It wasn't like I'd planned to go on the run and hideout in this town.

"Your sister wore nice clothes when she was here. I'm sure she'd want the same for you. Does she know you've been struggling and living in a dangerous area?"

"Not exactly," I mumbled. Or really, not at all. I hadn't tried to contact Lupita even once, and I was sure she was worried about me. If she'd thought for one second the Dixie Reapers had turned me away, she'd have found a way to either reach me herself, or she'd have sent someone after me.

"That's what I thought. If you'd told her you were refused entrance to the compound, I have no doubt she'd have a found a way for all of us to be murdered in our sleep. She never said your name, but she did talk about a little sister during one of our conversations. I could tell she was protective of you."

"Yeah, sometimes she takes it too far. Like going to prison for something she didn't do."

"We didn't understand at the time why she did it, but it's making sense now."

"I told her it was stupid," I muttered. "She should have just asked you to help me. Surely you aren't all big enough assholes you'd have told her no."

"Well, we can be assholes, but no. If we'd known you were in trouble, we would have helped, or at least tried to," Tank said.

"So what do we do now?" I asked.

"Right now, I'm going to feed you, and you're going to tell me exactly what you're running from. Obviously, it's your father and that Ernesto dickhead, but I need to know everything. If you want me to keep you safe, I need to know what I'm up against."

"Feed me?" I asked. "Am I a pet?"

"And there's the Montoya sarcasm. I knew you had to share something with Lupita other than the shape of your eyes."

My cheeks warmed. "Sorry."

"You are a legal adult, right? I'm not harboring a teen in my house?"

"I'm twenty-one," I said, glaring at him. Did he honestly think I looked like a kid? Sure, I still got carded when I went out for a drink, but I'd always thought it was just because they were legally obligated to ask for ID. It never occurred to me they thought I was underage.

"No, baby. You definitely have the curves of a woman, but I had to ask."

It made me wonder just how old he was. I figured if he'd chased after Lupita, he had to be at least close to her age. She was nearly thirty, but he seemed a bit older. Maybe thirty-five? I'd never been attracted to an older man before, but then I'd never met someone who looked like Tank either, or had his commanding presence. Just standing near him, I could almost feel the power coming off him. My father and Ernesto were both powerful men too, but they were cruel and heartless. There was a hint of warmth in Tank's eyes. Regardless of what he'd done, or would do, I could tell he was a good man. Maybe not by everyone's standards, but when you found out the man you'd called father all your life sold women and children, drugs, and guns, and murdered people in cold blood, it put things into perspective.

"Come on," he said nodding toward the kitchen. "You must be hungry. As big an asshole as that manager was, I doubt he's made sure you get to eat while you're at work."

"Um, no. We were permitted a break since I guess it's the law, but if we eat anything from the diner, he makes us pay full price."

Tank pulled out a kitchen chair for me and I sat. He opened the fridge and shifted some things around, then pulled out a covered dish.

"Ridley made this for me last night. I haven't had a chance to eat any yet. I think she said it's a cheddar potato casserole with chunks of ham. Sound okay?" he asked.

"It sounds really good. Who's Ridley? Your girlfriend?"

Tank threw his head back and laughed so hard I thought he might hurt himself.

"No, sweetheart. Ridley isn't mine. She's belongs to Venom, and he'd have my head if I even looked at her that way. She has a tendency to cook extra food here and there, and gives it to one of us bachelors. It was just my turn to get treated to a home-cooked meal."

"Why do you all have strange names?" I asked.

"They're road names, and the only ones we use. For the most part. I know the guys who are married or have claimed old ladies use their real names at home around their families. Isabella has slipped up often enough with her husband Torch. It's a little funny watching his reaction when it happens, but the second he looks at her, he goes all soft."

"He must really love her," I said.

"Yeah, he does."

"So you don't have a girlfriend or a wife? Or what did you call them? An old lady?" I asked.

"Nope. Completely single and free."

"Just the way you like it?" I guessed.

He shrugged. "I wouldn't mind settling down if the right woman came along. Been burned one too many times, I guess. I don't usually let women get close enough for something like that. Easier to just keep it casual."

"Lupita is the same way. I don't know if she's ever gotten serious with anyone. I've only been in this country for three years, and I've never heard of a boyfriend. I know she dates, but I don't think she sees anyone more than once or twice."

"What about you?" he asked. "When you came here, did you leave a boyfriend at home?"

"No. I've never..." I looked away. "I've never dated."

Saying those words out loud, especially to a man who had probably slept with a ton of women, made me feel inferior for some reason. It wasn't that I hadn't been asked out while I was in college. After finding out about my father, and learning about Ernesto, it was hard to trust anyone. What if my father had been using them? Or even worse, what if they were just as bad as

Ernesto? I didn't trust anyone anymore. Until now. Lupita trusted Tank, so that meant I could too.

Tank put the casserole dish into the oven, then headed to the front of the house when the doorbell rang. A moment later, he came back with another man following him. I recognized him as the guy who had turned me away that first night. He looked a little green, and I wondered just how much trouble he was in for not passing my message to Tank.

"Recognize her, Fenton?" Tank asked.

"Maybe," Fenton said, looking everywhere but at me.

"I know you recognized her car. You looked about ready to piss yourself when you saw me bringing her into the compound," Tank said. "Want to tell me about it?"

"I didn't know she was important," the man said. "We've had a lot of women trying to get inside, claiming to know one of you. I thought she was just another groupie trying to get into the compound. She said she was related to some woman named Lupita Montoya, but I didn't know who the fuck that was. Figured it was some club slut."

"Who gave you permission to decide who was allowed inside and who wasn't?" Tank demanded.

"I thought I was protecting the club," Fenton mumbled, looking at his boots. When his gaze locked on Tank's, the man turned so pale I thought he might pass out.

"I should kick your ass out and not let you come back," Tank said. "Do you have any idea what she's been through because you tossed her message away? There are powerful men after her, and she was fucking scared. She came here for help and instead she ended up in a shit motel in the bad part of town. You know damn well what happens over there."

Fenton audibly swallowed and went to move closer to me, but Tank blocked him.

"I just want to apologize to her," Fenton said, his voice strained. "I didn't mean to put her in danger. If I'd known she needed help, I'd have let her in."

Tank shifted to the side and Fenton came closer, then knelt at my feet. I could see how sorry he was, the compassion in his eyes wasn't something he could fake. He reached for me and Tank growled softly. It was enough to make Fenton drop his hand.

"I'm sorry I turned you away and didn't give your message to Tank. If I'd known you needed help and weren't just trying to sneak into the compound, I'd have let you through even if he wasn't here. I hope you can forgive me. You need anything and I'll be there."

"It's okay," I said.

"No, it fucking isn't," Tank said. "You want to stay and be a Reaper?"

"You know I do," Fenton said, rising to his feet. "I fucked up, and I know it. I'll do whatever it takes to earn back your trust."

"You can start by scrubbing the clubhouse top to bottom, including the toilets. All of them."

Fenton winced.

"Be glad I don't make you use a fucking toothbrush to do it," Tank said.

"Yes, sir. I'm sorry, Tank. Really. You know I'd never put a woman in harm's way. Not intentionally."

"That remains to be seen. Get the fuck out of here."

Fenton gave me one last apologetic look before disappearing. I heard the front door open and shut a moment later. Tank folded his arms and stared off in the direction Fenton had just taken, the tension rolling off him in waves. I stood and went to him, placing my hand on his arm. When his gaze landed on mine, I felt my breath hitch and my heart skipped a beat. I couldn't imagine my sister turning this man away. If he ever tried to pursue me, I knew it wouldn't take much to get me into his bed. I'd held out this long, but Tank was different from the others.

Not that he'd look twice at me if Lupita was more his style. I loved my sister, but we couldn't possibly be more opposite. Other than our coloring, there wasn't a damn thing we had in common. Unless you counted DNA. She was all fire and ready to bust someone's balls, while I was more the sit and read in the corner type. I'd never envied my sister until this moment. For the first time in my life, she had something I wanted. Well, she might not technically have Tank, but he'd have been hers if she'd given in.

"I'm fine, Tank. I know Lupita wanted you to protect me, but Fenton didn't know I was in trouble. Everyone makes mistakes."

"His could have gotten you killed."

"My father might not be a nice man, and Ernesto makes my skin crawl, but I don't think either would have killed me."

"Then why did you try to hide from them? Why do you need me if they're such upstanding men?" he asked.

"I didn't say they were upstanding, just that I didn't think they would kill me." I looked away and sat again. "If I'd married Ernesto, I'd have wanted to die by the time he was finished with me. He's not a good man. He's cold, heartless, and I think he enjoys hurting people, even women."

"You're safe here, Emmie. He can't get to you."

"You don't know him," I said softly. "He won't stop until he has me. I should have known I couldn't escape my fate. It was stupid to come here, to even leave Spain to begin with. I knew my father would look for me and eventually find me. I'm only prolonging the inevitable."

"You said you're here legally," Tank said. "Does that mean you're now a US citizen? Or are you on some sort of student Visa?"

"My sister helped me get a Green Card when I told her I needed to leave Spain. I don't know if she used her connections or what, but I'm considered a Lawful Permanent Resident of the US. It didn't happen overnight, but Lupita helped me through the process. I've been a student the last three years, until I moved here a few weeks ago. My sister helped me get set up at the school. I'm registered as Emmie and not Emelda, but just to be safe, she had agents watching over me. As far as I know, they were still around even after she went to prison. But without knowing for certain…"

"Worried your dad would track you?" he asked.

"Yes. Lupita told me to come straight here and not stop. I only took breaks to retrieve the directions she'd left for me and little pit stops along the way to refill the gas tank and buy some food."

"Your college isn't nearby?" he asked.

"A few hours. I didn't want to be too far from where Lupita was living. I had a dorm room, but I'm sure by now my roommate has reported me missing."

Tank's eyebrows rose. He pulled a phone from his pocket and made a call.

"Wire," he said. "I need you to find anything you can on Emelda Montoya, previously of Spain. Might check under Emmie Montoya as well. See if anyone is searching for her. She left school abruptly, and they may have called the police and filed a missing persons report."

He listened for a moment, then ended the call.

"Who's Wire?" I asked.

"One of my brothers. If there's any information out there on you, he'll find it."

"So, what do I do now?" I asked.

"Your new clothes should be here later today. When they get here, you should probably soak in the tub and try to relax. You look about ready to jump out of your skin."

"I don't think I've been relaxed since Lupita went to prison."

"Why did she turn herself in for those murders?" he asked. "She had to have known we would help you without her going to such extremes."

"She said she didn't want to give you a chance to say no."

He shook his head and walked over to the oven, then pulled the casserole dish out and set it on top of the stove. Taking down two plates, he scooped the food and put both plates on the table, then retrieved silverware and drinks for us. Tank claimed the chair next to me and the heat from his thigh nearly touching mine made my belly clench. Not once had I ever been tempted by a man. Not in Spain, and not since coming to the US. Until Tank.

It figured the one man who definitely wouldn't want me was the first guy who made me want to give up my V-card. It would never happen, but it didn't mean the man didn't tempt me. I'd never met a guy in his twenties who had Tank's confidence and air of authority. Maybe that was part of what drew me to him.

We ate in silence, with Tank mostly ignoring me. I did catch a glance here and there, but he was probably just making sure I was eating. Men like Tank didn't notice me. And the guys who did notice, only wanted in my pants. Except Ernesto. I shivered, scared spitless of what that man wanted from me. I knew he wanted me to be a virgin when he claimed me, but I didn't know exactly what my fate would be at his hands, just that it would be painful. A man like that didn't give a shit about anyone but himself.

The doorbell rang again and Tank rose to answer it. I pushed my plate away, unable to eat another bite. The food was really good, but I didn't have much of an appetite. Despite Tank's assurance that I was safe, I wasn't sure I believed him. I'd thought hiding in this town would be enough to stay under my father's radar, but I'd slipped up somewhere. I didn't use the same phone Lupita had given me, I didn't use my bank account, hadn't contacted my college, got paid under the table... Where had I gone wrong?

I heard Tank curse and a door slammed into the wall. I bolted out of my chair, knocking it over, and looked around the kitchen for an escape. Had my father found me? Was Ernesto out there, forcing his way into the house? My heart felt like it was going to hammer out of my chest and my body started shaking.

When Tank walked past with my sister in his arms, I gave a startled cry and ran after them.

"What's wrong? Why is Lupita here?" I asked.

He ducked into the room he'd given me and laid her out on the bed. She looked like she'd been beaten to hell, dark purple and black bruises covering every inch of exposed skin. Tears streaked my cheeks as I rushed to her side, but Tank held me back.

"Easy, sweetheart. You might hurt her more if you try to hug her right now," Tank said.

"What happened?" I asked, my voice breaking.

"I'm not sure. I opened the door and before she could speak, she pitched forward and passed the hell out."

Heavy footsteps entered the room. A giant blond man I'd never seen before gazed at Lupita with concern. The front of his cut said *Flicker*.

"I already called the doc," Flicker said. "She probably needs a damn hospital, but I don't know if she broke out of prison or was released. I'm not taking a chance on the cops picking her up."

"Agreed," Tank said. "Get Wire to do some digging. Tell him to drop everything else until we know if Lupita is in danger."

My heart clenched. It was obvious Tank felt something for my sister, and it hurt. At the same time, I was grateful he was going to help her and keep her safe. She moaned on the bed and her hand twitched, then she quieted and lay still. If her chest wasn't rising and falling, I'd have worried she was dead.

"Come on, Emmie. You don't need to see her like this," Tank said. "Flicker will keep an eye on her until the doc arrives."

Flicker nodded. "Won't leave her side."

I nodded and Tank led me from the room. He guided me into another bedroom, and as I looked around, I realized it was his. He pulled a T-shirt from a drawer and then tugged me into the bathroom. Setting the shirt on the counter, he then turned to the tub and started running water so hot that steam rose from it.

"You're going to take a bath and try to calm down," Tank said. "I know you're worried about your sister, but I promise we'll get her whatever help she needs. All right?"

"You care for her, don't you?" I asked softly, hating myself in that moment. My sister could be lying in there dying, and I was worried about Tank's feelings for her. It made me feel so damn low.

He gently gripped my chin and tilted my head back. My gaze locked on his and he stared hard for a moment, then his lips crashed against mine. I couldn't stop the whimper that rose in my throat and I pressed closer to him. Tank wrapped an arm around my waist and held me tight against his body as his mouth devoured mine. Feeling his hard body pressed against my rather ample curves made my panties wet. He ground his cock against me and I tangled my fingers in the hair at the base of his neck.

"Tank," I said softly as he drew away, but didn't release me.

"Zach. Call me Zach," he said, then he kissed me again. It wasn't until the water overflowed the tub that he pulled away.

He reached over and shut off the tap, then let the water drain.

"I thought you wanted me to take a bath," I said.

"Changed my mind. If I know you're in here naked, I'll be too damn distracted to get answers from Agent Montoya."

"Lupita," I said. "I'm sure she gave you permission to use her name."

"No, she didn't. And she sure as fuck doesn't know my real name." He licked his lips, then kissed me once more. "I've wanted you from the moment I walked into the diner three weeks ago and saw you, but you seemed scared, so I kept my distance."

He led me back into the bedroom, but didn't seem ready to release me just yet. I wasn't going to complain. I liked the feel of his hand holding mine, the way I'd felt pressed against him. And those kisses?

"Eating at the diner every day during my shift is keeping your distance?" I asked with some amusement.

"It was the best I could do. Staying away from you was impossible. Your sister is going to kick my ass, but I can't have you thinking I want her and not you. Yeah, I flirted with her, chased her a little, but I've never wanted a woman the way I want you, Emmie. Don't doubt for a second I want you in my bed."

"Go check on Lupita," I said. "I'll be there in a second. I just… need a minute."

He looked down at his cock, clearly outlined in the denim clinging to him. "Don't think you're the only one."

Flicker cleared his throat at the doorway, not looking at either of us. "Not to interrupt since it seems you're having a moment and all, but Dr. Myron is here. And Lupita is awake."

Tank pulled away from me, ran a hand down his face, then gave me one last heated look before he left the bedroom. I gave myself a moment to calm my racing heart, then went to check on my sister.

Chapter Three

Tank

Emmie stuck close to me when I checked on her sister, close enough I could feel the heat of her body through my clothes. My cock was still semi-hard, and there wasn't a fucking thing I could do it hide it. Lupita looked from me to her sister and a darkness flashed in her eyes, until Dr. Myron pressed on a rib, and then she grimaced and started cursing in Spanish. She'd stripped to a bra and panties, not caring who saw her partially naked. The woman was covered head to toe in massive bruises, and a few areas were swelling. I didn't know how the fuck she'd made it here in this condition, or why she was here for that matter. She hadn't said much of anything yet.

"I know you're in pain, and I'm sure the doc here will give you something good, but first I have a few questions," I said.

She nodded. "I know."

"Are you on the run?" I asked.

"I was given my freedom, but it came with conditions," Lupita said.

"What kind of conditions?" Flicker asked.

"The kind that mean I can never work in law enforcement again, which was a given after I was sentenced to prison. I also had to turn over some of the evidence I had against some pretty big fish in the government offices. In exchange for my silence, they set me free."

Flicker waved a hand toward her battered body. "So did you piss off the wrong person on the way here?"

"Something like that. One of the men decided he didn't trust me to keep quiet, so he hired some muscle to take me out." Lupita's lips twisted. "Didn't quite work out as they'd planned. They look worse."

"How did you get away from them?" Emmie asked. "You can't even walk!"

"Had some help." Lupita glanced at me and Flicker. "Hades Abyss. Fox happened to be in the area and heard me fighting them off. Came and saved my ass at the last second."

"He bring you here?" I asked.

"Dropped me at the gates. One of your Prospects helped me get to your door. Knew you'd take in little sis if I sent her your way." She smiled a little. "Figured you wouldn't be able to resist a chance to get in my good graces."

I glanced at Emmie and gave her a wink, hoping she didn't buy into Lupita's bullshit. Like I gave a fuck about being on her good side? She made it sound like I had a thing for her, and yeah, I'd chased her but just for fun. I focused on Lupita again. "We had a slight misunderstanding when she arrived, but it's squared away now."

"What kind of misunderstanding?" Lupita asked, her voice hardening.

"A Prospect thought she was just some groupie and wouldn't let her in. I was present when your dad and her supposed fiancé showed up where she was working. If I'd known about her sooner, I'd have brought her here," I said. "The Prospect has been dealt with."

Lupita leveled a glare at Emmie. "I told you to come to me if they turned you away. It wasn't safe for you to be outside of these gates."

I decided not to mention exactly where Emmie had been staying before now. Her sister would likely lose it if she knew her precious baby sister had been in the worst part of town, in a motel known for prostitution and drugs. Some things were just better left unsaid.

"I didn't have enough money to drive back," Emmie said. "It's fine. I worked at the diner for a short time, and then Tank discovered who I was and brought me here."

"Couldn't have one sister so you quickly made a move on the younger one?" Lupita asked. "I knew you'd watch out for her, but I didn't count on you trying to get in her pants. She's a virgin, you know? You'd chew her up and spit her out."

"I know you're in pain, and I'm sorry for what happened to you. My club is grateful that you stepped in and helped Wraith stay out of prison so he could be there for Rin and their kid, but I won't stand here and listen to you talk about Emmie like she's less than you."

"I love my sister," Lupita said. "If I didn't, I wouldn't have risked my life in order to ensure her safety here at the compound. Just figured you'd keep it in your pants. The way you came after me, Emmie doesn't exactly seem like your type. Or is anyone in a skirt good enough?"

"And I think it's time I give her that injection," Dr. Myron said. He had the syringe ready and before Lupita could protest, he jabbed the needle into her arm and depressed the plunger. She glowered at him and he pulled the needle free, capping it and putting it away. "I'll properly dispose of the syringe when I'm back at the office. That should kick in within a few minutes, and she'll be more pleasant. I think."

"Go check on Emmie," Flicker said. "I'll stay here."

I looked at Lupita one last time, then walked out with Dr. Myron. Before I was out of earshot, I heard Flicker tell Lupita to stop being a bitch. It made me smile that he not only had my back, but Emmie's as well. I walked Dr. Myron out, then went to look for Emmie. She was in the backyard, arms wrapped around her waist, and staring up at the blue sky.

"You okay?" I asked, stopping next to her.

"Is she right?" Emmie asked softly. "Are you interested in me just because you couldn't have her?"

I turned her to face me and pulled her against my chest. "No. Not just no but hell no. Yes, I chased your sister, but I wasn't seriously pursuing her. It was fun to verbally spar with her and see if I could get her to give in. I meant it before when I said it was never serious. I never wanted to keep Lupita and make her mine."

My shirt grew damp and I saw tears sliding down her cheeks. My heart felt like someone was squeezing the shit out of it. I hated that she was hurting, that her sister had put doubts in her mind. It didn't seem like Lupita to act like that or say those things, not the woman I'd come to know when she'd helped us out back in December a few years ago. I hoped it was just the pain talking. Regardless, she owed her sister an apology.

"Baby, look at me," I said, trying to tip her chin up, but she refused to budge. I sighed and held her. "You want to know what type of woman I prefer?"

"Yes. No. I don't know," she said, then sniffled.

I smiled a little, then cleared my expression so she wouldn't think her tears amused me. "I like petite curvy women. The kind with soft skin and ample curves. And this hair..." I tugged on the long strands. "Your hair drives me fucking crazy. I've wanted to sink my fingers into it ever since I first saw you."

"You're not just saying that?"

"Emmie, look at me. Please."

She looked up.

"I don't ever say things I don't mean. If you don't believe how much I want you, ask any of my brothers. They've been giving me shit for weeks about the number of times I eat at the diner just so I can see you. Does that sound like a man who isn't interested?" I asked.

"No. It doesn't."

"I meant what I said in the bathroom. I've wanted to ask you out, but you seemed scared. I'm a big guy and I worried that you'd run the other way if I approached you."

"It wasn't your size that scared me. I thought your club didn't want me here."

"I should go kick Fenton's ass," I mumbled.

Emmie giggled a little, then bit her lip. "He said he was sorry. Besides, we have other things to worry about. What are we going to do with Lupita?"

"She can stay in the guest room for now."

"I was supposed to stay in there," she said.

"Then I guess you'll just have to share a room with me instead," I said. She blinked at me a few times, then a slow smile spread across her lips, and quickly vanished. "You don't like that idea?"

"You heard her. I'm a virgin. I can't... I..." Her cheeks flushed. "I'm not experienced like Lupita, or like the other women you've been with. What if I do it all wrong?"

"Sweetheart, trust me when I say that you won't do anything wrong, but I'm not offering you a place in my bed just for sex. We just met, and even though I want you so fucking bad I ache, I'm not about to press you for more than you want to give."

"Lupita won't like it," she said.

"Lupita can go fuck herself," I said. "I'm only letting her stay in my house until she's back on her feet, then she can find somewhere else to go. If she can't be civil to you, then she's not welcome."

"You can't throw her out."

"Watch me," I said.

The back door opened and I glanced at the house to see King stepping outside.

"So, you know there's a half-naked woman in your house, right?" King asked. "How the fuck did you get lucky enough to have two women?"

Emmie stiffened in my arms and I wanted to kick King's ass. "Shut the fuck up, asshole. "

King took a step back and gave me a nod. "Didn't mean any disrespect. I only brought clothes for the one you're holding. I don't think any of it will fit the other one."

"Your sister hasn't been here long and she's already a pain in my damn ass," I muttered. "Come on, Emmie. Let's see if the drugs have kicked in yet and mellowed her. If not, I may have to tell the doc we need more. I've never wanted to throw a woman out on her ass until now."

I led her back into the house and heard Flicker speaking low and soft. I paused in the hall, drawing Emmie to a halt behind me.

"Why don't you let me take care of you, Lupita?" Flicker asked. "You don't really want to stay at Tank's, do you?"

"Shouldn't have kissed you," she said, her voice slurring.

"Probably not, and we both know I'm not your type, and you're sure as fuck not mine, but you're going to cramp Tank's style if you stay here."

"He wants to fuck my sister."

"I think it's more than that, and if you weren't hurting so much, you'd see it too. He's been obsessed with her for weeks, eating the same damn food every day just so he can be close to her. Give them some space, Lupita."

She mumbled something I couldn't hear and I decided to let them know they weren't alone. I stepped into the room with Emmie and King on my heels. She looked from me to Emmie and back again, her eyes glassy from whatever the doc had given her.

"You really like her?" she asked. "Not just a piece of ass?"

"No, she's not a piece of ass. I've wanted to ask her out for weeks," I said. "Then I found out who she was and I was going to keep my distance."

"Doesn't look like much distance," she said, eyeing our joined hands.

"I don't care if you approve or not. I was going to put some space between us because you'd entrusted her to my care."

"And now?" Lupita asked, her eyes getting heavy. I could tell she was fighting to stay awake.

"I won't give her up. Not for you or anyone else," I said. "But we're going to take things as slow as she wants. I'm letting her call the shots, except for where her safety is concerned. I'll do whatever it takes to keep your dad and that Ernesto fucker away from her."

"Good," Lupita said, then she succumbed to sleep.

Flicker looked from Lupita to me, then Emmie.

"You really taking her home?" I asked. "Because that is one unpleasant woman when she's in pain. I'd keep sharp objects and weapons away from her."

Flicker smiled. "I think I can handle her. It's only until she's better. I have no doubt she'd eat me alive if she stayed for too long."

"You kissed my sister?" Emmie asked.

"Um, more like she kissed me," Flicker said. "I think it was the adrenaline more than anything. I like my women a little less…"

"Balls to the walls?" King asked, eying Lupita. "Pretty sure that's the most badass woman I've ever met. I don't think anyone here could handle her, except maybe Tank, and he doesn't seem interested."

I stared at her and couldn't help but smile as an idea struck me.

"What's that look?" Flicker asked.

"I think our good pals Drey and Logan should be asked to babysit. Who better to watch over an ex-Fed than two DEA agents?" I asked. "Take her home, Flicker, but call those two and see what they say."

"You know, they were eyeing her back when that shit went down last year," Flicker said, smiling broadly. "Yes, I think maybe those two could handle her. If they liked Josie and all her sass, then Lupita may be just what they need. Good call, Tank."

"You need anything else?" King asked. "If not, Torch said he wanted me to handle something."

"Where'd you put the things I asked for?" I asked.

"In the living room. Didn't know where you were putting Emmie."

Flicker gently lifted Lupita into his arms and followed King out of the room, leaving me alone with Emmie. I stared at the bed that was now rumpled from her sister lying on it. I knew I should do the right thing. Put clean sheets on the guest bed and let her sleep in here, but it wasn't what I wanted. Now that I'd had a taste of her, I wanted her close.

"Zach." She tugged on my hand.

"Yeah, baby?"

"Are you sure you want me here?"

"In this room?" I asked, eying the bed again.

"No, in your house."

I looked down at her and gave her what I hoped was a reassuring smile. "There's nothing I'd like more than for you to stay here with me. If you want to be in here, I'll remake the bed. Or…"

"Or what?" she asked.

"You can stay in my room. No pressure to do anything more in there than sleep," I said. "I told you before, you set the pace. I don't want to do anything that makes you uncomfortable."

"Would you kiss me again?" she asked almost shyly.

I cupped her cheek and lowered my mouth to hers, giving her a soft kiss. The little vixen seemed to have other ideas and flicked her tongue against my lips. With a groan, I deepened the kiss and backed her into the hall, pressing her against the wall. The way she submitted to me, practically melting in my arms, made me want to strip her bare and thoroughly claim her. I held myself in check. She was so damn sweet and tempting that it wasn't easy to back away.

Her chest was heaving and her lips were swollen. The look she gave me nearly had me going back for more, but I took a step away from her. There were some things we needed to discuss before we took the next step, and I'd promised her time. Ripping her clothes off within minutes of the house emptying wasn't part of the plan, even though my cock felt like it was trying to tear through my jeans to get to her.

"There are some things we need to discuss," I said. "Before this goes further, I want to make sure we're on the same page."

She nodded. "All right."

I took her hand and led her to the kitchen. I pulled out a chair and waited for her to sit, then I put on a pot of coffee. I didn't know if she drank it, but I definitely needed a cup. While it brewed, I tried to decide how I was going to start this conversation. Even when I'd been a virgin, I hadn't slept with one. I'd heard it could hurt the first time, and I wasn't exactly a small man. Anywhere. But more than that, she needed to know this wasn't just a one-night stand for me.

I poured a cup of coffee and held it out to her, but she shook her head. I claimed the chair next to her and took a swallow. Staring into the cup, I didn't know how to say everything I was thinking. With my brothers, I'd just be blunt, but I thought she might need something more from me than just laying out the facts.

"Have you been kissed before?" I asked.

"Did I do it wrong?" Her brow furrowed and worry filled her eyes.

"No! Fuck, no. Kissing you was amazing, Emmie. I just didn't know how much experience you have. With men."

"None," she said, refusing to meet my gaze.

"So I was your first kiss?"

She nodded.

"You deserve someone far better than me," I said. "But I'm a selfish bastard and I want to make you mine. It makes me so fucking hard just thinking about being the only man to kiss you, to touch you."

"Zach, I've never trusted anyone enough to let them get that close, but Lupita sent me to you, and if she trusted you, then I knew I could too."

"Not so sure she trusts me right now," I muttered.

"She's never been so mean to me before," she said, tracing a pattern on the table with her finger. "I think she secretly wanted you and thought maybe you'd keep chasing her."

"I'm not going to lie to you, Emmie. I've been with a lot of women, some of them still hang around the club. And yes, I would have slept with your sister if she'd given in."

She pressed her lips tightly together.

"But Emmie, those other women? They never meant anything. They were a quick release, just a way to blow off steam and have some fun. I never wanted any of them for more than a night or two."

"Isn't that what I'll be?" she asked.

"No." I reached for her hand, wrapping my fingers around hers. "I want more than that with you, Emelda. I haven't had a girlfriend in a long-ass fucking time. Not since before your sister went to jail. The last time I tried to date someone, she ended up screwing me over. I never even got to the stage of calling her my girlfriend before I found out some things about her I didn't like. In fact, the only two times I've attempted a relationship with someone, I've ended up with cheaters and liars."

"I would never do that to you," she said, squeezing my fingers.

"I know, baby, and it's why I want to try again. With you. I want more than a few nights, or even a few weeks. We may not know much about each other, but I know enough that I want to claim you."

"Claim me?" she asked.

"What do you know about being part of a club?"

She glanced at my cut. "You mean your biker club?"

My lips twitched in amusement. "It's called an MC, baby. A motorcycle club. And yeah, that's what I meant."

"Not really anything. I know you all wear those matching cuts. I did try to watch a few episodes of some show about bikers, but I couldn't really get into it. It was kind of violent and all the men were cheating on their women. I didn't see the appeal."

I nodded, having a good idea which show she'd watched. "I can promise that I would never cheat on you. In fact, every guy here who has an old lady or wife hasn't cheated. Once we find the woman we want, we tend to be a faithful bunch. If I even thought of fucking another woman after making you mine, I have no doubt the Pres and the VP would both kick my ass."

"So when you say you want to claim me, you… want to marry me?" she asked, looking more confused than ever.

"One day. We're still strangers, Emmie. I wouldn't ask that of you right now. Just… if you come to my bed, I don't think I'll be able to let you go. If you're only wanting a quick fling, then tell me now."

"You want to keep me?" she asked. "You want me to live here? Be with you long-term?"

"Yes, Emmie, but only if that's what you want."

"I can't promise anything, Zach. My dad and Ernesto won't stop coming for me. They'll do whatever it takes to get their hands on me. I don't know what Ernesto plans, but he seems to want me badly. He's not a man who will back down."

"I will protect you, Emmie. I'll do whatever it takes to keep you safe," I said. "Those men will never lay a hand on you. If they do, I'll tear them apart one piece at a time until there's nothing left."

Her lips tipped up on one corner. "A little bloodthirsty, aren't you?"

"I'm the club enforcer, sweetheart. My hands are far from clean, and they never will be. I will always do what it takes to protect my brothers, even if it means burying someone six feet deep. Ernesto's blood wouldn't be the first I've spilled, and I doubt he'll be the last. It's something you need to consider before you decide you want to give this thing between us a try."

Emmie stood and came closer, easing down onto my lap. She placed her hand on my cheek and stared into my eyes, almost as if she were trying to look into my soul. I hoped whatever she saw didn't frighten her. A soft smile curved her lips, then she kissed me softly. As her lips moved against mine, she reached down and took my hand, then placed it over her breast. My breath caught for a second and I wanted to pull away, ask if she was sure about this, but she pressed my hand tighter to her.

I slid my hand down her belly, then up under her shirt. When I cupped her breast again, I could feel her nipple pebble through the soft fabric of her bra. I stroked the hard bud, then pinched just hard enough to draw a moan from her. She was so fucking perfect. If she hadn't had trust issues, I wondered if some other guy would have had the honor of hearing those sweet sounds before me.

"Can I see you, angel?" I asked, tugging at the hem of her shirt, but not removing it without her permission. The last thing I wanted to do was push too fast and scare her.

She gripped her shirt and eased it over her head, letting it drop to the floor. Her bra was plain white cotton, but the dusky mounds nearly spilling out of the scrap of fabric mesmerized me. She was more than a handful, and I couldn't wait to see her spread out, completely bare in my bed. I kneaded her breasts, rubbing her nipples with my thumbs.

"You're the most beautiful woman I've ever seen," I said, my gaze lifting to meet hers.

"I'm too round," she said, her cheeks flushing.

"No, you're perfect." I lifted my hips, pressing my cock against her ass. "Feel that? I've never been this damn hard in my life, and it's all for you."

She licked her lips and reached behind her. I heard a pop, and then her straps slid down her shoulders.

"Emmie, you don't have to. What we were doing was more than enough."

"I want more," she said.

I released my hold on her breasts and the bra slipped down. She tossed it aside and I couldn't help but stare. Had I said she was beautiful? I needed to upgrade that. The woman in my lap was a fucking goddess, and she was all mine. No way in hell would I let her walk out the door. My gaze clashed with hers and the heat I saw there was enough to nearly destroy what little control I had. When it came to Emmie, I wanted to tie her naked to my bed and enjoy her for days, give her so much pleasure she never wanted to leave. It was the first time a woman had ever made me feel like this, and it scared the fuck out of me.

Chapter Four

Emmie

The way he looked at me, the heat of his body and the touch of his hands, was enough to make me want to beg for more. I wanted to experience everything with him, wanted his lips on my body, his cock inside me. Even though I was a virgin, I'd read enough and watched some porn that I thought I was prepared for what would happen between us. When he cupped my breasts and took first one nipple, then the other into his mouth, sucking hard on the tips, then grazing them with his teeth, I shuddered and wished we had fewer clothes between us.

I wanted to see him, to explore every inch of his body. The thought of exposing myself like this to someone had always frightened me, but not with Zach. With him, this just felt incredibly right. I remembered my mother once telling me that when you met your soulmate it was something you just knew. She'd had a wistful look on her face, and I'd thought at the time she was speaking of my father. As I got older, I realized that she could have never loved my dad and had probably been in love with another man at some point. I didn't want to be like her, look back and realize I'd missed out on something great because I was too scared.

He rocked his hips against me and I felt the ridge of his cock. He felt huge and I worried a little that he'd be too big for me, but I trusted him not to do anything that would hurt me. He might be this big brute of a guy, and he claimed to have a violent side, but with me he'd been sweet and gentle. Even now, he kept his touch light enough that he wouldn't bruise me. From what I'd learned from my roommates at college, most guys didn't think about much other than themselves. At least the boys at school were that way. Maybe one day they'd become men like the one sending waves of pleasure through me.

"Zach," I murmured, holding him to me as he sucked at my nipple again.

I squirmed, wanting more but not knowing if I should ask. Would he think badly of me if I said wanted things to go further? He said we were strangers, and we were, but he didn't *feel* like a stranger. When he held me, it felt like I'd come home for the first time in my life, like I was exactly where I was supposed to be. I didn't think he wanted to hear that. Men didn't like crap like that, did they?

"Please," I begged. "Zach, I... I need..."

He nuzzled my neck, then licked at my jaw before kissing me. "What do you need?"

"More. I need more."

Heat flared in his eyes and he tapped my thigh. I stood on shaky legs and Zach slowly reached for my pants, pausing with his fingers over the button. I gave him a nod and he unfastened my jeans and pushed them down my legs. I stepped out of them and he groaned as he stared at my plain panties. Lightly, he ran his fingers across the front of them before giving them a tug. They fell to the floor and I stood before him completely exposed. He licked his lips as he stared at my pussy.

"You shave the hair off?" he asked, his voice rougher than before.

"One of the girls at college talked me into going with her for a wax. I liked the way it felt afterward, so I kept going back," I said. "Is that a good thing?"

"Really fucking good. I've heard it makes things more pleasurable for you."

"Zach."

His gaze caught mine and he gripped my waist, then lifted me onto the table in front of him. He pushed my legs wide and I could feel myself opening to him. He groaned and stared before running his fingers down my slit.

"So fucking wet," he said. "You ever played with yourself or used toys?"

My cheeks warmed. "No. At home I was too scared to try something like that, and at college I was never alone."

"You've never had an orgasm, even by your own hand?" he asked.

"No."

"Christ, Emmie." His eyes slid shut and his jaw went tight. "The things I want to do to you. You should tell me no, put your clothes on, and get the hell out of the kitchen. Go lock yourself in the bedroom or something."

"What if that's not what I want? What if I want you to do all those things to me?" I asked.

"You don't know what you're saying. If you could see the things I'm picturing, then you'd run."

"Zach, I'm a virgin, not an idiot. I've watched porn and read erotic books. As long as you aren't going to cause me pain, then I don't care what you do to me. I don't think BDSM would be my thing, but I trust you not to hurt me."

He growled and stood so fast his chair tipped over. "You shouldn't have said that, Emmie. I was holding on, barely, but I was managing. Giving me an open invitation wasn't your wisest decision."

I stared at him. "Maybe it's exactly what I want. I'm probably the only twenty-one-year-old virgin at school. I want you, Zach. I trust you."

He scooped me off the table and briskly walked to the bedroom. Zach eased me onto the bed, then shut and locked the bedroom door. I frowned and looked at it, wondering why we needed a locked door when it was just us in the house.

"I leave the front door unlocked in case anyone needs me," he said. "But if anyone barged in here and saw you naked, I'd have to remove their eyes and beat the shit out of them."

He quickly stripped off his clothes, and I eagerly scanned him from head to toe, taking in every inch of muscle and ink. I'd never thought of a man as beautiful before, but Zach's body was a work of art. One that I wanted to trace with my fingers and tongue. His cock was hard and erect, and a little frightening with how big it was. He must have noticed me staring and gave it a stroke.

"Don't worry, baby. I'll go slow. You want me to stop at any point, just tell me. Might give me blue balls, but I'm not going to take something you aren't offering. I'm an asshole, but I do understand the word no."

He crawled over me on the bed, caging me between his thighs and arms. Pre-cum dripped from his cock onto me and I had the urge to taste him. The way he watched me, I felt like prey. He was an intimidating man, all controlled power in a deadly package, but I'd never wanted anyone more in my life, and I didn't think I ever would.

"When you look at me like that, I feel like I can take on the world," he said. "I would gladly slay dragons for you, Emmie. Or Spanish mobsters."

I smiled a little. "Leave the poor dragons alone."

"But the mobsters are fair game?" he asked.

"Oh, yeah. Those you're allowed to slay. Even if I am related to one of them."

He kissed me, his lips firm but not forceful. His tongue stroked mine and my belly tightened as my pussy got wetter. Zach took his time, almost as if he were savoring me. My lips tingled when he started kissing a path down my body, stopping to pay attention to my breasts. He seemed fascinated with them, and for the first time, I didn't hate my body quite as much as I usually did.

When his shoulders spread my thighs wider, I gasped and bit back a moan. His beard tickled as he rubbed the inside of my leg before focusing on my pussy. He licked and sucked, making me feel things I'd never felt before. My body was tightening and getting hot. As his tongue flicked against my clit, it felt like my entire world shattered and I screamed out his name, my body bowing off the bed as the most intense sensations I'd ever felt rolled over me. He kept licking and teasing. One orgasm quickly turned into two and silent tears slipped down my cheeks from the force of my release. It left me shaken and blinking to clear the stars from my vision.

"Fuck, baby. I've never had someone come that damn hard so fast before," he said, settling over me again.

"Is that a bad thing?" I asked, swallowing hard.

"No. It's fucking perfect. You're perfect."

"Don't make me wait anymore. Make me yours," I said. "Show me what I've been missing."

He reached between our bodies and slowly sank a finger inside me. "So damn tight, baby. Let me stretch you a little or it's going to hurt like a bitch."

He stroked first one finger in and out, then a second. It burned a bit, and when he added a third finger it pinched. His thumb swiped over my clit, causing a spark of pleasure. He did it again and again, and soon his thrusting fingers weren't nearly enough. I could feel something building again. He twisted his fingers on the next stroke and I came.

Zach eased his fingers from me and I widened my legs, wrapping them around his hips. I felt his cock press against me, the head stretching me as he sank into me. Sweat beaded his brow and his jaw was tight. He didn't rush, pushing in one inch at a time, pausing if I gave any indication it hurt.

"Just do it. Get the painful part out of the way," I said.

"Emmie..."

"Do it," I said, gritting my teeth to prepare myself.

He hesitated only a moment, then thrust hard and deep. I sucked in a shocked breath and felt my eyes go wide. It felt a little like I'd been split in two, but Zach held completely still, his muscles straining. After a moment, the pain faded. If he hadn't been so huge, I didn't think it would have been all that bad. Zach was definitely big all over.

"I'm okay," I assured him. "You can move."

His gaze held steady on mine as he pulled back, then pushed inside. It was slightly uncomfortable for the first few strokes, and then that warm tingling started again. Soon I was begging him to go faster, harder. The headboard slammed into the wall with every thrust. He kissed me, thoroughly, as he drove into me again and again. I came apart, clenching around his cock as the breath was nearly stolen from my lungs, the world falling away. I felt the warm splash of his cum inside me. When he stilled, buried deep, I wished we could stay like that forever.

"Are you okay? I wasn't too rough?" he asked.

"It was perfect," I assured him.

He glanced up at the headboard and a weird look crossed his face. I craned my neck and couldn't stop the laughter that bubbled inside me as I saw the crack in the wall behind the bed. I'd heard people comment about breaking a bed during sex, but I'd never heard of someone breaking a wall. Maybe we'd set a new record.

As he pulled out, he looked down between my legs and cursed.

"What's wrong?" I asked, leaning up on my elbows.

"I forgot protection," he said. "I never fucking forget."

It felt like a weight settled in the pit of my stomach. Was he upset because he didn't want kids, or was he upset for some other reason? I hadn't really thought about protection either, but he'd said he wanted to keep me. If that were true, then kids would eventually happen, right?

Zach got up and went to the bathroom. I heard the water running and tried to swallow the knot in my throat. Maybe it hadn't been as perfect as I'd thought. I started to get up and grab my clothes, but he returned with a rag in his hands, his brow furrowed when he saw me.

"What are you doing?" he asked.

"I thought…" I looked away.

Zach came closer and knelt at the side of the bed, his hand on my thigh, and then he gently cleaned me. My pussy was sore and it stung a little as the warm, wet cloth swiped against me.

"You thought what?" he prodded.

"I thought you were mad and wouldn't want me in your bed anymore."

He reached up and cupped my cheek. "I'm not mad, baby. Not at you anyway. I'm upset that I didn't think to protect you against pregnancy. We haven't even discussed anything like that. I know some of the guys in my club got their women pregnant on purpose, but I would never do that to you."

"It wasn't because you don't want kids with me?" I asked.

"No, sweetheart, but I think it's too soon for either of us to be thinking about a family. We have plenty of time for that."

My hand splayed across my belly. "What if I'm already pregnant? Since I wasn't sexually active, I'm not on birth control."

"Then I hope we have a little girl as pretty as her momma," he said softly, giving me a smile.

He tossed the rag into the bathroom and I heard it hit the floor, then he nudged me farther onto the bed. Zach stretched out next to me and pulled me against his chest, cocooning me in his embrace.

"I promised to take care of you," he said. "Using a condom would have been a good step toward that. I can't change it now, and I can't say I'm all that sorry. I loved feeling you, all of you. I've never gone bare inside a woman before. And just so you know, I get tested regularly. I haven't been with anyone since my last test and I'm clean."

I snorted. "Obviously I am too since I'd never even kissed someone before you."

He pressed his lips to my forehead. "And you have no idea how happy that makes me, to be your first for everything. You've given me a gift I will always cherish, Emmie. Even if you decided to walk out of here tomorrow, I'd always remember this moment."

I lifted my head and looked at him. "You'd let me leave?"

He arched a brow.

"Yeah, I didn't think so," I said. "You don't seem like the type to give up something you want."

"I'd let you go. Give you a head start; then I'd come after you. By the time I was done, you'd never want to leave again."

I smiled. Maybe I should have been scared or creeped out, but it made me feel warm and tingly that he wanted me to stay. I had a feeling I was already losing my heart to him. I only hoped that one day he'd give me his too.

Pressed against his side, his fingers toying with my hair, I felt more content than I'd ever been. Being with Zach felt right on so many levels. Even if my sister wasn't happy about it, and I still had the dark cloud of my father and Ernesto hanging over me, in this one moment I was truly happy. I knew it wouldn't last, but I wanted to bask in the afterglow a little longer. I'd heard so many stories of how my friends at college had hated their first time. It had hurt, but once the pain had faded, it been an earth-shattering experience, one I would remember the rest of my life.

Someone pounded on the bedroom door, making Zach curse and get out of bed. He pulled his jeans on, then tossed his shirt to me. Once I was covered, he opened the door and glowered at a ginger-haired man on the other side.

"What the fuck, Wire? There's such a thing as a damn phone."

The man glanced at me before focusing on Tank again. "There are some things you need to know, especially since it looks like you slept with her already. Maybe we should step out of the room."

"Is this about Emmie?" he asked.

"Yes, but I don't think she needs to hear this. The news isn't good, Tank. Hear what I have to say, then if you want her to know everything, you can tell her."

Tank looked at me, his gaze assessing.

"It's okay," I said. "Go see what he found out. I trust you."

He left Wire standing in the doorway and sat next to me on the bed. Tank pushed my hair back behind my ear, then kissed me softly. The look in his eyes was tender and he gave me a slight smile before he got back up. He opened a dresser drawer and pulled on a fresh shirt, then followed Wire out of the room, pulling the door shut behind him.

I leaned back against the headboard and stared at the opposite wall. I didn't know what Wire had found that he thought might upset me, but I knew it had to be pretty bad. I already knew who my father really was, and I had no doubt that Ernesto was just as evil. Did they have a plan for me that I hadn't heard that day? Something other than a marriage? I'd thought having to live with that man, having to sleep with him, would be the worst thing I could ever live through. Now I had to wonder if my worst fears were more like a vacation compared to what the two of them had in store for me.

Lupita had believed that the Dixie Reapers could protect me, that Tank could. But she'd mentioned someone else. Casper VanHorne. Was he the key to everything? I wasn't familiar with the name, but if Lupita knew of him, and if he could handle my father, then it meant he wasn't a man to be trifled with. I didn't understand his connection to the Dixie Reapers, or why he'd help me. Maybe I should have asked more questions, or at least paid more attention to what happened around me before I'd left Spain.

My virginity had been important to Ernesto. That part had been clear in his comments at the diner. Was it just that he wanted his wife to be untouched? Or was it something more? Possibly something sinister? A shiver raked my spine as I thought about the kind of pain I'd have felt at his hands during my first time. No matter what happened, I was glad that Tank had been my first.

I looked over at the door and hoped that whatever Wire had found wouldn't change things with Tank. After what we'd shared, my heart would break if he tossed me out. He'd promised to protect me, and I hoped that he'd meant it, but what if Wire's news made him reconsider? My hands twisted in the blankets and my stomach churned as I waited. Lupita would have charged in there and demanded to know what was going on. But I wasn't Lupita.

I was just Emmie. Naive, timid Emmie who jumped at shadows.

I had a feeling that if I was going to survive whatever was heading my way that I would need more of a backbone. I hoped that deep down I had a lioness hiding inside me, but I worried I was more like a mouse.

Only time would tell.

Chapter Five

Tank

Wire's first bit of news had been concerning. No one was searching for Emmie, which meant her school hadn't reported her missing. I had a feeling her father had something to do with that, and it made unease claw at me. If he'd known where she was, why had he waited until now to come for her? She'd been in the US for the last three years, but he'd kept his distance. It didn't make sense, unless Lupita had managed to hide her that well. Even then, I thought something more might be going on, but unless we had a discussion with them it was doubtful we'd ever know. I had a feeling something big was happening now, and I didn't like it. Not with Emmie in the middle of it. And how had he known to find her at the diner today? Or that she'd been staying at the motel? Just how long had he been watching and waiting?

"What am I looking at?" I asked, flipping through the grainy pictures Wire had somehow obtained. They were from the first of three folders he'd brought with him. The man was always thorough with every investigation, but I wasn't certain what these buildings had to do with Emmie. I knew we didn't have any place like this in town.

He tapped on one. "See this? It's the compound of Fernando Montoya."

"Why is that name familiar?" I asked, brow furrowed. I knew Montoya was Emmie's last name, but I didn't remember meeting a Fernando Montoya.

"He's the man who bought Ridley from her stepdad, the one who sent her running straight into Venom's arms."

I looked from the picture to Wire, waiting to see if there was more to that statement. I remembered the asshole who was going to hurt Ridley, and I also knew what had happened to him. He'd been from South America, or so I'd thought.

"He's dead," I said.

"Yeah, but his brother isn't." Wire handed me another picture and my gut clenched. Now this man I had met, even though we hadn't shared names. "Meet Luis Montoya, father of Emelda and Lupita… and brother to Fernando."

"You have to be fucking kidding me."

Was it a coincidence that Lupita had come here that December two years ago? Had she known about the connection with us and her uncle? Worse, did she know exactly what had happened to him and our part in all of it? Emmie had said that Lupita went to prison over Wraith's massacre to ensure the Reapers would give our aid, but what if it went deeper than that? It made me question the federal agent's motives in coming here, and for sending Emmie straight to me. I'd always listened to my gut, and right now, it said something was really wrong with all this.

Wire slid another picture my way. "Ernesto Lopez. One of the highest paid assassins in Spain, and also the owner of several brothels around the world, some underground clubs, and this little gem…"

I flipped over the next picture and stared in horror. I'd done some fucked-up shit in my life, but this? Holy hell! Bile rose in my throat and I turned the picture back over, not wanting to look at it another moment. What kind of sick monster could do that?

- 220 -

"What does all this have to do with Emmie? Her father wanted her to marry the guy. You don't think he'd…" I waved a hand at the offensive picture.

"I more than think." Wire sighed. "Once I found out who he was, I did some digging, and managed to hack into one of his email accounts. I also poked around in the bank accounts I could find, but I'd be willing to bet he has a bundle in some unmarked offshore accounts. It seems he woke up from the love tap you gave him and was pissed as fuck. He ranted about the whore he was supposed to have married and made arrangements for her. Bidding has already begun. Looking at his bank records, he's done this sort of thing several times this year already. I'm not so certain that Emmie wouldn't have been auctioned off once he was finished with her, even if she had been a virgin when she'd married him. Or maybe he'd already had a plan in place, if she'd been innocent."

"Her father won't allow that. Will he?" I asked.

Wire pulled out a sheet of paper. "Luis Montoya. How do I put this? Let's just call him the most feared man in all of Spain and leave it at that. There isn't much he isn't dabbling in, and he honestly makes Ernesto look like a cherub. From what I can tell, Fernando was a decent guy in comparison to his brother. I honestly have no idea how your Emmie isn't scarred beyond belief from living with someone like Luis. We need to know what she's heard or seen."

"Jesus fucking Christ," I muttered. "We needed Casper VanHorne to take down Fernando. How the hell am I supposed to keep Emmie safe from two men who are even worse than the one Ridley ran from?"

"I know you like handling this type of thing on your own, but maybe this time you need to take a step back. You're obviously involved with Emmie, which I honestly saw coming. You've wanted her from the moment you first saw her. I knew it was only a matter of time before you gave in, but how far are you willing to go?" Wire asked.

"How far?" I asked.

Wire drummed his fingers on the table a moment, then slipped more documents my way. It took me a moment to realize what the hell I was seeing. I looked from the papers to Wire, who was staring at me with a challenge in his eyes.

"What the fuck? Are you serious right now?" I asked.

"She needs protection, right? And you'd go to any lengths to make that happen?" Wire asked.

"You hacked the county and state government systems and fucking married us? Jesus, Wire. You didn't even talk to us about it. What if she doesn't want to marry me?"

"Too late," Wire said. "In the eyes of the law, you're now legally married, and have been for the past week."

"This is fucked up and you know it. Sleeping with her is one thing, but this?" I slapped my hand down on the papers. "You need to undo this, right now."

"Don't want to marry her?" he asked.

"It's too soon! We don't even know each other."

"Pretty sure Venom and Ridley would tell you that's bullshit. And what about Torch and Isabella? Rocky and Mara? Need I go on? The Reapers know when they meet the right woman. In your gut, you know that Emmie is it for you. Forever. I just saved you some time and paperwork."

"And took the decision completely out of her hands," I said. "What the fuck does this solve anyway?

Do you honestly think either of those men are going to care if she's married?"

"No, I don't. But now that you're legally married, we can pull in Officer Daniels, and even the Feds, and tell them that your *wife* is in danger. Your possibly pregnant wife. If we put enough eyes on her, then it's going to be damn hard for either Luis or Ernesto to make a move. I know it's not an ideal situation, but I honestly think this is our best shot, at least until reinforcements can get here."

"What reinforcements?" I asked.

"I filled in Torch before I came here. The other clubs are sending help, and Torch put in a call to his father-in-law." Wire smiled. "I still can't say that with a straight face since Torch is older than Casper. Either way, the top assassin in the world will be arriving before long. We can use all the firepower we can get."

"And I'm supposed to do what? Keep Emmie locked up in this house indefinitely?" I asked.

"Not exactly."

I rubbed my forehead, feeling a pain starting to pulse in my skull. I didn't know how many more surprises I could take, not when it came to Emmie. Nothing had ever fazed me, but the thought of losing Emmie, of her being hurt or killed made me want to rip someone to shreds.

"Just tell me what the fuck else you've been up to while I was otherwise occupied."

"You won't like it," Wire said.

"I haven't liked any of this shit so far. It hasn't stopped you yet, so by all means, continue with the awesome news."

"Does she know you're an asshole?" Wire asked.

I flipped him off and watched as he pulled more shit out of his folders.

"This looks like a fucking fortress," I said, studying the pictures.

"Because it is. It's a secret government base, or it's supposed to be a secret. Let's just say that in exchange for me not letting the world know how easy it is to hack certain US government files, we have free use of it for as long as we need. Or rather, as long as Emmie needs it. I've made arrangements for you to take her there. Not to mention, I've been assured that if Luis Montoya and Ernesto Lopez were to vanish, then both our country and Spain would owe us a debt of gratitude. It seems they're trying to reach into the US now, and the Spanish have been trying to find a way to get rid of them for years."

"No," said a soft voice behind me.

I turned and saw Emmie, dressed only in my shirt. I had the insane urge to cover her up so Wire couldn't see her bare legs, or the fact she was braless. She came closer and looked at everything spread across the table.

"I've run whenever trouble came my way," Emmie said. "I don't want to run anymore. I'm tired of being a scared little rabbit."

Her gaze landed on something and locked. Slowly, she reached out and slid a paper closer. I groaned when I realized what the hell it was.

"We're married?" she asked. "How? I'm pretty sure I'd have remembered walking down the aisle, especially a week before you even spoke to me."

Wire waved at her. "That would be my doing. You can thank me later. I like cookies and pies, if you're into baking."

She blinked a few times. "You married us? I'm so confused right now."

"Just a few keystrokes," Wire said, which I knew was bullshit.

She reached for the gruesome picture and I grabbed her hand long enough for Wire to remove it. I didn't want that image in her mind. Bad enough I knew what that picture held, but Emmie? She'd have nightmares the rest of her life. Even if I hadn't known her long, I knew that she was a gentle soul, and that kind of brutality would be more than she could handle. Or at least more than she *should* handle. If I could protect her from the ugliness of the world, then I would.

I knew Wire was wondering just how innocent she was, now that we knew she was connected to Luis and Fernando Montoya. I didn't doubt for a moment that she was every bit as sweet as she seemed. Whatever Luis had done in his lifetime, I didn't think it had ever touched Emmie, until now. She was smart to run from Ernesto. Coming here may have saved her life. No, I knew it had. If she'd remained in Spain and married that monster, she would have died a horrible death at some point. I wasn't even convinced the man had ever intended to actually marry her.

"Emmie, what do you know about your father and Ernesto?" Wire asked. "Did you ever overhear anything? See anything?"

"Just them planning my engagement to Ernesto. I was never consulted. It was after I saw how cold he was that I decided to investigate a little. I discovered who he was, and who my father really is. My father had never been a caring sort, but I'd never realized he was a monster. It scared me and I ran to Lupita, hoping she could keep me safe," Emmie said. "And she did, for a long time. Even after she went to prison, she still managed to keep my dad away. I don't know what changed recently."

"And she sent you to me," I said.

"Yes. Do you know why?" Emmie asked. "She's never said much, except that you seem to have some sort of connection to a man called Casper VanHorne. It seemed important to her, even though I don't know who he is. I had to wonder why she waited so long to send me here if she thought you were my only hope of getting away from Ernesto and my father. I never asked, but maybe I should have."

Wire and I shared a look. Yeah, the ex-agent had some explaining to do. It seemed every move she'd made, even back in December two years past, if not further back, had been calculated. But to what end? Just to save Emmie, or something more?

"Casper is the man who killed your uncle," Wire said. "And Casper's daughter is married to our President, Torch."

"And now the pieces are falling into place," Emmie said. "Lupita didn't just get assigned to a federal office near your compound. She requested that location. I didn't understand why since she'd been living farther north before that. Now I have to wonder if she came here on purpose. When she sent me here, she mentioned Casper VanHorne. I didn't know who he was, or why she was so interested in him."

"Which means she made sure she was here when we needed her," I said. "I don't like it, but if she felt you were in danger, then I can understand why she would have gone to such lengths."

Assuming that was the only motive she had, but only Lupita could answer that.

"Where is Lupita now?" Emmie asked, seeming almost distracted for a moment.

"She went home with Flicker, remember?" I said. "He'll watch over her."

"Actually." Wire cleared his throat and looked away a moment. "Lupita walked out of here about an hour ago. An unmarked car picked her up, no plates, windows blacked out. No one knows where she went or what she's doing. She's no longer a federal agent, which means she's no longer on a leash. Flicker tried to stop her, but she said she had business to take care of."

Emmie's horrified gaze locked with mine. "You don't think she'd go after our dad and Ernesto, do you? I mean, the whole point in me coming here was so you would protect me. Wasn't it?"

"Wire, go do your thing. Find her, and then make sure she's all right. Whatever it takes. I may not know if I completely trust her right now, but she's Emmie's sister. Since you married us, that makes Lupita my sister-in-law, and Reapers take care of family."

Wire nodded and started gathering his files and papers. "I'm on it. You may want this though," he said, sliding the marriage license across the table.

I stared at the paper and wondered how Emmie felt about it. She hadn't said much in regards to our marriage, other than being surprised Wire had pulled such a stunt. Once he was gone, I pulled her down onto my lap and wrapped an arm around her waist. She leaned against me, tucking her head under my chin.

"So, wife… You know, I can just have Wire make it all disappear, if that's what you want. It isn't like we went through a ceremony and you agreed to marry me."

She curled her fingers into my shirt and turned her face into me, taking a deep breath. "I want to stay married. If that's okay with you."

"Em, we don't even know each other."

"I know enough," she said. "But if you don't want forever with me, then just say so. I'll move back to the guest room, and we can pretend that nothing happened between us."

"You could be pregnant," I reminded her.

"Maybe. Maybe not. I doubt many women get pregnant the first time."

"You'd be surprised," I muttered, thinking about all my brothers who seemed to have easily knocked up their women. I was starting to wonder if there was something in the water, or beer, that caused us to have super sperm. Hell, Preacher hadn't only knocked up his woman, but he'd given her twins! And I seriously doubted that Saint had been trying to knock up the woman he'd been seeing in secret.

"Is that why you want to stay married?" she asked. "Because you think I might be pregnant? People don't get married these days just because they have a baby. It's not the nineteen fifties anymore, Tank."

I glared at her. "Just how old do you think I am?"

She shrugged. "Thirties? I figure you're at least ten years older than me."

"Jesus," I said, shaking my head. I didn't think this conversation was going to go over well. I closed my eyes and hoped she didn't freak the hell out. "Baby, I'm forty-five. There's over twenty years between us, not ten."

She turned to face me, her eyes going so wide it was almost comical. "But you don't look older than thirty-six!"

"Good genes, I guess," I said. "So is this a problem?"

"Zach," she said softly. "I don't care how old you are. Age is just a number, right? If it doesn't bother you, and it doesn't bother me, then what does it matter how many years there are between us?"

"Guess it doesn't. Just so you know, I tend to stick to women thirty and older. I don't make it a habit of chasing after women your age."

"Just makes me special," she said, smiling.

"My sister is going to give me so much shit," I said.

"Why? Because you're older than me?" she asked.

"Her husband knocked her up and ran off. He didn't show back up for two years. It wasn't the age difference I had such a problem with, but more the fact he acted like an idiot. She's going to give me grief, because I always told her I'd never go for a woman as young as you. Hell, I hadn't even planned on settling down, not after the shit I went through before."

I could tell she had questions, but I didn't think she'd ask. Yet. Sooner or later, I'd have to tell her about my past, and why I didn't trust women easily.

"Does she live here? Will I get to meet her?" Emmie asked.

"She lives with the Devil's Boneyard in the Florida panhandle. Once everything is settled with your dad and Ernesto, maybe we can take a trip there. No way I'm inviting them here. Not enough space."

"Do you own this house? Or does it belong to the club?" she asked.

"It's mine. Sort of. Torch gave each of us a house. I hadn't planned on having a family other than Josie, so

I took one of the smaller ones. It would be easy to build on if we needed to."

"Where would your sister and her family stay if they came to visit?" Emmie asked. "If we don't have space here, I'm sure there are other Reapers with family who don't have room for visitors either."

"What are you getting at?" I asked.

"Is there an empty house that could be set up as a guest home of sorts for visitors? Or maybe there's room to build something? A small row of townhomes or something?" Emmie said.

"Not a bad suggestion. When all this is over, we'll talk to Torch about it. He's always open to new ideas, especially if it's for the well-being of the club and our extended family. There are a lot of club members who have relatives through marriage to other MCs. Torch always lets them visit whenever they want, but you're right about us needing a place for everyone to stay. If we didn't have to use one of the bedrooms for guests, then we could use both bedrooms for any kids we have."

"Kids plural?" she asked. "What if I only want one?"

I rubbed my beard. "Do you? Only want one?"

"I don't know. It was nice having a sister, until Lupita moved away. It gave me someone to rely on, even if she was quite a bit older than me."

"It's not something we have to settle right now, baby. I need to go see Torch and see what he makes of all this mess with your family. I know that Casper VanHorne is on his way here, but I'm not sure how we're handling everything. I need to know for certain that no one will come for you."

"Then you go take care of business. I can occupy myself for a while. If you have the Hallmark Channel I can find something on there; they always have good movies playing."

I kissed the top of her head. "Watch whatever you want. If there's a channel I don't have, let me know and we can order it. I should shower and change before I head over to the clubhouse."

She stood, then paused, biting her lower lip. "Zach, I know that this marriage blindsided us, but I'm glad it's you I'm married to."

"Me too, sweetheart." I gave her a smile, then stood and brushed a kiss against her lips before I left the room. If I didn't go shower now, I might be tempted to do something else, like toss her over my shoulder and make love to her all day long.

Chapter Six

Emmie

There was a strange flutter in my stomach every time I thought about the piece of paper Wire had left behind -- a marriage certificate. Mine! It baffled the hell out of me that he'd been able to do something like that, and I still wasn't quite convinced he'd done it as a way to save me. I'd heard him tell Tank that it was obvious the biker wanted to keep me. There was a huge difference in keeping me and marrying me. Tank was right. We were still strangers, even if we had been intimate already. I really wasn't sorry that Tank was all mine.

It was completely insane, but with him I felt safe and like someone truly cared what happened to me. With the way Lupita had recently acted, I wasn't entirely sure that she loved me as much as I loved her. Did she really see me as being so pathetic that a guy like Tank wouldn't want me over her? He'd shown me exactly how much he wanted me.

My hand went to my belly when I thought about the possibility of carrying his baby. We'd been careless, and I knew it was wrong, but at the same time the thought of being pregnant with his child made me feel warm and fuzzy inside. I'd always wanted a family of my own, ever since I'd realized mine was so badly broken. Even before I'd found out who my dad was, I'd known that our family wasn't like other families. My dad had never been the type to give hugs, or praise for that matter. It was like I didn't exist, until he could use me to further a business deal. My children would *never* feel unwanted or unloved! I'd do everything I could to give them the best life possible. Not the kind money buys, but the kind built on love and affection.

The front door flew open so hard it banged into the wall, and several female voices drifted to me before the women stepped into view. I was thankful I'd gotten dressed after Tank left. I'd never expected people to just barge in without knocking. My jaw dropped a little when they just bustled right in and made themselves at home. Who were they? Each of them wore one of the black cuts like Tank did, except theirs said *Property of* and a name.

"Um, hi," I said cautiously.

The blonde that seemed to be the ringleader smiled broadly. "We couldn't wait another second to meet you. I'm Ridley, Venom's wife."

"Finally," one of them muttered.

I didn't have any idea who Venom was, even though the name was familiar. Tank must have mentioned him. For that matter, the name Ridley left me with the feeling I'd heard it too. Right now, all I could do was focus on the women staring at me. I now understood what a zoo animal felt like, or a fish in a bowl. What did they want? Why were they here?

"I'm Emmie," I said, even though I had a feeling they already knew that.

"Wire told us all about you," said a woman with long black hair. "I'm Isabella, Torch's wife."

Now Wire I was familiar with, thanks to the marriage certificate I couldn't stop thinking about. If he'd told them about me, did they know that…

"Where's your ring?" the third asked. "I'm Darian by the way, Bull's wife."

"Ring?" I asked and looked down at my hands. Huh. I hadn't even thought about a wedding ring.

Then again, I doubted that Tank had either, since neither of us had known that Wire married us over the computer. Who the hell did that? And how?

"Wire said you and Tank are married," Isabella said, then she pursed her lips. "That sneaky little shit. He did that hocus pocus with his computer, didn't he?"

I nodded, not knowing what else to say.

"He may be more devious than any of us realized," Darian said. "And if he was able to do that all along, why didn't he do that for any of us?"

"Speak for yourself," Isabella said. "I for one loved my wedding to Torch. It's a memory I'll cherish always."

Ridley snickered. "Yeah, right. What you remember is what happened *after* the wedding. Pretty sure half the compound heard you."

Isabella's cheeks flushed. "Hush. Like you and Venom are any better. You've been together over nine years and have three kids, but you're still all over each other."

Ridley shrugged and smiled. "So, Emmie. Tell us all about you."

"Um." I looked at the three women, feeling a bit overwhelmed. "I'm Lupita's sister. The FBI agent who helped you back about two years ago?"

Darian's eyes went wide. "The one in prison?"

I blinked. Did they not hear that Lupita had been at the compound? I wasn't sure it was my place to say anything, so I kept quiet.

"Okay, so your sister is a badass. That doesn't tell us anything about you, except who you're related to," Isabella said.

"I worked at the diner until Tank brought me here yesterday." Had that only been one day ago? It seemed like weeks, or even months, had passed in that time. "I was a student before things turned ugly."

"We heard about your dad and the man claiming to be your fiancé," Darian said. "No worries. The guys will handle it. They've protected each of us at some point. It's how most of us ended up here. Except Isabella. Her dad made a deal with Torch for services rendered."

Isabella snorted. "Thanks. Make me sound like a prize to be won."

Ridley nudged her. "I'm pretty sure Torch thinks you *are* a prize."

"Why are you here?" I asked, just blurting it out. Not that it wouldn't be nice to have friends, but these women didn't know me, hadn't even known I existed until now. I didn't understand what they wanted. People weren't nice unless they wanted something, right?

"Ridley, I told you that you should have prepared her," Darian said. "Good thing we didn't bring the entire crew."

"There's more of you?" I asked. I wasn't certain if the idea intrigued me, or scared me. The three women in front of me seemed to be a force to be reckoned with, and envisioning more of them was a bit frightening. Lupita was powerful and strong, but these ladies had a presence that might have even overwhelmed my sister.

"Oh, yeah. Wraith just married Rin about two years ago. It was so romantic. They had a Christmas wedding! Let's see… Preacher and Kayla are together, then there's Tex and Kalani. Hmm. Rocky and Mara, although she tends to keep to herself. Who am I missing?" Ridley asked.

"Zipper and Delphine. Not to mention Laken is married to Ryker, and while he's not a Dixie Reaper, she's Flicker's sister," Isabella said. "I'm sure you already know that Tank has a sister, Josie, but she's with the Devil's Boneyard. They're close, so I'm sure he's mentioned her."

"Their VP is my dad," Darian said. "You'll see the Boneyard crew around here pretty often. They don't live that far off either."

I felt like I'd fallen down a rabbit hole, except unlike Alice, I was pretty sure I was going to land on my head when I reached the end. Too many names to remember, and way too much information to process all at once. I still didn't entirely understand the MC thing, and it sounded like it was a big group. Would I fit in? These women seemed confident and strong, and I felt very far from either of those things.

"Told you we should have waited," Isabella said under her breath but just loud enough for me to hear. "I think we've broken her."

"No, I'm… just thinking. I only met Tank yesterday and now Wire says we're married. I don't know anything about Tank or the Dixie Reapers, much less any other clubs. I feel a little… lost."

"It will be fine," Darian said. "I ended up here completely by accident. I didn't even know my dad was a biker at that time. We'd never met. But the Dixie Reapers welcomed me and made me family, and they welcomed my dad too even though he's from another club."

"It's kind of their thing, but don't let on that you know," Isabella said. "They take in strays. The guys can be completely badass and tough when they need to be, but when it comes to women and kids? Complete teddy bears. Well, innocent women anyway. Cross the MC or hurt a kid and the guys won't care if the person is male or female. Justice will be served."

"And not in the legal way," Ridley said, "but you get used to it. As long as the guys stay out of jail, I really don't care how they handle things. They get the job done, and as far as I'm concerned, they're providing a service to this community. Anyone they put six feet under deserved it and probably hurt innocents."

"So they're like modern day superheroes but without the capes?" I asked.

Darian snickered. "I can't wait to tell Bull that one. Wonder if I can convince him to dress up as Thor for Halloween this year?"

"With that long blond hair and beard? He'd be a good one, or maybe a Viking marauder," Ridley said.

"Really?" Darian asked. "You want to arm Bull with a broadsword? Or an ax?"

"Well, you were going to give him that hammer thing Thor carries around. That's just as bad," Ridley said.

"Thank you, ladies," Isabella said. "I now know what the club's next charitable event will be. Superheroes visiting the children's ward at the hospital. Maybe they can make it a regular thing."

"Yeah, like you're getting Venom or the other guys to dress up in those leotard things," Ridley said. "But if you do, I'm taking pictures. Lots of pictures. They may even make it onto social media, or the local paper."

I couldn't imagine Tank dressing up in one of those things, but it did make me laugh. The more the women talked, the more at ease I felt around them. They seemed happy, and it gave me hope that maybe I could find that same happiness with Tank. In all the times I'd pictured myself settling down, it had never been with a biker, or anyone as hardened as Tank. But like the ladies said, hard exterior and soft teddy bear inside.

"I know Tank doesn't want you leaving the compound," Ridley said, "but sometimes we hang out at the clubhouse during the day. The sluts aren't around then."

Wait. What?

"Sluts?" I asked.

"Um." Ridley looked at the other two before focusing on me again. "There are women who hang around the club, sleep with any of the guys who ask, in hopes of becoming an old lady. Or maybe some of them just like the thrill of being used by bikers. Whatever the case, at night, the clubhouse tends to have mostly if not fully naked women running around."

Well, that was news to me, and not the good kind. Tank had said he was with a lot of women before me, but I hadn't realized they were still here. Did he still see them every day?

"And Tank goes there at night?"

"He used to," Darian said. "I'm sure that he won't now that he's married. And even when the guys go who have wives or old ladies at home, they make sure the sluts leave them alone. Once a Reaper settles down, they never want another woman."

I hoped they were right. Tank might not have married me of his own free will, but the fact remained that according to the state records, we were in fact husband and wife. I just didn't know if that meant anything to him. It seemed like he wanted me in his life, and wanted me as his wife, but what if someone better came along? I'd never been as secure as Lupita, and now it was going to bite me in the ass. I just knew if Tank went to the clubhouse at night, I'd worry myself to death that he was with another woman. I hated being that type of person, but I didn't know how to shut it off. Maybe after we knew each other better, I'd feel more secure that he wouldn't cheat on me.

"You shouldn't have said anything," Darian muttered. "He obviously hasn't told her much about this way of life."

"Better to know than find out the hard way, right?" I asked.

"If Tank didn't rip into Wire, then I'm sure everything is fine," Isabella said. "He's never been shy about expressing his opinions. The fact you don't have a lawyer here writing up divorce papers tells me that he wants to be married to you, which means you're the only woman he wants."

"What if I'm not enough?" I asked. "He wanted Lupita, and I'm nothing like her. She's all strong and mouthy, and I'm just... not. What if he regrets being stuck with me?"

"Ladies, out," Tank said from the doorway, his voice deep and commanding.

I hadn't even noticed him standing there, and now I felt like an idiot. My cheeks burned with embarrassment as the women scurried out. After the front door shut, he moved closer, dragging a chair over, and took a seat across from me, close enough our knees were nearly touching. I couldn't look at him, feeling completely humiliated. How much had he heard? Was he angry with me?

He reached for my hand and slid something onto my finger. I blinked at the sapphire that sparkled in the light. It was plain white gold with a big stone in the center, and had a diamond encrusted band paired with it. I stared, not sure what to think, feel, or even say. I'd been thinking he didn't really want me, and he'd been out buying me a ring? How had he even known what size to get? It was a perfect fit.

He held another ring out to me, this one a man's ring in white gold. I took it from him and lifted my gaze to meet his. He was watching me intently, but didn't say anything. Tank held out his left hand and I slid the ring onto his finger. My heart was hammering in my chest and my fingers tightened on his.

"Emmie, I think there are some things we need to discuss," he said.

Right. Like what I should and shouldn't say around the other ladies. Or anyone for that matter. I felt like such an idiot. Even though I didn't know Tank very well, it had been wrong of me to voice my concerns about his intentions in front of the women in his club. I should have gone to him if I was worried.

"I'm sorry," I said. "I shouldn't have said what I did."

"Why are you having such a hard time believing that I want to be with you and only you?" he asked.

"Have you seen you? You're like every woman's fantasy, and I'm… I'm like a female version of the Pillsbury Doughboy. My sister is graceful and strong, and very independent. She's the kind of woman who can make a man beg."

"And you don't think men would beg to be with you?" he asked.

"Why would they?"

He abruptly stood and tugged on my hand. Without a word, he led me back to the bedroom, then kicked the door shut. When he opened the closet, there was a full-length mirror hanging on the inside of the door. Slowly, he began to remove first my clothes and then his. I tried to look away, but he turned my chin until I was staring at our reflection.

"What do you see?" he asked.

"A woman who needs to lay off the cookies?"

His gaze held mine in the mirror, and I could tell he wasn't pleased with my answer. He slid his hands down my sides to my hips, then one palm gave my ass a squeeze.

"I fantasized about this ass for weeks. It's perfect, and it made me hard just thinking about you bent over and begging to be fucked." He moved his hand back to my hip. "And these curves? They're gorgeous. *You're* gorgeous, Emmie. I could worship your breasts for hours, and I love the way your softer body presses against me when I'm inside you. I'm glad you're not stick thin. There's nothing wrong with those women, but I like a woman who gives me something to hold onto."

"Zach..." My heart gave a ping. No one had ever said something like that to me before. Even though I hadn't dated, I'd heard enough comments about putting down the donut or getting a salad that it had made me doubt myself. Guys had hit on me and made lewd suggestions, but none had ever asked me out. I'd given those people power over me. "I never felt beautiful until last night. The way you looked at me was something I'd dreamed of often and thought I'd never have. Guys only ever wanted to get into my pants, and even those were few and far between. Especially if they met Lupita. I've never been on a date."

"If you had walked in with your sister the first time I met her, I never would have even glanced her way. You've held me captive since the first moment I saw you, Emmie. The guys teased me about the number of times I ate at the diner, just so I could be near you." He shrugged. "And I may have followed you back to the motel after every shift to make sure you made it into your room safely."

Tears pricked my eyes. "You did that for me? Even before we'd spoken?"

He nodded.

I turned in his embrace and placed my hands on his broad chest. I could feel the *thump* of his heart against my palms. Slow and steady. The warmth in his eyes wasn't lust, but something a little more. The hard cock trapped between us said enough about how much he desired me, but I was starting to think that maybe what we had went beyond that. It seemed unthinkable since we'd only met yesterday, but maybe Wire had been right. When you know, you just know. If the right person comes along, maybe it doesn't take weeks, months, or years to be certain.

"No one has ever made me feel as special, or as wanted as you do. I think part of my self-doubt is that I'm worried it's all too good to be true. That I'll wake up tomorrow and find out it was a dream. You seem too perfect, Zach, and it scares me. The only men I've known were people like my father, or the players at school who just wanted notches on their bedposts. You aren't like them."

"Em, don't make me out to be something I'm not. I'm no angel. I've killed people, and those I left alive wished they were dead. I've run guns and drugs, slept with more women than I care to admit."

"And maybe to some people that makes you a bad person. The way you look at me, the tender way you touch me, shows me that there's more to you than all that other stuff. Maybe it's a side that only I get to see, and I'm all right with that. I could easily fall for you, Zach."

"Good," he said as his head lowered toward mine. He stopped when our noses touched. "Because I'm already falling for you, Em."

When he kissed me, it felt like I was burning from the inside, and my toes curled as I melted against him. Zach was everything I'd ever wanted, and never dared to dream I'd have. To some, he might be dangerous and deadly, but the only danger I faced was having him break my heart.

He lifted me and carried me over to the bed, then gently laid me down. His heated gaze caressed me from head to toe before he lowered his body over mine. I welcome his weight as he pressed me into the mattress, his cock already hard and leaking pre-cum. Zach kissed me until I was breathless. My heart felt like it was racing and I was already trembling. Just the power of his lips was enough to make me beg for more.

"You deserve a man who will take all the time in the world to worship every inch of you," he said, his voice deep and rumbling. "Someone who will leave no doubt that you're the most desirable woman in the world."

"Zach, if you take all the time in the world, I might combust. I already want you."

"I don't want you to ever doubt how beautiful you are, or how perfect. And just to make sure you learn that lesson, I'm going to make sure you take everything I have to give."

What did that mean? I blinked up at him and before I could process what was happening, he'd rearranged me on the bed and shackled my hands to the headboard. I stared at the cuffs before looking at Zach again.

"Where did those come from? I don't remember them being there before."

"They weren't," he said. "I hung them on the headboard before I left to see Torch. I know you didn't think you'd be into this sort of thing, but I'd thought we could play with them. I'd have stopped the second you weren't into it. Now they'll serve another purpose."

"And that would be?"

"To keep you from moving too much. Unless you want your legs tied, I'd suggest you hold still."

My heart skipped a beat. Tie my legs? I wasn't sure if I was extremely turned on by the idea, or slightly disturbed. Since I hadn't had sex before Zach, I didn't really have any experience with bondage. Despite the fact I liked to read rather spicy books, finding myself in this position didn't feel at all the way I'd thought it would. I trusted him, but the thought of being helpless made my twist my hands and squirm a little. If it were anyone else, I'd be really damn scared right now.

His gaze softened a moment as he stared at me. "You okay, baby? I can unfasten them if you want. I would never ask you do something you don't enjoy, not in the bedroom anyway."

"No, they're fine. I'm just... not used to something like this."

"Then I guess I'd better take your mind off it." Zach flashed me a grin, then lowered his head to my breasts, licking first one nipple, then the other. He grazed the second one with his teeth and a shiver raked my body. He took his time, lavishing attention on one breast, then the other, before moving back again. My nipples were throbbing, and so was my pussy. My hands clenched as I jerked at the handcuffs, wanting to hold him closer to me.

"Patience, sweetheart," he murmured as he kissed his way down my body.

I felt like I was on fire, and as his shoulders spread my thighs wider, my breath froze in my lungs. The first swipe of his tongue against my wet folds had me keening and tightening my legs against him. He only chuckled when I squeezed him, then went back to teasing me without mercy.

He flicked my clit, then traced around it. My legs trembled and I tugged on the cuffs again. Zach gripped my hips and speared me with his tongue, thrusting it in and out. I whimpered and begged, wanting to come. When he sucked my clit into his mouth, I screamed with the force of my release, stars bursting behind my closed eyelids. It felt like I'd left my body before I came crashing back down. My chest heaved with every breath as he rose above me, his hips pressing against mine.

"Zach," I said softly.

His gaze held mine as he sank into me, stretching me slowly. When every inch of his cock filled me, I wrapped my legs around his waist. Zach pulled back, then drove into me with enough force the headboard smacked against the wall. Every thrust was harder and deeper than the last, until he was slamming into me. My body was tightening and I knew I would come even harder than before.

"So close," I said. "Don't stop!"

He growled and took me even faster. I cried out his name as I came again, squeezing his cock until I felt the warmth of his cum inside me. His strokes slowed, but he didn't stop until my breathing turned ragged and I felt boneless. As he kissed me softly, I felt his hand at my wrists, and then the cuffs were unlocked.

I glanced up and tried not to snicker as I saw the crack in the wall had gotten even bigger. If he was going to keep breaking the wall, we'd have to either pad the sheetrock or move the bed to the center of the room.

"Any doubts that I think you're the most desirable, most beautiful woman I've ever seen?" he asked.

"No," I said softly. "I'm sorry I doubted you before. It wasn't you that I was doubting, not really. It was me. I've never had anyone notice me when my sister was around, and I guess I worried the same would happen with you."

"You're mine, Emmie. My wife. Reapers don't divorce, so you're stuck with me forever. I gave you the option to have Wire make it all vanish, but I'm taking that off the table. If you wanted out of this marriage, you had your chance. I will always be faithful to you, and I expect the same in return. We may not have said vows, but it doesn't make you any less mine."

"There's no one I want but you, Zach."

He kissed me and cuddled me close. With his name on my lips, I fell asleep. There was nowhere safer than being in his embrace.

Chapter Seven

Tank
Two Weeks Later

I'd spent every waking moment waiting to hear from Emmie's father and that Ernesto fuck, and planning how I would take them out. My nights were filled with making my sexy wife scream my name. I'd patched the bedroom wall and let Emmie pick out a paint color. Slowly, my house was becoming a home. At her suggestion, I'd placed the bed at an angle in the corner of the room, and I'd bought some of those foam noodles the kids played with in pools. I'd cut them down to size, then sliced them open and fit them around the posts of the bed where it might hit the wall. Since then, we hadn't had an issue with cracked walls.

The bedroom was now a slate blue, and she'd ordered matching bedding online. I hated that I couldn't take her outside of the compound, but I wasn't going to take a chance with her safety. Every Dixie Reaper -- patched members, officers, Prospects, and even the old ladies -- had been shown pictures of Luis Montoya and Ernesto Lopez. Not only were we keeping a sharp eye for them sneaking into the compound, but anytime someone left they watched their surroundings. The ladies were on lockdown, which had pissed off Ridley to no end, but she understood.

Since none of the kids could leave the safety of our fenced compound, Torch and Venom had ordered playground equipment and set up a park area away from the clubhouse. They'd spared no expense and even added benches and a covered pavilion for future family gatherings. I couldn't drive by the new spot without smiling. Over the last nine years, things had changed drastically for my brothers. There were still some wild parties at the clubhouse, but fewer and fewer members were partaking. Quite a few of us had settled down and had families. Even though Saint was still single, since he'd become a father, I'd noticed he didn't go to the clubhouse as often. Isabella and Ridley had both offered to watch his daughter, but he always declined.

At one point, I'd have laughed if someone said we'd all start settling down. No way the wild bunch of men I called brothers would ever give up all the free pussy they could have. I'd have been wrong. With the right woman, all that other pussy just didn't mean a damn thing. Not once since I'd laid eyes on Emmie had I even entertained the thought of being with another woman. She was it for me.

"I thought VanHorne was supposed to be here," I said, as I looked around the table at my brothers. Torch had called Church nearly a half hour ago, but so far no one had said a damn thing. "Wasn't he arriving weeks ago, but we haven't seen him?"

"He's here," Torch said. "Just because you can't see him, doesn't mean the man isn't around. He stopped in to visit Isabella and his grandkids, but he hasn't really made his presence known. The last thing we want is for these fuckers to go to ground."

"So someone has seen Ernesto and Luis?" I asked.

"Do you really think I'd let those sick bastards wander around our fucking town without knowing their every move? They've been watched. So far, they haven't done much of anything, but I'm sure that won't last. From what I hear, they're getting tense and I have no doubt they'll make a move soon," Torch said.

"You're not using Emmie as bait," I said.

"We didn't ask to," Venom said. "Nothing changes where the ladies and kids are concerned. They're all on lockdown until this is handled."

"But?" I asked. There was always a fucking "but" in there.

"We're going to set up a meeting with them. As far as they know, we're willing to listen to what they have to say. They'll be allowed into the compound, patted down, then escorted straight here. Guards will be stationed not only outside the door, but around the clubhouse as well. There's no way those fuckers are going to get anywhere near Emmie," Venom said. "And the dumb shits probably won't realize they're walking into a trap."

"You didn't think as Sergeant at Arms I might have needed to be consulted on this? Making sure this type of thing runs smooth is kind of my job," I pointed out.

"It is," Torch agreed. "But I also think you're too close this time. No one is disputing that you're Sergeant at Arms, or the best choice for that position, but just this once we're asking you to take a step back. At least as far as planning goes. You can be present at the meeting, as long as you keep your cool."

Right. Like two unarmed men wouldn't be temptation for anyone? Especially the sick fuckers who would be seated at this very table? I wasn't going to make that promise. If I saw my chance to take them out, then I'd do it. Anything to make sure Emmie was safe, as well as the other women that fucker Ernesto was selling off to brothels and butchers. The guy really made my stomach turn, and I could handle some fucked-up shit.

"They won't give up their weapons," Flicker said. "I've been checking out these guys, and there is no way they'll walk in here completely unarmed. If we're going to meet them, I say we do it somewhere public. Remember when Josie was bait for her father?"

"Yeah and a lot of innocent people could have been hurt," Saint pointed out. "If anyone had opened fire, women and kids could have been killed. Too risky. I don't trust those guys to give a shit about bystanders. A bloodbath wouldn't matter much to men like those two. We might have done some fucked-up shit over the years, but only to those who deserved it. It's part of why I love this club so much."

"I'll second that," Tempest said.

"Whatever y'all decide to do, I'm behind you one hundred percent. When I needed space, you left me alone. And then I came here with Mara, and you stepped up to help when we needed it. Whatever it takes to keep Tank's wife by his side, count me in," Rocky said.

"I want to know what VanHorne thinks of all this," I said. "He took out Fernando Montoya. After having dealt with the family before, maybe he has some insight. We brought him in for a reason, right?"

"I told you he's already been checking into things," Torch said.

The doors burst open and Wire rushed in, a sheaf of papers in his hand and his hair standing on end. His gaze scanned the room and landed on me, then he vaulted over the damn table and dropped the papers in my lap.

"Did you know about this?" Wire asked.

I shuffled through the papers, and my heart nearly stalled when I realized what I was looking at. Had Emmie known? Or would this come as just as much of a shock for her? It explained why Luis had been ready to sell her off to the highest bidder and he hadn't attempted the same with Lupita.

"Emmie isn't really a Montoya?" I asked.

"No. Her mother had an affair with Carlos Gomez during a trip to South America. His family is relatively poor and runs a shop in Rio. It's where he met Emmie's mother. When Emmie was born, she wasn't in Spain. She was born in a hospital in Rio, and as you can see, her father is listed as Carlos Gomez," Wire said.

"And then somehow, for whatever reason, Emmie's mother got Montoya to adopt Emmie and give her his name?" I asked.

"That's what the papers show. There's more. Did you notice the account information in the Cayman Islands?" Wire asked.

"It's in Emmie's name. I don't think she's aware that she has all that money available to her. If she'd known, she wouldn't have been working at the diner, right?" I flipped through the papers again. "So Ernesto wanted Emmie to get his hands on her money, Luis wanted to get rid of the bastard daughter his wife had birthed, and... what? Ernesto was just going to sell Em once he had her money? I'd have thought Luis would want to get his hands on the cash. Guess maybe he hated Emmie more than he wanted that damn money."

"Pretty much," Wire said. "Although, to be honest, I'm not sure he's aware of the account. Ernesto has some contacts and might have run across the information on his own. He wouldn't want to share that knowledge with Luis, if he thought the man would try to keep the funds himself."

"Do you think Lupita knows all this? She's older than Emmie and would remember her mom being pregnant. She may have heard something over the years," Venom said. "I think we need to bring her in and ask some questions."

Flicker snorted. "Good luck."

"What's that supposed to mean?" Torch asked. "I know she came here and showed up at Tank's place. And I know you took her home."

"Then you should also know she vanished by the next morning," Flicker said. "I don't know who picked her up or where she went. I haven't heard from or seen her since. As far as I know, she's not been in contact with anyone here. Tank? Has your wife heard anything?"

"Emmie hasn't had contact with her either," I said.

"Great. We have a crazy ass, deadly woman wandering around and no one knows where the fuck she is or what she's up to," Torch said. "Tank and I have discussed it, and we believe that Lupita came to our compound for a reason. Something other than keeping Rin safe. She wanted us to owe her favor, but it's all a little too tidy. Why go to jail for a crime she didn't commit? Considering the lengths we went to in order to protect Rin, she had to know we'd help Emmie if she asked."

"So we need to deal with Ernesto and Luis, and worry that Lupita has an agenda too?" Flicker. "Wait. You let me take a woman into my home that you think had ulterior motives for being here? Assholes!"

"We didn't realize that everything didn't quite add up until after Lupita had been here and left," I said. "I wouldn't have let you put yourself in danger. Besides, Lupita seemed to get along just fine with you. She did seem a bit pissed that I was with her sister."

"Um, yeah about that..." Flicker glanced away before meeting my gaze again. "She liked you chasing her. The reason she asked Emmie to find you and not anyone else is that she thought Emmie wouldn't be even close to your type. Even though she didn't want to settle down, I think she's ticked off you picked her sister over her. And now that we know Emmie is only her half-sister..."

"This is getting too fucked up," Torch said. "Whatever happened to the days we only had to worry about a gun deal going bad? No, we all have to fall for women who come with a shit ton of trouble."

"Seems to be working out just fine," Tex said. "Kalani was worth it. I'm sure you feel the same about Isabella, and I know Venom is glad to have Ridley."

"And for the record, Kayla wasn't in trouble when I claimed her," Preacher said.

"No, she was just knocked up," Saint said.

A few of the guys snickered. Saint hadn't been patched in when Preacher had knocked up his sister, Kayla. He'd still been a Prospect at the time, but he hadn't been the least bit happy. It had all worked out. Anyone who saw Preacher and Kayla couldn't deny the man adored her. She'd been exactly what he needed. And as screwed up as this current situation was, I had to admit that Emmie was worth every bit of trouble. She might not be the type of woman everyone had assumed I'd be with, but she was perfect for me. Torch was right. We all ended up with women who came with a bunch of problems, but I knew none of the married men around the table would have it any other way.

- 253 -

"We should let Casper know this latest bit of info," I said.

"He already knows," Torch said.

A shadow emerged from the corner of the room and every one of us around the table jolted. There were quite a few ex-military men I called brother, and it was unnerving the assassin had gotten the drop on us. It proved that he was right for this mission. If he could sneak up on an entire room full of Dixie Reapers, then surely he could handle Luis and Ernesto. And if he couldn't, then I didn't know what else to try, but I'd have to think of something. No way would I let Emmie become a victim of either man.

Casper had aged a bit since I'd last seen him, but he apparently hadn't lost his skills. The man was considered the best assassin in the world. Or maybe the deadliest would be an accurate description. It was often said that if Casper VanHorne was coming for you, then you'd better have your affairs in order. A gold band glinted on his finger, but he was dressed head to toe in black aside from that bit of jewelry. I'd found it slightly odd that he'd gotten married a while back, but none of us had ever met his wife. As far as I knew, Isabella and Torch hadn't met her either.

"You let me handle Lupita Montoya," he said. "And I'll be taking care of the little problem of Ernesto and Luis too. With pleasure. There are plenty of people who want those two dead, and many who would pay for the proof they aren't breathing anymore."

"When you say handle…" Not that I trusted Lupita right now, but she was my sister-in-law. I felt like I should be watching out for her, as long as she didn't intend my wife any harm. If she came for Emmie, nothing would save her from my wrath.

"I'm not going to kill her, if that's what you mean, but she won't bother you again. Not until I know for certain she doesn't have something devious in mind," Casper said. "I may not have met your Emmie, but my daughter lives here and my grandchildren. I want to make sure they're safe."

"How are you going to handle Ernesto and Luis?" Flicker asked.

"Everything is already in place for those two. By tonight, they won't be a problem for anyone. Nothing I do will trace back to the Dixie Reapers, so you'll all be in the clear. Keep Emmie close tonight, Tank."

I nodded, having every intention of doing that very thing.

"Casper, not that I doubt your prowess when it comes to this sort of thing, but how exactly are you taking care of them?" Rocky asked.

"They've been spending their evenings at a strip club in the seedier section of town. I've paid off the owner to give me access to the men. When they aren't looking, I'm slipping them a bit of arsenic. I know it seems like a classic murder mystery novel or film, but it works. I'll be gone before they even know I'm there," Casper said. "And the dose will be high enough they'll die quickly."

"You aren't worried about it being detected in an autopsy?" Preacher asked.

"No. Those two have enough enemies, the police will never narrow down who killed them. And I'm not even on their radar as a possibility. Everything will be fine. Just keep Emmie safe until then," Casper said.

"Who's with Emmie now?" Torch asked.

"Fenton. He wanted to make amends for sending her away the first night she came here," I said. "Calder said he'd hang around the outside of the house just in case something went down."

"Go check on Emmie," Venom said. "We can wrap things up here, and someone will be touch to let you know if anything new is discussed in your absence. She's your number one priority right now."

"Thanks, VP."

I hauled myself out of my chair and left the clubhouse. The bike ride to my house was short, and I found Fenton and Emmie in the living room. The Prospect was staring out the windows and Emmie was reading a book Mara had sent over. Once the Reaper ladies had heard Emmie liked to read, they'd started leaving books on our porch at random times. Even though Mara tended to keep to herself, she'd left several books in the last few days, each with a note for Emmie to keep hope that everything would work out.

"Thank fuck you're here," Fenton muttered.

"Trouble?" I asked, my body going tense.

"No. Not for me anyway," he said, glancing at Emmie.

She hadn't lifted her nose from the book yet, even though she knew damn well I was here. It wasn't like her not to greet me, and I knew something was off. The tension in my body didn't ease as I studied my wife, wondering what had happened while I was gone.

"The two of you need to talk, so I'm going to head out," Fenton said. "And um… Calder and I won't say a word about…"

He glanced at Emmie again and I stared at my wife once more, hard enough she finally glanced up at me. I heard the front door slam, then Fenton's bike start up a moment later. Emmie set her book aside but didn't move. There was a nervousness to her that I hadn't seen since that first day I'd brought her here. I knew her father and Ernesto hadn't gotten into the compound, so what could have her fidgeting and not wanting to hold my gaze? Whatever it was, Fenton and Calder knew about it. They'd have told me immediately if she were in danger.

"Something I need to know?" I asked.

"Maybe?" Her hands twisted in her lap.

I moved closer and sank onto the couch next to her. Reaching for her hands, I stilled her fidgeting. Her hands were cold, and I could feel the tension coiled inside her.

"Emmie, whatever it is, we'll face it together. What happened today?" I asked.

"I noticed that... I'm late." She stared up at me, almost expectant.

"Late? For what?"

She blinked. "Are you serious right now? I'm late. You know, *late?* As in I missed my period? It was due a week ago."

All right, so maybe I hadn't been that quick on the uptake with that one. I still didn't understand why she seemed so nervous. It wasn't like I'd made it a secret that I was in this for the long haul.

"Calder went and picked up some pregnancy tests for me. I know those over the counter ones aren't always that accurate, but I took three different brands of those early detection ones. All three came back positive." She squirmed in her seat. "Did you hear me, Zach? You're going to be a daddy."

Yeah, I'd heard her, and I still didn't understand why she was so nervous. Maybe finding out she was pregnant while her dad and Ernesto was still running loose wasn't exactly ideal, but I wasn't going to let those fuckers anywhere near her. They'd have to get through me, and all my brothers. "Why were you worried about telling me you're pregnant?" I asked.

"Like you've pointed out before, we're strangers. We might be married, but… what if things don't work out between us?"

I smiled a little. "Sweetheart, I'm here, right beside you, until the end. I'm not going anywhere, and I'll never want to either."

Chapter Eight

Emmie

Tank sat beside me, looking like I hadn't just dropped a bomb on him. I was pregnant. That was a huge thing, right? The kind of thing that sometimes sent men running. He looked completely calm and like we'd just been discussing the weather and not life-altering things like babies. I would have thought a big biker like Tank would be impulsive, might even be volatile, and definitely not the type of guy to calmly hold my hand when I told him we were having a kid together. He wasn't anything like I'd thought he would be and was constantly surprising me.

The phone I'd brought with me started ringing in the other room. It was the first time I'd received a call since I'd landed in this small town, and my pulse leapt at the implication. No one had that number, except Lupita, as she'd been the one to give it to me. Well, I'd given it to the guy at the front gate, but he'd thrown it away. I hadn't heard from my sister since she walked out of here two weeks ago, nor had she tried to come see me. If Lupita was calling, did that mean she was in trouble?

I jumped off the couch and went running for the guest room, where I'd left the phone on the dresser. I picked it up and saw a number I didn't recognize. My hands shook as I answered, hoping it wasn't bad news but fearing for the worst.

"Hello."

"Emmie."

The sound of Lupita's voice made me clutch the phone tighter.

"Just listen," Lupita said. "Don't say a word, and don't tell that hulking giant who you're talking to."

Why did she want to keep Tank in the dark? My brow furrowed as unease settled in the pit of my stomach. Lupita didn't sound like her usual self. There was tension in her voice, and an urgency. But more than that, she sounded… almost like she was on some sort of drugs. Her words weren't slurred, but her speech was faster and choppier. Almost like she was spitting the words out.

"I was wrong," Lupita said. "The Dixie Reapers can't save you, but I know someone who can. You need to leave, Emmie. Now. Right now. Meet me outside of the compound. When you leave the gates, turn left and head into town. At the first stop sign, hang a right and you'll see a park. I'll be waiting at the picnic tables. Get out of there before it's too late."

The line disconnected and I stared at the phone. What was going on? It was strange that she wanted me to leave the compound. So far, my father and Ernesto hadn't been able to get to me. Why would she want me to leave? Wouldn't I be in danger if I were out in the open? Something felt off, but Lupita had never done anything to hurt me before. At least, not before she'd showed up at the compound. Until that day, she'd always been my loving older sister. Maybe she really did know something and thought she was helping me. Should I have told her about the baby?

"Who was that?" Tank asked as he filled the bedroom doorway.

Lupita had said not to tell him, but that felt wrong. Tank had protected me, cared for me… hell, I was married to him. Why would she want me to leave and not tell him?

"It was Lupita," I said, putting someone ahead of my sister for the first time in my life. "She… wants me to leave the compound and meet her at a park."

"Did she say why?"

"She said the Dixie Reapers couldn't protect me. She asked me to sneak out and not tell you I'd spoken to her, or where I was going."

"And yet you're telling me everything," he said.

"It felt wrong, what she asked. And she didn't sound right."

Tank nodded. "Did you know that Lupita is your half-sister?"

I blinked, then blinked again. *What?*

"Wire found a birth certificate that had been buried deep. Your real father is from South America. Your mother had an affair with him, and for whatever reason, Luis Montoya adopted you and gave you his name. Lupita would have been old enough at the time that she may know about it," Tank said.

"Why would they keep that from me?" I asked.

"I don't know. But the way Lupita acted when she was here, her sudden break from prison when she should have been locked up longer, and now this phone call? It's not all adding up, Emmie. I don't know what your sister is up to, but I don't like it. I'm not sure she's really trying to help you, and I won't put you in the path of danger."

"What do we do?" I asked.

"I don't know. When you don't show at that park, she's going to contact you again. Or she may try to come here and get you herself."

"Do we want that to happen?" I asked.

"I think we do," Tank said. "I don't like the thought of you being bait, but if Lupita shows her face here, I'm going to make myself scarce. I'll be lurking, and you'll be perfectly safe, but I don't want her to know I'm here. I want to see what she says and does. You're right. The Lupita who showed up here isn't the same one who was here two years ago."

"So now we just sit and wait? See what she does?" I asked.

"Exactly. Just know that you'll be protected, Emmie. I won't let anything happen to you." He placed a hand on my belly. "Either of you."

"What do we do while we wait?"

"How about I feed you?" he asked with a smile. "It's my experience that pregnant women need to eat more, and have strange cravings. Anything in particular you want?"

"Um, I think it's too soon for cravings, but I am hungry."

"Let's go see what I can throw together in the kitchen. Once all this is over, you can go shopping with me. I know being stuck inside the compound can't be easy."

I followed him through the house and sat the table while he pulled ingredients from the cabinets and fridge. I saw some pasta, shelled shrimp, walnuts, garlic cloves, olive oil, and a few seasonings, but I didn't know what the heck he was making. I was sure I'd love it. He had yet to cook anything I didn't like. For that matter, he had yet to set me loose in the kitchen. I wondered if he thought I couldn't cook. I didn't really have any experience with it, but surely I could read a recipe and figure things out.

Tank added some oil to a pan and started boiling water for the pasta. While the noodles cooked, he added the shrimp and other ingredients to the pan. Whatever he was making smelled incredible, but I didn't see any sauce. I'd never had pasta without it before, but I was willing to give it a try.

When he was finished and had plated our food, I took a hesitant bite. The subtle flavor was really good. It didn't take me long to clear my plate, and Tank filled it a second time. He gave me a wink as he sat back down and my cheeks flushed. I'd never had a problem eating more than my share, but he seemed to enjoy the fact I could eat more than one helping.

"Good?" he asked.

"Nope. I hated it. That's why I'm on serving number two."

"Smart ass," he said.

"I thought you liked my ass."

"Among other things."

I could hear my phone ringing again in the guest room, but I ignored it. It had to be Lupita. No one else had the number. The ringing stopped, then started up again a moment later. My hand tightened on my fork, and Tank leaned over and brushed a kiss against my cheek. I took a deep breath, then let it out. The phone went off several more times before going silent again.

"I'm going to clean up the kitchen and leave the house," Tank said. "I'll be watching, and so will my brothers. Lupita will be allowed inside the compound, but none of us are going to trust her until we know what's going on."

I went into the living room and picked up my book again. Not that I really saw the words on the page. I was nervous, and a bit scared. My sister wasn't acting right, and I didn't know who the new version of Lupita was or what she wanted. Would she hurt me? Had my entire life been one huge lie? I obviously wasn't really a Montoya, for which I was grateful. But I'd never thought my sister would turn her back on me.

I clicked on the TV and tried to watch the movie that played. Every noise made me jump. The front door opened and shut, and my body tensed. My gaze jerked to the living room door and I saw Lupita, or I thought it was my sister, stumble into the room. Her hair was stringy and lank, her healthy glow was long gone, and there was a wildness to her eyes. She glanced around, looking like a cornered animal, before advancing farther into the room.

"We have to go, Emmie. We can't wait," she said, her words just as rapid fire as before. The way her hands trembled, the pallor of her skin, and her overall strung out appearance told me I had been correct. Lupita was on drugs, but I didn't know if they were voluntary.

"What happened?" I asked. "Lupita, you're scaring me."

"The Dixie Reapers aren't who we thought they were," she said. "You're in danger, Emmie. Have to save you. Can't let them get you."

"Save me? Lupita, I'm fine! I'm happy here."

Her head jerked around as her gaze scanned the room, but she twitched and jerked like she needed another fix of whatever she was on. I had never known my sister to do drugs. Even when she'd been sick, it had been a battle to get her to take a prescribed medication.

"Lupita, look at me. Please," I said.

Her gaze swung toward me, and I could tell that my sister wasn't really there. I didn't know what had happened to my sister, but I wanted to find out. It didn't matter that she may have hidden the truth from me, that I wasn't really a Montoya. Lupita had protected me when she could, and now I needed to do the same for her.

"Lupita, I want you to listen carefully. The Dixie Reapers are good men. Tank is everything you said he was, and so much more. I'm safe here, and so are you. Stay with me. We can wait for Tank together. He'll help you, just like he's helped me," I said.

A motorcycle backfired somewhere nearby and Lupita gasped, spinning toward the window. While she was distracted, I skirted around her and made my way to the front door. I pulled it open and whisper-yelled for my husband.

"Tank! I need you," I said.

My big biker materialized from the darkness, along with Flicker and the giant I'd recently met called Rocky. The guy was so massive, he was even bigger than Tank. I had no doubt my husband could take him down, if the need ever arose.

"Something's wrong with Lupita. I think someone drugged her," I said in a whisper. "She looks about ready to crawl out of her skin, and she keeps saying I'm in danger and can't trust you."

"I'll call the doc," Flicker said, pulling out his cell phone.

Tank and Rocky moved past me into the house, and I heard Lupita start to scream. My heart pounded as I stepped up to the living room doorway. Rocky had his arms around Lupita as she kicked and snapped her teeth at Tank.

"You can't kill me!" she yelled. "I won't let you hurt my sister!"

"Agent Lupita Montoya," Tank said, his voice deep and commanding. "Cease and desist. We aren't going to hurt you sister. Or you."

The laugh that came out of Lupita sounded like the craziness that came out of patients in psych wards in the movies. She looked completely unhinged and sweat was starting to coat her skin. The drugs were probably working their way out of her system, and I had a feeling that she was going to crash hard. I looked at Tank, knowing that he would do whatever he could for Lupita.

Lupita let out a string of Spanish that made me wince.

"What the fuck did she say?" Rocky asked.

"Um, you don't want to know," I assured him. "Maybe we should restrain her with something other than you?"

Rocky snickered.

"Take her to the guest room," Tank said. "I have some rope. We'll tie her to the bed until the doc can get here."

I hurried out of the way as Rocky half-carried and half-dragged my sister down the hall. He lay across her once he had her on the bed, and I closed my eyes as Lupita did her best to attack the huge man. Tank came into the room carrying a few lengths of rope. I wasn't sure I wanted to know what he'd used them for, since he hadn't used them on me. Once he had secured Lupita's hands to the headboard and had run a rope under the mattress to tie her feet, he stepped back and so did Rocky.

Lupita cursed and screamed, twisting and trying to break free. A tear slipped down my cheek as I watched her. Who had done this to my sister? And why? My heart broke as my once strong sister thrashed and cried out, trying to break free. She'd grown thinner over the past two weeks, and I was worried she wouldn't survive whatever had been done to her.

I wanted to calm her, but when I approached the bed, Tank pulled me back. His arm banded around my waist and I turned to bury my face against him. I let the tears fall and clutched at him. Whoever had hurt Lupita, I wanted them to pay! It killed me to see her this way.

"Doc will be here in a few minutes," Flicker said as he stood in the doorway. "She may need to go to the hospital. Who knows what she's on."

"She was drugged," I said, pulling my face away from Tank. "Lupita didn't even like taking aspirin. There's no way she did drugs of her own accord. Someone did this to her."

"And we'll find out who," Tank said, running his hand up and down my back. "Your sister is safe now, Emmie. We'll make sure she's taken care of and treated by the doc. It would be better not to involve the hospital, but we will if we need to."

"Maybe you should take Emmie back to the living room?" Flicker suggested. "Rocky and I will watch over Lupita. Nothing will happen to her, but your wife seems distraught."

Tank lifted me into his arms and carried me out of the room. I gave Lupita one last look before the wall blocked my view. When Tank entered the living room, he went to his favorite chair and sat down, settling me across his lap. He tangled his fingers in my hair and kissed me softly.

I snuggled against him and breathed in his scent. I knew that Tank would do whatever he could to help Lupita, but it didn't keep me from worrying about her. What if the damage done by the drugs was permanent? What if she didn't survive?

The front door opened and the doctor I'd met before walked in. There was an old-fashioned bag clutched in his hand, and he didn't even stop to spare us a glance. He made his way down the hall, then I heard Flicker talking to him.

"You remember Doctor Myron? He's helped out the club a few times, and he's the one we called for Lupita before. All the Reaper ladies see him for their medical needs, so your sister is in good hands," Tank said.

"Why would someone do this to her?" I asked. "I thought it was me they were after."

"Maybe they believed you'd run to Lupita when she called. Whoever hurt her had to have done it as a way to get to you. I'm betting they wanted to lure you away from the compound. If you'd have gone to the park, someone would have possibly snatched you. I don't think any of this was about Lupita. I think she was just a tool for them. And something tells me that she was released from prison not because of her cunning but because someone pretty powerful thought they could use her."

"Why do men like my father and Ernesto have to exist? How does someone become so evil?" I asked.

"I don't know, sweet girl. I guess in order for there to be a balance in the world, there needs to be a bit of evil. Someone smarter than me could probably give you a good reason. I think some people are just born bad, and others become evil through abuse or other trauma."

It felt like we waited forever before the doctor came back from checking on Lupita. The expression on his face wasn't overly worried so that eased some of my fears.

"I think she's going to be fine, but it will take a while. She's going to have a rough detox with the symptoms she's showing, but the worst should be over in a few days. I can't say for certain what she's on without doing some lab work, but my best guess is heroin. Even then, there are several different types. They could have mixed it with any number of things, including fingernail polish remover or over-the-counter meds."

"Can you take a blood sample and run the tests so we'll know for sure?" Tank asked.

"I can. I do my lab work in-house, but I'm not set up to house her while she detoxes. I can understand why you don't want to take her to the hospital. I have a friend who was a medic in the Army. He has a nursing degree and I'm sure he'd be happy to watch over Lupita," the doctor said.

"You know anything like that would have to be cleared by Torch. We'd have to find a place to set him up. I only have the one guest room," Tank said.

"I was thinking more that she would stay with Jeb while she's recovering. He lives down on the coast, and has plenty of room for Lupita. The Gulf Coast might be good for her right now," the doctor said. "Even though the crucial part of her detox will only last a few days, her recovery could take a bit longer. Without knowing what mixture she was given, if this is even heroin, it's hard to say what effects it will have on her body and mind. Some types can leave lasting psychological harm."

"Let him help her," I said. "I want my sister back. Whatever it takes."

Tank sighed and nodded. "All right. How are you going to get her there?"

"I can give her some Narcan. It's not a permanent fix, and it won't last long. It might be just enough time to get her strapped down for transport. Jeb has some connections and can get her safely to his place. I just need the okay for an ambulance to come through the gates. Privately owned and operated," the doctor said. "Anyone who handles the transport won't breathe a word of this to the authorities or the hospital, but there will be a certified EMT to sit with Lupita in case she needs medical attention."

"Please, Tank," I said. "If this Jeb person can help Lupita, let him. Give him whatever he wants. She's my sister."

"Fine. I'll call Torch and make sure the Prospect manning the gate knows to let in an ambulance when it arrives. I wish we had more time. There are plans in place to take care of Ernesto and Luis, but they could still be roaming free right now," Tank said. "I'll need the name of the driver so the Prospect can ask for ID before letting them through."

"I'll call Jeb now and get the ball rolling," the doctor said.

Tank brushed a kiss against my cheek. "Why don't you go to the kitchen and make some coffee? I have a feeling we might need it. As much as I know you want to see Lupita, I think it's best if you stay out of that room right now."

I wasn't sure I agreed with that assessment, but I went to the kitchen anyway. I gazed down the hall at the open bedroom door and heard Lupita yelling and cussing at poor Flicker. I hated seeing her like this and wished I knew what had happened. She never would have taken drugs voluntarily. Had they tricked her into taking something?

I set up the coffeemaker and sat at the kitchen table while it brewed. My hands fisted on the wooden surface as I heard Lupita get more and more out of control. She sounded completely irrational and paranoid. Lupita had always been the one to watch out for me, and now it was my turn to return the favor. I only hoped we were doing the right thing. I knew why Tank didn't want to involve the hospital or police, but it didn't mean I liked the thought of Lupita suffering more than she had to. Hopefully, this Jeb person would be able to take care of her properly.

I hadn't met a lot of male nurses, but I hadn't been to the hospital very often. I wondered why he'd chosen that instead of becoming a doctor. Maybe I'd get a chance to meet him at some point. It would be nice to know who was taking care of my sister. But Tank seemed to trust Doctor Myron, and I trusted Tank. So if the doc said this Jeb guy was the one for the job, then I had to believe him. It wasn't like I had a lot of options. I could tell that Dixie Reapers didn't trust my sister very much right now, and I could see why, but deep down I didn't think she would ever do something to hurt me.

I wondered if she'd already been on the drugs the day she'd arrived here, all banged up and saying mean things. That hadn't been at all like the sister I'd known and loved all my life. How long did it take for drugs to start changing a person? I'd never researched it before, and without knowing what Lupita was taking it was hard to know which drug to study.

The coffeemaker beeped and stopped gurgling. I poured a cup for Tank and another for the doc. I carefully carried both mugs into the living room, then handed them off and returned to the kitchen for more. I didn't know how Flicker liked his coffee, or Rocky, so I just poured it the way Tank liked it and carried two mugs down the hall. When I reached the bedroom, I hesitated. Was I ready to see Lupita tied down? Flicker stuck his head out of the room and gave me a slight smile.

"You okay, Emmie?" he asked.

"Yeah, I just…" I thrust the mugs toward him. "Thought you and Rocky might want coffee."

"Thanks." He took one of the cups and sipped it. "Perfect."

I scurried back down the hall, too chicken to peek in on my sister. She was quieter, but I wasn't entirely sure that was a good thing. In the living room, Tank was pacing with the phone against his ear and the doc was sitting down enjoying his coffee.

"Both sisters are here," Tank said. "What the fuck do you mean you lost Ernesto and Luis?"

I tensed. Whoever he was talking to must have been keeping tabs on my father and would-be-fiancé. The fact this person didn't seem to know where they were wasn't a good thing. I didn't think they could get inside the compound, but what if I was wrong? I'd believed I'd been safe all this time because they couldn't reach me behind the gate. If I was wrong, then they could be lurking nearby right now, just waiting to make their move.

"Find them and do your fucking job, Casper. If they get inside the gates, it's not just Emmie in danger. They could go after your daughter and grandkids. These sick fucks don't care who they hurt," Tank said, then ended the call. He stared at his phone a moment. "It was much more satisfying to hang up on someone when you could slam the phone down onto the cradle. Pushing a button is anticlimactic."

The doc snickered. "I think you're showing your age. Emmie over there probably never used a landline in a house. Only offices have those these days."

No, I hadn't, but I wasn't about to volunteer that information.

Tank sighed and ran a hand through his hair before moving to the window. He cracked the blinds with his fingers and peered outside. It was dark and I couldn't see a thing, but the inky blackness had an ominous feel to it tonight. Probably had more to do with the fact I knew my father and Ernesto were missing than anything else.

"What are we going to do?" I asked.

"I can't let anyone into this compound without knowing exactly where those two are hiding," Tank said. "It's too dangerous. They could threaten or bribe their way inside that ambulance. I know you want your sister to get the care she needs, but we need to wait, Em. I won't risk you, or the women and children inside the gate."

"I wouldn't ask you to," I assured him.

"I'll text Jeb and let him know to hold off on sending the transport just yet. I'll let him know when it's safe to extract Lupita," the doc said.

I moved closer to Tank and wrapped my arm around his waist, then leaned against his side. The strength I felt in his body helped ease my fears a little. He was so strong I was certain he was nearly invincible. If my father and Ernesto did manage to get to me, I didn't doubt that Tank would protect me. I just hoped he didn't die trying. A world without my big teddy bear wasn't a place I wanted to live in, not even for a second. He was all big and gruff, barking orders at other people. With me, he was sweet and tender.

"I'm starting to think we need a panic room inside the compound," Tank said. "Big enough for all the women and children. Then when shit goes down, we won't have to worry quite so much. I don't like the thought of you sitting here, an easy target if they get into the house."

"I trust you to keep me safe," I said. "And I'm not completely helpless. I may not be as fierce as Lupita, but she did teach me enough that I can get away if the need arises."

"Let's hope we don't have to test your skills today, or any other day," he said.

I stood with Tank, keeping vigil at the window. I hadn't met the mysterious Casper, but I hoped he would get the job done and make sure Ernesto and Luis couldn't hurt anyone ever again. I didn't care if that meant they were buried six feet under. They were completely rotten to the core, evil and vile. The world would be better off if they didn't exist.

Chapter Nine

Tank

Every time the shadows outside shifted, I went on alert, fearing the worst. Emmie had fallen asleep in my chair about an hour ago. It tugged at my heart that she trusted me to keep her safe even with all the craziness going on. I couldn't help but smile a little every time I looked at her. I'd sworn to never get involved with a woman, and then Emmie had shown up at the diner. The moment I'd seen her, I'd been hooked. Even if she'd been too spooked for me to talk to her, I think deep down I'd known that she was the one for me. I only regretted that I hadn't had the courage to talk to her sooner.

Lupita was back to screaming and thrashing, her need for whatever drug she'd been given nearly driving her mad. I feared what would happen to her if we couldn't get her out of here soon, but I didn't dare make a move just yet. With Ernesto and Luis unaccounted for, I didn't want to take a chance on letting anyone in through the gate. As the Sergeant at Arms, I took my duties seriously, and keeping the women and children safe was number one on my list. Especially Emmie.

"Never thought I'd see you settle down," the doc said.

"Didn't plan on it, Doctor Myron. Then I met Emmie." I shrugged. Wasn't more to say on the subject. Maybe Wire had been right. When a Reaper met his perfect match, he just knew.

The doc grinned. "You know, as often as your club uses my services, you should probably start calling me Garret. I've been treating your ladies for close to a decade now. I think we've moved past using my title all the time."

"Thanks for trying to help Lupita, Garret. She means a lot to my Emmie," I said.

"I could tell." He glanced at my wife. "Everything all right with her? With everything going on, I never thought she'd fall asleep. Hell, someone could have slipped me a sedative and I probably still would be awake."

"She's pregnant," I said. "Or at least that's what those over the counter tests say. Just found out today so we haven't had a chance to book an appointment with your office. I know the other ladies around here were more tired when they were expecting. Either that, or the stress finally got to her."

"That would do it. Both the stress and the pregnancy. I've witnessed pregnant women fall asleep in the strangest places. With everything she's been through, it wouldn't hurt to bring her in for a check-up. She'll need prenatal vitamins too."

"I'll set something up once this nightmare is finally over. I'm sorry you're trapped inside the compound," I said. "Your partner know you'll be home late?"

Garret smiled. "Phillip is aware of the situation and is concerned about Lupita. He's probably worried about me too, but he'd never say as much. I'm sure he'll be in touch here and there, and he's supposed to contact Jeb about Lupita's care once we know what drugs she was given. It's possible it was just one, but they may have mixed them. Her signs lead me to believe it's heroin, but it could be something else. And there are a lot of ways for heroin to be prepared. Too many options to make a guess."

"This club owes you a lot. Both of you. We appreciate you always being there when we need medical attention for our women. Wouldn't trust anyone else with Emmie, and I'm sure the others feel the same about their wives."

"These women hold a special place in my heart. They're all so strong in their different ways. They're each remarkable and I'm blessed to have gotten to know them, and the Dixie Reapers," Garret said. "If I'd ever met a woman as fierce as the ones all of you seem to find, I might have been persuaded to swing both ways."

I, for one, was thankful he preferred men. Not that I thought Emmie was going to leave me, but if the guy was going to be looking at her even partially naked I didn't think I'd have been quite so cool about it if he were straight.

My phone buzzed in my pocket and I pulled it out. *Incoming.*

"Rocky says there's someone heading this way, and I doubt they're friendly. He didn't say how many there were, or how the fuck they got inside. If this shit keeps happening, we're going to have to up the security on the perimeter."

"I didn't even notice him leave. Quiet for such a giant," Garret said.

"Comes from his military training. Know anything about guns?" I asked. I didn't know what was about to go down, but I wanted to be armed just in case.

"Yes."

He didn't elaborate, but I gave a nod and went to the bedroom. Inside the closet was a custom-made gun safe. I placed my hand on the scanner and unlocked it, then loaded the Colt Night Cobra I'd only had a few months and handed it to Garret before arming myself. The Glock 9mm I'd had for years was my go-to weapon. I hesitated as I looked at my Tresna 9mm AR, but I didn't want to use it so close to Emmie. I'd never seen her around gunfire before and didn't know how she'd react. Part of me wanted to lock her in the bedroom, but I worried they'd come in through the back and snatch her. Being out in the open might not be very safe, but I wanted to keep an eye on her.

I made sure Flicker was carrying, and then I went to stand near the front door. As crazy as these bastards were, I doubted they'd do something so cliché as come in the back way, even though I wasn't about to leave Emmie in that part of the house unprotected. Men like Luis and Ernesto weren't exactly sane, and anything was possible. It didn't take long before I was proven right. Except it wasn't the door they used. They came crashing through the living room window, sending shards of glass everywhere. I should have woken Emmie before now to at least let her know what was going on, make sure she could get out of the way if need be, but time wasn't on my side.

Emmie bolted upright in the chair and let out a scream as Ernesto snarled at her.

"You've caused me no end of trouble," he said. "Come quietly and quickly. Maybe I'll make your death painless."

"You're not touching my wife, asshole," I said, taking aim and unloading half my clip. Out of the corner of my eye, I saw Emmie dive behind the chair and out of sight. It gave me the freedom to focus solely on the bastard who wanted to harm my woman, but I hadn't counted on the fucker being so damn fast. He dove out of the way before I'd even gotten off the first round. Two of the bullets grazed him, leaving flesh wounds, and the others missing completely. The coffee table was toppled and Ernesto did his best to hide behind it. I wasn't exactly known for missing and it pissed me off. Then again, I wasn't dealing with an ordinary man either.

I went after Ernesto as he lunged from his hiding place and charged toward Emmie, and I saw Garret corner Luis. With the doc taking care of Emmie's father, I was able to concentrate on taking down Ernesto. Six shots left in my Glock. I blocked out everything around me, silencing the noises. Even if I'd wanted to take cover, there just weren't any options for a guy my size in this room. As my gaze held Ernesto's, my finger squeezed the trigger. The moment he started to move, I shifted my aim. The bullet hit just to the right on his chest. Not close enough to his heart, but it was sufficient to slow him down. I sent three more shots into him, with the last being a headshot. His sightless eyes stared up at the ceiling as his body crumpled to the floor.

Once I was certain he wasn't getting up, I turned to face Luis. The doc hadn't fired yet, though he looked ready to shoot at any moment. Montoya held his hands up and sweat beaded his brow. His gaze went to the fallen Ernesto and I watched as he swallowed hard. As I moved closer, a wet spot stained the front of his pants, which amused me to no end.

"How did you get in and how many others are there?" I asked.

"None! It was just us," Luis said, sweat beading on his brow as he stared at my gun.

"How the fuck did you get in?" I repeated.

"Fence. We... we cut the fence about two miles from the gate. No one was watching that area and it was dark."

Fuck. We'd definitely had to up our security. Too many crazy people were managing to get inside the compound. If we couldn't keep our women and children safe, then what was the damn point of having a fence?

"Did I or did I not tell you to leave Emmie alone?" I asked. "I told you that she was mine and you couldn't have her."

"I had a deal with him," Luis said. "You understand. It was just business. Perhaps we can make a deal! Anything you want. Whatever I have, it's yours."

"I already have the only thing I want. Emmie." I place my finger on the trigger. Only two bullets left, but I just needed one. "Any last words?"

"I'll sign everything over to Emelda!" he shouted. "Let me live, and it's all hers. Yours. The two of you can have it all."

"I have no need of your money or your house in Spain," I said.

Emmie came out of hiding. Her body trembled and she stayed near the chair. "He has a will," she said.

"And what's in it?" I asked.

"In the event of his death, everything goes to Lupita. I'm fine with that. He's not really my father so none of it was mine to begin with," she said.

"So if I kill him, then she inherits everything?" I asked.

Luis pressed his lips together and that wet spot grew bigger. How the fuck was this man who inspired such fear pissing himself just because I held a gun on him? I didn't think it was the first time a firearm had been pointed in his direction. With his winning personality, I'd be willing to bet it happened on a daily basis.

"Yes," Emmie said. "Lupita gets it all."

"Sounds fair." Without any warning, I pulled the trigger, hitting Luis right between the eyes. His blood and a bit of brain splattered the wall before his body fell to the floor. I sighed and looked at the mess. Between the broken window and all the gore, it was going to take a lot of work to make this place livable again. I couldn't ask Emmie to stay here. Hell, she might never want to live here ever again.

Flicker came down the hall, putting away his gun. "Torch and Venom are outside. They said not to shoot when they come through the door."

"Where the fuck is Casper?" I asked. "He was supposed to take care of these two, not leave them to make a mess of my damn house!"

"I'm right here, dickhead," Casper said as he came through the broken window. "Not my fault you idiots couldn't keep them outside of the compound. Looks to me like someone needs to ride fence and figure out where they slipped through."

"Ride fence?" Venom asked as he entered through the front door. "Does this look like a fucking ranch? Isn't that what cowboys do? Ride the fence lines?"

"What the fuck else would you call it?" Casper asked.

"It will be handled," Torch said as he joined us. "Definitely time to up our security."

"And install a panic room big enough for the women and children," I said. "Somewhere they'll be safe if this shit keeps happening."

"I don't mean to be one of those really weak, pathetic women, but… I think I may be sick," Emmie said.

I watched as she paled and swayed on her feet. I handed my gun off to Garret and reached for my wife. Pulling her against my chest, I helped her out of the living room and away from the carnage. She pushed at me and I released her, just as she threw up all over the hall floor. I winced and started to wonder if we should just burn the damn house and start over. She wiped her mouth with the back of her hand and groaned.

"Take her outside," Garret said. "The fresh air will help."

"You can put the guns in the bedroom. I'll clean them, then lock them up later," I said. I picked up Emmie and carried her out to the driveway. She wobbled a bit as I set her down, but the color slowly started coming back into her cheeks.

"I'm sorry," she said.

"For what?"

"Being so weak."

I tipped up her chin. "Baby, you are far from weak. You came down here all by yourself with those men on your trail, and when you couldn't get inside the gates, you took care of yourself. Two men died in there. Anyone would have lost their lunch over something like that."

"You didn't," she said.

"Not my first rodeo," I said.

"Is it safe for the ambulance to come through?" Garret asked from the doorway.

"Yeah. Ask Venom to clear it with whoever is watching the gate," I said.

Torch came out and looked at the house before turning his gaze on me. "Should have known whatever house I gave you would end up destroyed at some point."

"Hardly destroyed. It's a broken window."

"And a lot of blood, among other things." Torch looked at it again. "Any sentimental value to it?"

"Nope. Thought about burning it down and starting over."

He chuckled. "That would be one heck of a bonfire."

"I can't sleep in there tonight," Emmie said softly. "I'm sorry. And I know I keep apologizing, I just… could we please stay somewhere else?"

Torch focused on her. "You want a family, Emmie?"

Her hand went to her belly and Torch gave me a knowing look.

"There's a house two down from Venom," Torch said. "Big yellow thing with a white porch. Four bedrooms, two living areas. Already has a fenced yard in back too. Why don't the two of you take it?"

"Why haven't you already given that house to someone?" I asked.

He snorted. "Because… like I said, it's two doors down from Venom."

"And? I know the VP can be an asshole, but what Reaper can't say the same?"

"It's not Venom," Torch said. "Think about it. Two doors down. From Ridley. And those hellions they call kids. Every fucker I've offered that place to has run the other direction."

Emmie coughed to cover a laugh.

"We'll take it," I said. "Besides, we'll have kids of our own soon enough. Maybe ours will take after my sweet Emmie and they'll have a calming influence on Venom's little monsters."

"Let's hope for one kid at a time," Emmie said. "I've never been around kids and I'm terrified I'll screw ours up. If I have to handle two at once, I may lose my mind."

I winked at her, knowing damn well my dad had only ever sired one kid at a time, but that didn't mean there weren't twins or triplets hiding in either of our family trees somewhere. So far, Preacher was the only one with twins. I was up for it if that was Fate's plan for us. As long as Emmie was their mother and I got to sleep with her in my arms every night, then that's all that mattered to me. Even if she gave me all girls, that would be fine too. At least until they became hormonal teens. Then I'd have to hide somewhere. I wasn't afraid to admit I was terrified of teen girls. Couldn't shoot them even when you really wanted to.

"I'll stay with Emmie while you gather some clothes," Torch said. "The yellow house is furnished. I'd hoped it would lure someone over there. You can get your other stuff later."

"What's going to happen to this place?" Emmie asked.

"I'll have someone tear it down to the studs and start over. We could just fix the living room floor and busted window, but the house needs a fresh start. Might be a good home for whoever patches in next," Torch said.

I snorted. "We keep adding brothers, we're going to need more houses. Good thing we have plenty of land."

I left Emmie in Torch's care and went back into the house. Venom was on the phone and from what I could hear, he was ordering a clean-up crew to come in and handle the bodies. Garret was in the guest room with Lupita, and had apparently given her something since she seemed calmer. I gave him a quick wave and kept going. In the bedroom, I pulled a duffle off the top shelf of the closet and put a few changes of clothes for myself and Emmie into the bag, along with toiletries I thought we might need. I locked my guns back into the safe, promising myself I'd give them a proper cleaning tomorrow. Right now, Emmie needed me.

When I got to the driveway, Emmie was gone and so was Torch. I looked around, but didn't see either of them. Flicker came over, his hands in his pockets.

"He had a truck here already. Took Emmie to the new house," Flicker said. "Probably for the best. That shit inside could fuck up anyone, and she saw it go down."

Shit. He was right.

I strapped the duffle to the back of my bike and drove it over to the house Torch was giving to us. The lights were on inside and I had to admit it looked like a nice home, good place to raise a family. And then little Farrah let out a war cry and dropped out of the tree, nearly landing on my head. I sighed and looked down at her. The imp just grinned at me, until she tried to stand.

"You broke it, didn't you?" I asked, eyeing her foot.

Her lip quivered, but she lifted that stubborn chin of hers and tried to stand up again. I could see the pain etched on her face, but the little shit had too much of her daddy in her to give up. She took two hobbling steps before I picked her up and carried her down to Venom's house. Ridley was on the porch, hands on her hips, as she scanned the darkness.

"Farrah!" she called out, until she spotted us heading her way. "What the hell has that girl done now?"

"Think she broke her foot when she launched herself out of the tree," I said.

"What tree?" Ridley narrowed her gaze on her daughter. "I told you not to climb the tree in the yard."

"I didn't," Farrah said.

"You didn't climb that tree right there?" Ridley asked, pointing to one at the corner of the property.

"Nope," Farrah said.

"She dive-bombed me from the tree in front of the yellow house," I said, giving a nod in the direction I'd just come. "Torch gave the house to Em and me, seeing as how mine isn't in the best of shape right now."

The kid gave her mom a disgruntled look. "I waited forever for someone to come by. You took too long to look for me."

"So you were going to jump out of the tree at your mom?" I asked.

Farrah grinned, then grimaced in pain.

"Jesus," Ridley muttered. "Can you put her in my SUV? I'll have to ask Isabella to watch Mariah so I can take this one to the ER. Venom is just going to love this shit."

I carried Farrah over to Ridley's vehicle and set her down on the backseat. Ridley came out a moment later with Mariah, and as they drove off, I wondered if my life was about to become that eventful. I doubted it. Unless my kids took after me. I was hoping they'd be more like Emmie. I didn't think I could handle a miniature version of myself. The world wasn't ready for that, and I damn sure wasn't.

I walked back to my new home and found Emmie standing on the front porch. The truck was gone, which meant Torch had either gone back to my place until things were sorted, or he'd gone home to his wife and kids. Hopefully, he'd taken that useless shithead, Casper, with him.

"You like the house?" I asked as I removed the duffle from the bike. I walked up the porch steps and she wrapped her arms around me.

"I love the house," she said. "It's perfect."

"I guess all this room means your sister will be visiting frequently," I said.

"After Lupita has recovered, I wouldn't mind a visit. I don't think she'll make a habit of it. She's going to have to figure out who she is now that she's no longer an agent or a prisoner. Her life in law enforcement is over, and I know my sister. She's going to flounder at first until she finds another cause to support."

"We'll help her however we can," I assured her.

"Zach?" she said softly.

"What, sweetheart?"

"I love you. I know it's only been a few weeks, and people will say that's way too fast, but…"

I shut her up the only way I knew how. I pressed my lips to hers, and was grateful when I tasted mint. She smiled against my mouth.

"You didn't even know I'd brushed my teeth," she said. "That could have been really, really gross."

"Nah. Kissing you is never gross." I smiled down at her. "And I love you too."

She glanced over her shoulder through the open door of our new home. "You know. We have lots of space now. Tons of new rooms to explore. Maybe even christen?"

I swatted her ass. "Then I guess you better get inside and get naked."

Emmie smiled at me a moment, then it slid from her face. "I know something really horrible happened tonight, and yes, it was scary. I'm sure later I'll have time to think about everything and I might freak out. But right now, I just want to forget. I want to make a happy memory, something so wonderful that it will overshadow the evil from tonight."

"I can do that. Have you checked out our new shower yet?" I asked.

She grinned widely again. "Yep. Dual showerheads, and really big. We could probably fit three of you in there, maybe four."

"Go start the shower, Em. I'll be there in a minute. Just going to lock up for the night."

She went inside and headed upstairs. I watched her ass sway and sighed at the beautiful sight. After I made sure the house was secure, I tossed the duffle onto the bedroom floor and found a very naked, very naughty Emmie in the shower, with her hand between her legs.

"I told you to get the shower ready, woman, not start without me."

"You were too slow," she said as her fingers stroked her clit.

I stripped off my clothes and opened the shower door, stepping under the hot spray. My cock was already hard and aching just from looking at my sexy as fuck wife. I reached for her, and Emmie plastered herself against me. I kissed her long and hard, groaning when I felt her nipples harden even more. It still amazed me how responsive she was, and how eager.

"Please, Zach. We have all night to take things slow, but I need you right now."

I placed my hand against the tiled wall, but it felt cold. There was a bench along the opposite wall of the shower. I walked over to it and sat, then pulled Emmie down so that she straddled me. With my hand wrapped around my cock, I guided the head between her slick folds and watched as she lowered herself.

"Fuck, baby! You feel so damn good," I said.

"I never knew what I was missing," she said. "But I'm so glad I waited for you, Zach."

That made two of us. She lifted and lowered herself, moving slowly at first. I reached between us and rubbed her hard little clit. Her pussy grew slicker, hotter, and soon she was riding me with fast, jerky movements. I could tell she was close. I used my other hand to tweak her nipples, pinching first one, then the other. Her pussy squeezed me tight as she screamed out her release, slamming down onto my cock again and again. When she panted for breath and her body started to grow limp, I gripped her hips and thrust upward. I fucked my gorgeous wife until I filled her with my cum, and even then I still wanted her.

No matter how many times I felt Emmie wrapped around my dick, I knew I'd always need more. I didn't think the craving I felt for her would ever go away. If anything, it seemed to grow stronger every day.

"Love you, sweet angel," I said.

"Love you more."

I smiled and kissed her again, my cock already growing hard once more. Yeah, every day with my wife would be an adventure, and I couldn't wait to see what life had in store for us next. It just preferably wouldn't involve a lot of blood. I much preferred hearing my Emmie scream in pleasure, and I was going to keep her screaming all night long, until we were both too exhausted to do anything but sleep.

Epilogue

Emmie
Four Months Later

I glared at my smug husband, who was grinning like he'd won the fucking lottery. We'd just left my latest doctor appointment, and we'd finally been able to see our precious baby growing inside me. At least, we were supposed to see the baby. As in *one* baby. Nope. Of course not. It seemed my hunky biker had super sperm. He'd not only knocked me up right away, but he'd planted triplets inside me. "I hate you," I said.

"No, you love me. You know you love me. I think this is proof right here," he said, patting my stomach.

I swatted at him, but he just laughed and danced out of the way.

"Three babies, Zach. What the hell am I supposed to do with three babies? I don't even know how to take care of *one*!" My voice was rising with each word, panic starting to set in. Oh shit. Three! I couldn't do this! I didn't know the first thing about kids. What if I broke them?

"Hey," he said softly, wrapping his arms around me. "Breathe, sweetheart. We've got this. You aren't alone. No one at the compound has had triplets before, but Preacher has twins. I'm sure he and Kayla can give us some pointers. And there are a ton of babysitters whenever you need a break."

"What if I'm a bad mom?" I asked, my voice so quiet I didn't think he'd heard me.

"You are going to be the best mom ever," he said. "How could anyone as sweet and loving as you not ace being a mom? We'll read every baby book out there, listen to whatever advice the others offer --"

"Ridley said to buy stock in alcohol," I said before he finished his sentence.

"Okay, so we'll listen to everyone's advice except Ridley." He muttered something about making sure Venom knew Ridley had a drinking problem, which made me laugh.

"Want to go shopping?" I asked. "Maybe if we go to one of those big baby stores I'll see all the cute things and won't feel quite so… scared."

"We can do that," he said. "We'll need three of everything."

I arched a brow and looked at up him. "You seem rather calm. You did hear the part where we're having three *girls*, right? Daughters, Zach. You're going to have three. At the same time."

He audibly swallowed and nodded. "Yep. Need to start stocking up on more ammo. And more guns. Motion sensor lights around the house might be good too, you know, in case they end up being more like me and sneak out at night."

"I think we have a while until that happens," I said. "Let's focus on not breaking them right now."

"We've got this," he said again, but I thought this time it might be more for his benefit than mine.

The nightmares I'd had for weeks since Zach had killed Ernesto and Luis had stopped. It wasn't their deaths that scared me, but the horror of what might have happened if they'd lived. I always woke after one and reminded myself the evil bastards were gone. Now I worried my husband might wake up screaming at night, and for a very different reason. Watching my big teddy bear turn into a protective papa bear was going to be entertaining. Especially when the girls were old enough for boys to start coming around.

Oh, yeah. The future was looking bright indeed. As long as I didn't drop the girls before they had a chance to grow up. It was a real fear, but I'd conquer it. With Zach by my side, I knew that anything was possible. He believed in me, so I would too. And on the days I didn't think I could handle it, I'd remember all that we'd been through already and remind myself that I was stronger than I thought.

I glanced up at my husband again and fought back a smile. And I might have to remind him just how strong he was too. The big guy was already scanning the area and scowling at any little boys who could be potential threats to his darling daughters when they were older. Our life was going to be amazing, and I couldn't wait to spend the rest of mine loving the incredible man walking beside me and the little girls we'd created together.

Harley Wylde

When Harley is writing, her motto is the hotter the better. Off the charts sex, commanding men, and the women who can't deny them. If you want men who talk dirty, are sexy as hell, and take what they want, then you've come to the right place!

An international bestselling author, Harley is the "wilder" side of award-winning scifi/fantasy romance author Jessica Coulter Smith, and writes gay fantasy romance as Dulce Dennison.

Harley at Changeling: changelingpress.com/harley-wylde-a-196.

Jessica at Changeling: changelingpress.com/jessica-coulter-smith-a-144.

Dulce at Changeling: changelingpress.com/dulce-dennison-a-205.

Changeling Press E-Books

More Sci-Fi, Fantasy, Paranormal, and BDSM adventures available in e-book format for immediate download at ChangelingPress.com -- Werewolves, Vampires, Dragons, Shapeshifters and more -- Erotic Tales from the edge of your imagination.

What are E-Books?

E-books, or electronic books, are books designed to be read in digital format -- on your desktop or laptop computer, notebook, tablet, Smart Phone, or any electronic e-book reader.

Where can I get Changeling Press E-Books?

Changeling Press e-books are available at ChangelingPress.com, Amazon, Apple Books, Barnes & Noble, and Kobo/Walmart.

ChangelingPress.com

Printed in Great Britain
by Amazon